Heart of the Sandhills

STEPHANIE GRACE WHITSON

THOMAS NELSON PUBLISHERS®
Nashville

A Division of Thomas Nelson, Inc.
www.ThomasNelson.com

Published in Nashville, Tennessee, by Thomas Nelson, Inc.

Unless otherwise noted, Scripture quotations are from The Holy Bible, KING JAMES
VERSION.

Scripture quotations noted NKJV are from THE NEW KING JAMES VERSION.
Copyright © 1979, 1980, 1982, 1990, 1994, Thomas Nelson, Inc., Publishers.

Whitson, Stephanie Grace.
    Heart of the sandhills / Stephanie Grace Whitson.
        p. cm. — (Dakota moons ; bk. 3)
    ISBN 0-7852-6824-3
    1. Women missionaries—fiction. 2. Dakota Indians—fiction. 3. Married
people—fiction. 4. Minnesota—fiction. I. Title.

PS3573.H555 H43 2002
813'.54—dc21   2001054370

Printed in the United States of America
02 03 04 05 PHX 9 8 7 6 5 4 3

Dedication

ROBERT THOMAS WHITSON
1946-2001

Walk Slowly

If you should go before me, dear, walk slowly
Down the ways of death, well-worn and wide,
For I would want to overtake you quickly
And seek the journey's ending by your side.

I would be so forlorn not to descry you
Down some shining highroad when I came;
Walk slowly, dear, and often look behind you
And pause to hear if someone calls your name.

—By Adelaide Love

Other books by Stephanie Grace Whitson

Prairie Winds Series
Walks the Fire
Soaring Eagle
Red Bird

Keepsake Legacies Series
Sarah's Patchwork
Karyn's Memory Box
Nora's Ribbon of Memories

Dakota Moons Series
Valley of the Shadow
Edge of the Wilderness
Heart of the Sandhills

One

"But seek first the kingdom of God and His righteousness, and all these things shall be added to you. Therefore do not worry about tomorrow, for tomorrow will worry about its own things. Sufficient for the day is its own trouble."

—MATTHEW 6:33–34 (NKJV)

SHE FOUND HIM LEANING ON THE CORRAL FENCE, ONE foot on the bottom rung, his elbows resting on the top. Instead of tugging playfully on the long braid that hung down his back, as was her habit, she lifted his arm and slipped beneath it, nestling against him and murmuring, "Stop worrying, Daniel. They are coming to see *you*—not the things you own."

Daniel Two Stars tightened his arm around his wife. Pulling her against him, he nuzzled the top of her head with his chin. Then, he changed the subject. "I was remembering that night at the old mission. The moon was so bright it cast shadows on the ground—just like tonight."

Gen sighed and crossed her arms atop his, stroking the back of his hands. "The first time we kissed," she offered. "And, I think, probably the first time I let myself think I might like you more than a little."

Daniel tightened the pressure around her momentarily and then bent down to kiss her cheek. "You liked me long before that little kiss on Miss Jane's front porch," he teased. "You used to look for excuses to walk by the mission sawmill when I was working."

"I did not!" she protested. "It wasn't *my* fault the sawmill just happened to be on the way to everything else."

"All I know," he said gently, "is that first summer every time I looked up from my work a pair of blue eyes was watching me."

"I was worried you would leave with Otter and go back to your old horse-thieving ways." She spun around and hugged him fiercely. "I knew you were a better man than that. Even then I knew." She looked up at him, abruptly returning to the subject and the reason Gen suspected Daniel had not been sleeping well. "The children are coming to see *us*, Daniel. Not the house. Not the barn. Not our things."

Daniel gently disengaged himself and pointed to the moon. "Far away in New York they see that same moon. But that is all that is the same between us now." He leaned against the top board of the corral fence. "Aaron has grown to be a young man since he left Minnesota." He shook his head. "Thinking of marriage. Imagine that."

"He's only seventeen. His ideas about Amanda Whitrock are romantic daydreams, that's all." Gen added abruptly, "And they are ridiculous daydreams, at that."

"You said yourself he grew beyond his years because of the outbreak," Daniel reminded her gently. "You only protest because you don't like that girl he writes about." He changed the subject. "I look at the photograph Jane and Elliot sent us and I can't believe that young woman standing next to Aaron is Meg."

He chuckled softly. "I wonder if her temper still matches her red hair."

"She still has a temper," Gen said. "But once she realized little Hope was staying with us, she stopped pretending to be the spoiled baby of the family. Mothering Hope grew her up a lot."

"Hope doesn't know me at all," Daniel said. "All she knows is that grand house in New York where servants set her breakfast before her in silver dishes." He turned and looked up the hill. "They will be expecting a house like that," he said, nodding toward where Jeb Grant's two-story frame house stood overlooking the valley and the two log cabins below.

Gen could almost see their cabin shrinking in the moonlight as Daniel compared it to Jeb Grant's and Leighton Hall. She spoke up again. "Aaron and Meg don't care about those things, Daniel. They will never forget what you did for them—those nights when you protected us. Nothing will ever change that—or their love for you. And you can be assured Hope knows all about you. About us." She swallowed to keep her voice from wavering as she considered that Hope, the baby she had left behind, the child she loved so much, might not recognize her anymore.

"They love a memory," Daniel said. He beat his chest, mocking himself. "The Indian hero who saved them during the outbreak of 1862." He shook his head. "What will they think when they learn that hero is a poor man who doesn't even own the land he farms? What will they think when Jeb Grant rides down to inspect the fields and they see I am little more than a servant to a white man—just like the servants who bring them meals and wash their clothes?"

"Stop it." Gen stomped her foot impatiently and hit him lightly on the shoulder even as she flung a desperate, wordless prayer to heaven, asking for help to encourage him. "Stop talking about my husband as if he were nothing." Her voice was tinged with impatience. "The man I love *is* a hero. Three years ago he saved the lives of a half-breed girl and three white children. He was repaid with prison and nearly hanged, but he never gave up. And now, it is 1866 and he is rich in everything that matters. He has worked hard and harvested a fine stand of corn, his friends respect him, and"—she reached up and, laying her hand alongside his cheek, made him look at her—"he pleases his wife who will adore him until the day she dies." Standing on tiptoe, she kissed him, gently at first, then not so gently. When Daniel returned the kiss and pulled her against him, she wrapped her arms around his neck.

"What would I do without you, little wife?" he whispered.

Gen planted a kiss on his weathered cheek. "That, best beloved, you will never have to discover. I almost lost you once. I'm never letting you go again." A cool breeze made her shiver. She linked her arm through his. "Now stop brooding and take me inside. I'm cold."

"Stop ordering me around," he teased, quoting with mock seriousness. "*A contentious wife is a continual dripping.*"

"I am not being contentious," she taunted back. "I merely want you to obey the scripture that tells husbands to love their wives . . . oh, and the one that talks about husbands rejoicing in the wife of their youth."

"I can do that," Daniel muttered. He swept her up into his arms and carried her the short distance to their cabin door, setting her down just inside.

"Yes, I know," Gen said, taking his hand and leading him into the darkness.

⌒

With her arm bent beneath her as a pillow, Genevieve LaCroix Dane Two Stars lay on her side watching her husband sleep. The chill wind that had sent them shivering indoors had brought snow. Gen could hear the wind picking up as it hurled icy flakes against the northern wall of their little cabin. When a gust of wind swept across the top of the chimney and launched itself downward, a shower of sparks revived the flames and briefly illuminated her husband's face. Gen reached out to touch his lower lip, to follow its curve to the corner of his mouth and then across the jaw and finally into the mass of glossy black hair spilling across his pillow.

They had been married just a little over a year and still she woke often, having dreamed again that these months of happiness were the dream, that Daniel truly had been hung as one of the criminals from the uprising back in '62. Sometimes she saw him hanging on the gallows. Sometimes she watched in an agony of grief as the soldiers covered the thirty-eight bodies in a shallow mass grave, their heads covered by sackcloth hoods, and then one of the hoods slowly fell away to reveal a face—his face, her beloved Daniel's.

In some dreams, she was still married to Reverend Simon Dane but then, instead of being a good wife and nursing him through illness, instead of being faithful and mourning his death and mothering his children Aaron and Meg and their adopted child Hope, she ran away and found herself in some awful place where men abused her. Whatever the dreams, they all had the same theme. She was a worthless woman, and Daniel was not alive after all.

Now, lying next to her living, breathing Daniel Two Stars, Gen moved closer, praising the Lord who had reunited them, willing away her evil dreams with prayers. She prayed for the children who were to come in the spring and visit them here in Minnesota. She prayed for Elliot and Jane Leighton, who were joyfully keeping their promise to Simon to raise his children in New York and let Genevieve return to Minnesota. She prayed that Elliot would succeed in his efforts to sway Washington officials to help the Dakota still in Minnesota. She thanked God that the Dakota in Crow Creek, South Dakota had been moved to a new home in Nebraska and prayed that it would be a good place for healing between the nations.

She thanked God again for Simon Dane, who had taken her into his heart and then, in death, had given her a new life with Daniel. She had been a good wife, Simon had said in a letter dictated to Elliot from his deathbed. She had been a good wife and now she must go home to Minnesota where Daniel Two Stars waited for her. The children would be fine. They wanted her to go. And finally, months after Simon died and after a talk with Aaron, the man-boy who had grown up before his time, she had come home to Minnesota.

Genevieve thanked God for home, a tiny log cabin on Jeb Grant's sizeable farm. Ironically, it was land that used to belong to Daniel and his friend Robert Lawrence back in the ages before the madness called the Minnesota Sioux Uprising of 1862. Now Robert and Daniel plowed fields that were no longer theirs in return for a portion of the crops and the right to live in two small log cabins with their families.

Only a few weeks ago a Mr. Adams had stopped at the farm with questions for Jeb Grant. It seemed that Jeb had contacted the famous Bishop Whipple, a friend of the Dakota, and Bishop Whipple had in turn contacted Mr. Adams. Adams came in person to get Jeb's written recommendation for Daniel Two Stars and Robert Lawrence to receive part of a fund appropriated by Congress that would help the remnants of the Dakota tribe still in Minnesota.

"Be glad to write you a recommendation," Jeb had said, shifting nervously from one foot to another, " 'ceptin' I cain't write." He had turned to Daniel and said, "I'll tell you what to write and you put it down." He looked at Mr. Adams. "That all right with you?"

Mr. Adams had agreed, and so it was that an educated Dakota Indian wrote his own commendation upon which an illiterate white man made his mark so that more white men would see and believe that there were at least two Dakota men in Minnesota who had never scalped a child or outraged a woman.

"I'll be back before planting next spring," Mr. Adams had promised. "You may get more than money, and there's talk of trying to get farms up by the old reservation."

But Mr. Adams had ridden away with the papers extolling the virtues of Daniel Two Stars and Robert Lawrence and had not been heard from again. As she lay beside her husband, Gen could not imagine even a tiny corner of Minnesota being given up for Indians to inhabit. She had not realized when she came back from New York how universally despised they would be. Even though he could not read, Jeb sometimes brought down a newspaper from town, and what she read in it caused Gen to shudder. *Savages. Murderers. Fiends.* Looking at her husband sleeping next to her, she shook her head at the ignorance being displayed in those newspapers. Sometimes it worried her, thinking of the hatred lying so fertile just beyond the boundaries of Jeb and Marjorie Grant's farm.

She thanked God for Jeb and Marjorie Grant, good people with good memories of Indians in their home state of Kentucky. Two years earlier when Daniel and Robert were serving as army scouts and discovered a half-dozen ancient Dakota fleeing the Crow Creek reservation and trying to return to their homes in Minnesota, Daniel had brought them to Jeb, begging him to let them stay on his place. Jeb had agreed. The fact that two of the old women helped Marjorie bring twins into the world helped their cause. But Crow Creek and old age had taken their toll, and the little cemetery on the hillside behind Jeb's barn had grown steadily until now all the ancients had gone to the spirit land, leaving only Daniel and Genevieve Two Stars and Robert and Nancy Lawrence.

White settlers were trickling back into southwestern Minnesota—settlers who were well read in the stories of Indian depredations but illiterate when it came to the subject of Christian natives who had defended white captives, often at risk of their own lives. Gen had begun to notice that neither Daniel nor Robert ventured far off Jeb Grant's farm of late, and when they did, they rarely invited their wives along.

Gen struggled to be content. *In everything give thanks,* the Scriptures said. She closed her eyes and gave thanks. *Daniel is mine. We have a roof over our heads. The Grants are kind. We are not hungry. Daniel is mine. Robert and Nancy are such good Christian friends. The children are happy in New York. They will come to visit. Daniel is mine.* Always, her prayers circled back to the wonder of having the love of her life near.

"You be careful," Nancy had teased her once. "You worship the water that man walks on. One of these days he's going to sink. What are you going to do then?"

"Why, I'll dive in and pull him up," Gen laughed and returned to her work.

Everything was very nearly perfect, Gen thought. Except for the neighbors who didn't understand. And Daniel's worries about what the children would think of him now. Lying in bed listening to the wind blow outside, she closed her eyes and argued with herself. *Things will change when Elliot and Jane come. Daniel will see that the children don't care nearly so much about possessions as they do about seeing us. And the neighbors will see the children and finally accept who we are. Please, God, let the people see who we are. Make them see past our skins and into our hearts. All we want is a place to be. Just a place to be. Is it too much to ask?*

She lifted her head and looked at her husband again. *So handsome,* she thought. Such a beautiful man, even with the premature wrinkles around his eyes, the deepening crease between his eyebrows. *Worry,* Gen thought. He was always worrying. She had thought the news that Elliot and Jane were bringing the children for a visit in the spring would have been cause for rejoicing. Instead, Daniel worried more.

We'll put up a tent, Jane had written. *It will be such fun. Just like the old days when the mission held its annual meeting on the prairie. You won't believe how the children have grown. And they are so excited about seeing you again.*

Daniel's worries were groundless, Gen thought. But she didn't know how to make him believe it. He would just have to see for himself. She would spend the winter working on the quilts she was making for each of the children. Aaron's was almost finished, a simple blue-and-white nine-patch, small enough to include in his bedroll if he ever lived his dream of being an army interpreter.

Gen thought ahead to spring. She pictured the children arriving just as the crops were rising out of the ground, as the garden was planted, and as the wild roses she and Nancy had transplanted were blooming. She told herself the children's visit would be a celebration and at last Daniel would see that nothing mattered but their love for one another and their love for the Lord. *He will see,* Gen thought. She nestled against him.

Without opening his eyes, Daniel drew her closer, settling her head on his shoulder. "The storm is worse," he murmured, half asleep.

When Gen shivered slightly and curled one leg over his in an attempt to get warm, he opened his eyes, raised up on one shoulder and looked down at her. He said nothing, only pulled the worn comforter up around her shoulders before finding a more creative way to keep her warm.

Two

"It is an honour for a man to cease from strife:
but every fool will be meddling."

—PROVERBS 20:3

"No!" THE SHRILL DENIAL SPLIT THE EARLY AFTERNOON quiet in Leighton Hall's garden. From where she knelt beside a rosebush in one corner of the garden, Margaret Marie Dane looked toward the house just in time to see Amanda Whitrock flounce down the back porch stairs and storm in the general direction of the white gazebo on the opposite side of the garden.

"But Amanda," Aaron pleaded from the back stairs, "it's not until next summer. I'll be here all this winter. We can still go to the winter festival together."

"I don't care!" Amanda shot back over her shoulder. "You'll miss my birthday party—and it's the most important one! A girl only turns sixteen once in a lifetime, Aaron Dane." She disappeared into the gazebo.

Aaron hesitated on the back stairs and caught a glimpse of his sister hunkered down in the rose garden. With a woeful glance toward the gazebo, he stepped off the porch, thrust his fists in his pockets, and sauntered towards Meg.

"Somebody's angry with Aa—ron," Meg sang softly as he approached. "Somebody's angry with Aa—ron and her name is Mandy Dane." She snipped a white rose off a bush and twirled it in the air at her brother.

"Be quiet," Aaron snapped. "She'll hear you. She's still Amanda Whitrock for now. And you know she *hates* being called 'Mandy'." He reached for the rose.

Meg snatched it away. "If you want to give Amanda Whitrock a rose, give her one of *yours*." She gestured towards a pink blossom nearby.

"The pink ones aren't as pretty as the white ones," Aaron complained. He looked doubtfully towards the gazebo, somewhat cheered when a flash of color betrayed the fact that Amanda was watching for him.

"Too bad," Meg said, and straightened up. "I'm not giving *her*," she nodded towards the gazebo, "one of Gen's roses."

"She's just sad we're going to be gone next summer, that's all," Aaron explained.

"She's being a brat," Meg declared, "because she isn't getting her way. Sometimes she acts like she's four years old. No," Meg corrected herself, "I take that back. Hope acts *better* than Amanda most of the time. I never saw *anybody* as spoiled as Amanda Whitrock in my entire life," Meg said. "Why do you even like her, anyway?"

Aaron shrugged. "She's the prettiest girl in the class," he offered weakly, "and she likes me."

Meg rolled her eyes. Snipping off one more rose, she handed

Aaron her clippers. "Here," she said, heading towards the house. "Just remember. *No white roses.*"

With a sigh, Aaron bent to clip a small pink bud off a bush. On his way to the gazebo he set Meg's garden scissors on a white swing. Taking a deep breath, he headed towards the gazebo holding the small pink blossom before him like a penitent worshipper bearing a votive offering to his gods.

Captain John Willets pushed away the map he had been studying and leaned back in his chair. There had to be worse things in a soldier's life than boredom, but at the moment he could not think what they might be. He'd done his best to keep from being sent back to Minnesota, but to no avail. General Sibley wanted a seasoned man at Fort Ridgely as long as there was danger of hostile Sioux breaking back into Minnesota from the West. That man, General Sibley had said unequivocally, was John Willets. And so John had come, convincing himself that perhaps they were right, perhaps the string of scout camps along the frontier was not quite enough.

The need for extra vigilance had been brought home to Willets just this past May when a group of hostiles broke through the frontier defenses and murdered four members of a homesteader's family. It had sent panic all across Minnesota again, and for a while the garrison was alive with activity. But then the halfbreed responsible for the murders was caught and imprisoned at Mankato—and subsequently lynched and hung by a mob. That ended any significant Indian trouble, and it had been months since anything of interest had happened at Fort Ridgely—unless, of course, one considered the arrival of Miss Charlotte Parker of interest. Which, to be quite honest, Captain Willets did. Just now, as he sat behind his oversized desk inside the stone building that served as a combination headquarters and surgeon's residence, John gave himself over to the contemplation of Miss Charlotte's warm brown eyes and tiny hands. Something about a small woman called out the protector in him. Always had. And Miss Charlotte was not only small, but she gazed up at him with the trusting, liquid-brown eyes of a gentle doe.

In the contemplation of Miss Charlotte Parker, John Willets temporarily forgot his boredom. But then the fire burned low and a cold wind blew down the chimney and sent the map sliding off the desk onto the floor. When John bent to retrieve it he once again followed the line of the Missouri River west to where all things interesting were happening possibly at this very moment, and the lovely image of Miss Charlotte Parker was replaced by even more tempting images of supply trains and maneuvers and negotiations in the dusky light of campfires attended by men with names like Little Thunder and Bad Wound, Swift Bear and Spotted Antelope. As he put another log on the fire in his office, Captain Willets crouched down to warm his hands, thinking that it was going to be a very long winter—a few cotillions with the fleet-footed Miss Charlotte Parker notwithstanding.

"Cap'n Willets." A familiar voice sounded from the door.

"You got supper already, Pope?" Willets asked without getting up.

"No, sir. It's not that, sir. I was over at the sutler's store and—," Edward Pope cleared his throat. "Well, there's a settler over there and he's hoppin' mad. I heard him say somethin' about Indians. Just thought you might want to know, sir."

Willets stood up and turned around. Smoothing his unfashionably long blond hair with one hand, he reached for his hat with the other. He smiled. "Thank you, Pope. I'll see to it." He made his way across the parade ground and had just rounded the officers' quarters when he was nearly bowled over by a giant of a man who looked oddly familiar but whom Willets did not recognize even when the man introduced himself as "Marsh. Abner Marsh. Got to talk to you about some Injuns."

"Indian trouble? Here?" With a look in Edward Pope's direction, Willets lowered his voice. "We'll talk at headquarters," and without waiting for Marsh to reply, he headed back across the parade ground and inside.

When Abner Marsh ducked to clear the top of Willets's office door, he remembered. This was the man who had had some horses stolen before the outbreak and had come to the fort for help. Willets had led a company of men to the Marsh homestead where they found a dead Dakota warrior in Marsh's barn. As it turned out, Marsh had already recaptured his horses from the thieves in an act at once so daring and stupid Willets had been unsure whether to admire or chastise the man. He had ended up doing neither, returning to Fort Ridgely to bury the unidentified warrior in a corner of the fort cemetery plot.

"You had a place up by Acton," Willets said, motioning Abner Marsh into a chair. At Marsh's surprised expression, Willets smiled and passed a hand over his blond goatee. "I've changed—had a full beard back then. But I'm the one who came up to your place after your horses were stolen."

Marsh squinted at Willets momentarily, then nodded and grunted. "Hope I get more help this time than I did then." He leaned forward. "Got me a new place down by New Ulm. Nice place. Good water. Rich soil. Only problem is, still got Injun trouble." Looking around the room for a spittoon and finding none, Marsh sent a brown stream of liquid into the corner behind Willets's desk before continuing. "Neighbor named Jeb Grant. He's got four of 'em livin' on his place. Two bucks."

Willets smiled. "As it happens, Mr. Marsh, I know Daniel Two Stars and Robert Lawrence. They scouted for the Army. And they both did excellent service on behalf of whites during the outbreak. You have nothing to be concerned about with Daniel and Robert."

Marsh's jaw set momentarily, then he spit tobacco again.

With a glance into the corner, Willets said abruptly, "Would you mind if we finished this conversation outside?" Without waiting for a reply, he headed for the door.

Marsh followed Willets outside. Clenching his fists at his sides, he stepped towards Willets and stared down at him. "I want those Injuns off Grant's place. I got a wife and two young daughters. They was scairt half to death in that other mess. I ain't gonna' have 'em worried again."

Willets looked away and stared across the parade ground towards the place where his Dakota scouts had once camped. Looking back up at Marsh, he forced another smile. "All those two men want is a place to peacefully raise a family. Which is, I gather, what you want as well. They've both paid quite a price for just being Indians. And in my humble opinion, they both deserve to be left in peace for the rest of their days. If you want to know the truth, you'd sooner have to worry about Sitting Bull riding a thousand miles and personally attacking your place than any trouble from Two Stars or Lawrence."

Marsh raised his voice. "You tellin' me the United States Army ain't gonna lift a finger to protect lawful citizens?"

"No sir, I'm not saying that. The Army will always protect citizens," Willets said, forcing reasonableness into his voice. "I'm just telling you that you don't have a problem. And the Army cannot just ride onto private property and remove people who were invited to live there. Jeb Grant obviously wants them. And with all due respect, Mr. Marsh, I remind you that Mr. Grant's rights are on an equal par with yours. He has the right to hire farm hands of his choosing."

"Now you listen here," Marsh said, shoving Willets back against the stone wall of the building. "You may think that uniform of yours gives you permission to order me around. It don't. I pay your salary, and—"

A half-foot shorter than Abner Marsh and at least fifty pounds lighter, John Willets was no threat physically—at least that was what Marsh reckoned. Except that one minute he was pressing Willets against the wall and the next minute he had landed in the dirt on his backside.

From where he stood peering out from behind the barracks, Edward Pope laughed. "I told you Cap'n would handle 'im," he said to the two other privates with him. "I seen him whip a prisoner bigger'n Abner Marsh once. He's got moves so quick you don't know what hit you. No sirree, you better think again before you mess with Cap'n Willets." Pope laughed and headed off to fix a mess of his famous soup for the captain. The other two soldiers continued to watch.

"Here's a word of advice, Mr. Marsh," John said from the doorway of his office. "It does not help your case when you try to smash the face of the man you want help from." As Marsh scrambled to get up, Willets repeated, "Daniel Two Stars and Robert Lawrence are good men. I would take it personally if anything happened to them." He tugged on the brim of his hat. "Now if you'll excuse me, I have housekeeping to do. Someone used the corner of my office for a spittoon." Behind him, he heard Abner Marsh muttering under his breath about Injun lovers and cowards. He straightened his shoulders and went inside.

⌇

"Mornin', Abner." Jeb Grant nodded to his neighbor and climbed down from his wagon. With a farmer's inherent interest in the weather, he commented on the season's early snow even as he limped to the front of the wagon and hitched his team before heading towards Ludlow's Variety Store.

But Abner Marsh was not about to engage in meaningless small talk about the weather. "Got somethin' to talk to you about," he said. "Thought you'd be in town, it bein' Saturday and all."

Jeb hesitated before following Marsh to the side of the building. He nodded towards where a group of men were unloading bricks. "Good to see the town gettin' built up. Bodes well for the future."

Abner cast a brief glance towards the pile of bricks. He could hear the sounds of hammering and sawing from somewhere nearby. But where Jeb saw progress, Abner saw a need to rebuild a town that had been a prime target of Sioux attacks in the uprising of 1862. "How long you gonna keep Injuns on your place?" Abner asked abruptly.

Jeb pulled on the brim of his hat, scratched his ear, and seemed to be considering the question. "Can't say as I'm keepin' any now, Abner. Daniel and Robert are workin' for me. They more than earn their way. Reckon they'll stay as long as they want to stay." He squinted up at Abner. "I'm personally hopin' that'll be a long time."

"Government gave 'em a reservation out in Nebraska. That's where they should go."

"Why should they do that, Abner?" Jeb asked quietly. "Minnesota's always been their home—for longer than you or me been here, even."

"I got a wife and two girls to worry about," Abner grumbled. "We got to be careful. That trouble last spring proves it."

"Daniel and Robert got nothing in common with them hostiles that caused that trouble." Jeb forced a smile. He put his hand on Abner's shoulder. "You can't just lump people all together like that. I never liked Germans much 'til one saved my hide at Shiloh." He waved his hands around him. "Now I'm livin' near a whole town full of Germans and it don't bother me at all." He thumped Marsh on the back. "Give it time, neighbor. You'll see there's nothin' to worry about."

Marsh's spittle stained the light covering of snow at Jeb's feet. He wiped his mouth with his shirtsleeve. "I'll give you 'til spring plantin' to get 'em off your place," he said. "Come spring, if they're still there, I won't be responsible."

"You threatenin' my friends, Abner? That ain't neighborly."

"It ain't only me, Jeb," Abner said. "I been talkin' to Baxter and Quinn. They don't like it either. We kinda got you fenced in on this, Jeb."

Jeb looked past Abner towards his wagon. If Baxter and Quinn agreed with Marsh, he really was fenced in—literally. Between the three, they owned all the land surrounding Jeb. And he had been wanting to buy one of those sections from Earl Baxter. Trouble over Daniel and Robert took on a new level of importance. "Just calm down, Abner," Jeb said. He put one foot up on the board walk that stretched in front of the store. "I got to get my supplies and get home. Why don't you and Sally come up to the house after church on Sunday? Meet Daniel and Robert and their wives." He nodded. "We'll invite the Baxters and the Quinns, too. Once you all meet the Two Starses and the Lawrences, you'll know for sure there's nothing to get all riled up about."

Marsh shook his head. "Sally was in a family way when the mess happened back in '62. Lost the baby. Never been the same since. And she won't be makin' Sunday calls on some of them that done it."

"I'm sorry about what happened, Abner. I truly am. But we got to move on. Quinn was on the other side in the Rebellion, but I don't hold it against him. We're all Americans again and I'm willing to let it go." Jeb stepped up on the boardwalk just in time to see Reverend Donohue coming out of Ludlow's. "Let it rest, Abner. Everything will be fine. You'll see." He called out to Reverand Donohue before turning back to say, "You change your mind about comin' over, you're welcome any time. Marjorie makes real good pie. It's worth a visit." Without waiting for a response, he headed for the Reverend.

The Reverend Elmer Donohue advised a worried Jeb Grant to pray. Being new to the West and having never seen an Indian himself, but having heard his share of stories, he also suggested that perhaps Brother Marsh was right and that the, um, Dakota *guests* currently staying on the Grant farm could be encouraged to seek another domicile in the spring. Jeb listened to the reverend's meaningless, misinformed litany, finished his shopping at Ludlow's, and headed home, thoroughly discouraged.

❧

Although the early snow melted within a few days, its arrival infused every settler with an uneasy sense that they had better be about getting prepared for the onslaught of an early and harsh winter. After all, they reminded one another, hadn't the squirrels been lining their nests with an unusually thick layer of leaves? And weren't the horses' winter coats coming in thicker and sooner than normal? In the wake of such signs, Robert Lawrence decided to take Nancy along for what he expected would be their last trip into town before spring. When he returned, Robert pulled his team up in front of Daniel and Gen's cabin.

Daniel met them at the wagon. "Gen's up at the Grants' helping Marjorie make some apple pies," he said to Nancy. "I'll get her."

"I'll walk up there," Nancy said. She nodded at Robert and headed off up the road.

"Wait," Daniel called out. "Let us drive you."

Nancy put one hand on her belly. She laughed. "The baby won't be here for many moons." Her face grew sad, and inwardly Daniel felt a sympathetic pang, wishing he had not been the cause of bringing her two lost children to Nancy's mind. But Nancy recovered quickly and cast a bright smile in his direction. "You men need to talk. Gen and I will be back in time to make you something to eat." Without waiting, Nancy headed off up the road.

"What is it?" Daniel asked his friend, frowning.

Robert reached into the wagon for a newspaper and held it out to Daniel, who leaned against the wagon and began to read the article Robert pointed out.

> *I have recently learned, with much surprise, that the Sioux Indians who were the perpetrators of the Minnesota Massacre of 1862 have been moved from their location at Crow Creek down into one of the settled counties of Nebraska, directly opposite white settlements in Dakota.*
>
> *You are aware that these Indians murdered more than one thousand defenseless men, women, and children in the state of Minnesota. Now an order has been signed for the release of those hostile savages and they have been turned loose to seek revenge by a system of robbery, rapine, and murder upon our unprotected citizens . . . If these Indians are allowed to remain near our settlements, our citizens will either be compelled to abandon their homes for the security of their lives and property or wage a war of extermination against them . . .*

When Daniel finished reading, Robert spoke up. "The new reservation is in Nebraska. Plenty of timber, good land, they say."

"We aren't reservation Indians," Daniel said abruptly. "Not anymore."

"Maybe we should be," Robert answered. "If the new reservation is good. If—"

Daniel interrupted him, quoting from the newspaper article. "If the whites in the area don't 'wage a war of extermination against the savages'?"

"There are more letters in that paper," Robert said. "Many of the settlers here are beginning to worry about us. There's a letter from Quinn. He calls us *hellhounds*."

Daniel sighed. Leaning against the wagon, he studied the earth at his feet for a moment. "Elliot Leighton writes that Congress is going to give at least some of the Dakota scouts farms. He hopes that when he and Jane bring the children out in the spring they will be able to help us move to our own farms. Then all of these worries with Jeb's neighbors will be resolved."

"No one in Minnesota is going to give Indians free land," Robert argued.

"It isn't free," Daniel snorted. "It was *our* crops and *our* live-stock that fed the soldiers and the rescued captives for weeks. *Our* furniture fueled their campfires."

Robert interrupted him. "None of that matters. They don't care." He gripped the sides of the wagon and stared up the road towards New Ulm. "Someone threw a rock at Nancy this morning. Called her a fat sow and a few other things I won't repeat." He stared at Daniel. "Thanks be to God Nancy didn't hear the entire speech. Or at least she pretended not to hear."

Daniel swallowed hard and looked up at the sky, thinking. finally, he looked back at Robert. "I am sorry, my friend."

Robert shook his head and sighed. "We can be grateful winter is coming on. That will help keep our women close to home without frightening them."

Daniel nodded his agreement. "And in the spring when Elliot arrives with news that we are moving all these worries will be over."

He and Robert began to unload the sacks of winter provisions from the back of the wagon. They worked in silence, pretending not to worry, all the while wondering why God did not see fit to grant them peaceful lives.

Unaware of Robert and Nancy's mistreatment in New Ulm and unable to read the newspaper for himself, Jeb Grant discussed

Abner Marsh with his wife. Between them, they decided to keep both Abner Marsh's hostility and Reverend Donohue's indifference to themselves for the time being.

"Winter's coming on," Marjorie said, "and things will settle down."

Jeb mused, "Maybe that land they been promised will come through in the spring. Maybe they won't ever have to know." Jeb picked up one of his twin boys. "One thing we aren't going to do is let the bigots decide who our friends are." He hugged his son fiercely and then set him back down. "We just got to pray harder, I guess."

And they did.

Three

"For the word of God is quick, and powerful, and sharper
than any two-edged sword, piercing even to the dividing
asunder of soul and spirit, and of the joints and marrow,
and is a discerner of the thoughts and intents of the heart."

—HEBREWS 4:12

JEB AND MARJORIE GRANT EXPERIENCED ANSWERED PRAYER
in a unique way. As the old-timers had predicted, winter had
arrived early and was to stay long in their part of Minnesota, making traveling even the few miles into New Ulm impossible for days
at a time. Temperatures plummeted, hovering at fifteen to twenty
degrees below zero for days at a time. The first of many snow-
storms was so severe that the Lawrences and the Two Starses could
not see one another's homes for nearly sixteen hours. Nearly thirty
inches of snow remained on the ground for the entire month of
December. Abner Marsh and his neighbors were so busy trying to
keep their livestock—and, at times, themselves—from freezing to

death, they had little time to worry and no time to talk about the four Indians living a few miles away. For the first time in their married lives, Jeb and Marjorie were sincerely thankful for terrible weather. And then, something else happened that appeared to answer their prayers for peace.

❧

While Gen and Nancy spent nearly every day together, they were often unable to scale the deep snowdrifts separating them from the Grants' house only a quarter of a mile away. One morning Robert surprised the women by pulling up to Gen and Daniel's cabin standing on a makeshift sleigh he and Daniel had made by taking Robert's wagon off its frame and lashing the box to a crude pair of wooden runners carved from two saplings.

"Marjorie said to come and fetch you," Robert announced as he and Daniel stepped inside to warm up. "I think she said something about quilting." The men exchanged knowing grins as Gen scooped up her basket of finished quilt blocks and packed her sewing kit. In less than an hour the women were ensconced in Marjorie's kitchen, chattering away while Marjorie hand-cranked her sewing machine at top speed to finish the quilt top Gen was making for twelve-year-old Meg Dane.

"I can't believe how many pieces you have in these blocks," Marjorie said as she finished the last row. "Where did you get the idea?"

Gen smiled. "When my Papa made me leave home and go to school at the Danes' mission, he told me to look at the moon every night. He said he would be looking at that same moon, knowing it would bring us closer. Ever since then, when I'm lonely for someone, I look at the moon and imagine them doing the same." She paused. "Even now that Papa is gone, and so many other people I love are in heaven, I like to look at the moon and imagine them doing the same—from the other side." She hurried to finish. "More than once I've looked up and prayed for Meg, imagining her in the rose garden we planted together before I left New York." She blushed. "I wanted to do something to represent the moon. But just plain circles don't make a very pretty quilt. Daniel was teasing me one day and said I should put two stars inside each moon. When I tried it, this is what happened."

"It's beautiful," Marjorie said.

"I hope Aaron isn't jealous," Gen worried aloud. "I did a simple nine-patch hoping he could include it in his bedroll when he's a soldier."

"Well, you made Aaron's while we were harvesting the garden and doing all that canning and preserving last fall, " Nancy interjected. "If there had been three feet of snow on the ground, you could have made *him* a Two Stars pattern!" She added, "Aaron won't mind. Men don't care about things like that."

"Done!" Marjorie called out, holding up Gen's completed quilt top.

After lunch, the women lowered Marjorie's quilting frame from the kitchen ceiling where it hovered over the table when not in use. With four iron C-shaped clamps they anchored each corner of the large frame to a chair back. Then they stretched out the backing fabric, a collage of odd-shaped pieces of tan fabric gleaned from worn-out skirts and shirts. Once the backing was basted to the thin strips of ticking nailed to each of the quilting frame boards, the women spread a flannel sheet and the newly finished quilt top over it to complete the fabric sandwich.

"I can't reach the center!" Nancy panted as she strained to reach across her pregnant belly to baste her section of the quilt together. The women laughed while they ran extra-long stitches from the center to the edges of the quilt so the calico would remain in place without bubbles or bumps while the women quilted with smaller stitches.

While the women worked, Jeb, Daniel, and Robert came and went, stomping in to thaw out, leaving to haul feed to the horses or to shovel steaming piles of manure out of the barns. They dug tunnels to Marjorie's chicken coop and came in to report the loss of five hens—not to the cold, but to a fox. They set traps near the chicken coop and then headed for the pond to harvest ice. Marjorie's two-year-old twins, Lee and Sherman, fell asleep beneath the quilt. When Gen offered to help her carry them up to bed, Marjorie grinned. "Let them sleep. Won't do any harm and then I won't have to worry about them waking up and raising a ruckus upstairs."

She went upstairs and came back with a thick tied comforter that she set on the open oven door to warm.

"Let me," Gen said, when the comforter was warm. She bent down and ducked beneath the table. Tucking the warm blanket around the twins, she watched them sleep, caressing first one, and then the second little head and sighing.

"In God's time, my sister," Nancy said gently, peering beneath the edge of the quilt at Gen.

With a wistful smile and a nod, Gen emerged from beneath the quilt. Inspecting the tip of her left middle finger she muttered, "I don't have a callus yet. My finger is nearly bleeding."

"I'd say that's a signal it's time to bake cookies!" Marjorie said.

"Can we?" Gen asked, surprised.

Marjorie nodded. "I've been saving back the makings for a special occasion. I'd say this is it." She stood up and stretched, arching her back and rubbing her neck. While Gen and Nancy released the C-clamps holding the quilting frame in place and sent it back up to the kitchen ceiling, Marjorie bustled to the pantry. "I like to went crazy all these weeks cooped up in this house alone. I was crying to the Lord about it just this morning. In fact, I told Jeb I was going to make my own snowshoes and head out after lunch if he didn't figure a way to get the team out and get me some female company." She plopped a flour sack on the table. Her eyes teared up as she looked from Gen to Nancy. "I'm being silly, I know. But I just got to tell you two you mean a lot to me." She blushed furiously and headed back to the pantry.

❦

"Finally!" Marjorie opened her front door wide and waved Gen and Nancy inside. "I thought you'd never get here."

She and Gen followed Marjorie through the drafty house towards the warmth of the kitchen. At the doorway they both stopped short. Three other women sat around the quilt. At the sight of Gen and Nancy, they all cast piercing glances in Marjorie's direction.

Putting a reassuring hand on each of her friend's shoulders, Marjorie spoke up. "I know we've all been lonely with the string of bad weather, and when I sent Jeb out to round you ladies up for a day of quilting, I thought it'd be a good time for you to meet Genevieve Two Stars and Nancy Lawrence. They learned to quilt from the same missionaries that won 'em to the Lord," she said. While she made introductions, she pulled out the chair next to a blonde-haired woman. "Nancy, you sit here next to Lydia."

When Nancy didn't move, she felt Marjorie's hand on her back, gently guiding her to the designated chair.

Lydia pulled her hands away from the quilt top and shifted her chair away an inch or two, but she was blocked by her neighbor, a stoop-shouldered woman Marjorie had introduced as Lydia's sister Violet.

"Harriet," Marjorie said to a stout, dour-faced woman on the opposite side of the quilt, "now that we're all here, I'll just pop those rolls you brought in the oven." She directed Gen to the opposite side of the quilt. "You sit next to Harriet. I'll pull up another chair in minute." And so, while Marjorie slid a pan of rolls into the oven and clattered around making coffee, five very uncomfortable women sat motionless around a half-finished quilt while Marjorie filled the air with chatter.

"Show them, Gen," Marjorie said as she put a pot of coffee on to boil. "Show them the quilt we made for Meg."

Gen had wondered why Marjorie had sent word for her to bring what they had come to call the Two Stars Quilt with her, but she had obeyed, folding it into a basket slung over her arm. Now, as she exited the kitchen and went to retrieve the basket from where she had set it inside the front door, she heard Marjorie say, "Meg is the missionary's daughter I told you girls about. One of the children Gen's husband protected during the— the unpleasantness."

When Gen returned to the kitchen and held Meg's quilt up, the woman named Lydia let out an admiring "Oh."

Marjorie spoke up. "Isn't it stunning? I've never seen anything like that. Her husband teased her about putting two stars inside the moon. Don't you just love what Genevieve did?"

"How did you ever think to combine gold with the dark blue?" Lydia asked.

Gen touched a piece of gold fabric while she said, "The scraps are from Daniel's work shirts. The gold was in a package a friend sent from New York last fall. She said all the women back there are using it." Gen self-consciously folded the quilt back up.

Harriet demanded, "Let me see it." When Gen handed the bundle over, Harriet turned back a corner and leaned over, peering at the quilt's surface through the glasses perched on the end of her nose. "Who did you say taught you to quilt?"

"First, Mrs. Dane up at Lac Qui Parle Mission." Gen accepted a cup of coffee from Marjorie, but remained standing. When Harriet only harrumphed a response, Gen added nervously, "I'm afraid I wasn't a very good student. I didn't like sewing very much. Then the Danes lost their house in a fire and we had to move to Hope Station. One of the mission teachers—Miss Jane

Williams—and I used to sit out on her porch and quilt in the evenings. I—I pretended to be interested at first, and then one day I realized I really *was* interested. After a while I decided I even enjoyed it."

"Nice stitching," Harriet said, thrusting the quilt back at Gen, who nearly spilled her coffee before managing to wrap her arm around the bundle and return it to the basket.

Gen mumbled her thanks and perched on the edge of Marjorie's chair. Once again, an awkward silence reigned. With nervous glances at one another, Violet, Harriet, and Lydia picked up their needles and began to quilt. Gen noticed for the first time that Violet's odd, stoop-shouldered posture was forced by a melon-sized hump between her shoulders.

Marjorie settled into a chair at the opposite end of the quilt between Lydia and Harriet. "You can see we're just crosshatching. I thought I'd read a bit while you women quilt, if you don't mind." She beamed at them. "I'm so thankful the Lord gave us this break in the weather. And I mean to thoroughly enjoy it . . . heaven only knows when we'll all be able to do this again."

Violet glanced timidly at Harriet and croaked that she too was grateful for Jeb's sleigh bringing the women for a day's quilting and that she, for one, had been so lonely this winter—and wouldn't it be lovely if Marjorie were to read to them for a while?

Harriet opened her mouth to comment but shut it again firmly when Marjorie produced her Bible and, with trembling fingers, began to flip pages. With a distressed glance in Nancy's direction, Gen concentrated on threading her needle. Tying a single knot in the end of the thread, she slipped the needle between the layers of the fabric sandwich, popped the knot beneath the top layer, slipped the needle back on top, and began to rock her needle back and forth, back and forth as she quilted small, even stitches a quarter of an inch from the seam in the quilt.

"I been reading straight through the New Testament all this

winter," Marjorie said quietly. "I'll just start where I left off in Galatians." She began to read about the law and grace, about things Gen didn't understand. But then Marjorie read a passage that made Gen and Nancy duck their heads and quilt furiously.

"For ye are all the children of God by faith in Christ Jesus. For as many of you as have been baptized into Christ have put on Christ. There is neither Jew nor Greek, there is neither bond nor free, there is neither male nor female: for ye are all one in Christ Jesus."

Harriet shifted in her chair. Lydia got up and refilled her coffee cup, rattling the cup and saucer noisily. Violet paused and reached up to rub her neck, grimacing slightly and leaning back as best she could against the hump on her back. The aroma of fresh-baked bread wafted through the room. Still, Marjorie read . . . *"Bear ye one another's burdens and so fulfill the law of Christ. For if a man think himself to be something, when he is nothing, he deceiveth himself . . . As we have opportunity, let us do good unto all men, especially unto them who are of the household of faith . . . And as many as walk according to this rule, peace be on them, and mercy . . . "*

Marjorie finished reading. "Mmmm . . . those rolls smell good!" She got up and opened the oven door. The aroma of cinnamon filled the little room as the icy clouds of suspicion hovering above the quilt began to thaw.

❦

"You women have a nice time together?" Jeb asked later that evening as he settled down beside the kitchen stove to enjoy a piece of dried-apple pie.

Marjorie leaned over and kissed him on the cheek. "Thank you for collecting Harriet and the others, dear. I know it was asking a lot to have you take the team all those miles." She sighed. "I only wish Abner would have let Sally come. Genevieve showed the women her Two Stars quilt. Lydia especially admired it." She settled opposite her husband at the table.

Jeb took another bite of pie and a sip of coffee. He looked up at the underside of the quilt suspended above the kitchen table, studying it for a moment before reaching across the table to pat the back of Marjorie's hand. "Looks like you got a good bit accomplished today, Marjorie." He smiled. "Just what was it you said that broke the ice?" he questioned. "I mean, when I saw Gen and Nancy headed up onto the porch, I was waitin' for Harriet Baxter to come barrelin' right out and order me to take her home."

"Why, I didn't really say anything," Marjorie said. "I just poured coffee and read the Good Book."

Jeb chuckled. *The Good Book.* He leaned back and stretched. His chair creaked dangerously. "Don't suppose you happened upon any of them passages about lovin' your neighbor as yourself?"

"I just read what I read, Jeb," Marjorie said, blushing. "I wouldn't have wanted them to think I was preaching at them."

Jeb went to the window and looked out. "If the weather holds and you want to have another quiltin' you just let me know. I'll be glad to round 'em up any time you want company. Who knows, maybe if we pray on it we can even get Abner to let Mrs. Marsh around that quilt a time or two."

Four

"Forsake the foolish, and live;
and go in the way of understanding."
—Proverbs 9:6

Historians would remember the winter of 1866–67 because of the Fetterman Massacre in the West. Farmers would remember it because of the record-breaking cold and subsequent loss of livestock. Merchants would remember the most dismal season on record thanks to deep snows and below-zero temperatures for days at a time. But Marjorie Grant would always remember the winter of 1866–67 as the winter she proved that just as the pen was mightier than the sword, a quilting bee could prove to be mightier than prejudice. For that was the winter that Mrs. Abner Marsh came to quilting. She accepted a cup of tea from the hand of Genevieve Two Stars and hoped aloud that Nancy's delivery would be an easy one. And, as she said quietly to Marjorie one day, Sally determined to make the best of things with the neighbors—and to find a way to convince Abner to do the same.

And if it were not for an event in the far-off West, things could have been different. The long winter could have provided time to cool Abner Marsh's temper. His wife's exposure to Genevieve and Nancy could have been the beginning of a change in Marsh's heart. The spring arrival of the white children from the East who loved Daniel and Gen Two Stars could have made Abner Marsh and his neighbors willing to just let things be and get on with their lives.

Unfortunately, while Marjorie Grant was introducing the neighbors to her Dakota friends, events in the West conspired against the uneasy peace between the Marshes and the Grants, the Baxters and the Two Starses, the Quinns and the Lawrences. The West was where Colonel Henry Carrington, charged with building three garrisons to protect the Bozeman Trail through the only prime hunting grounds left to the Sioux Nation, listened to a thirty-three-year-old Captain who loved to boast that with eighty men he could cut through the entire Sioux Nation. While cutting through the entire Sioux nation was not feasible that December, Carrington trusted Fetterman to find a way to end a Sioux attack on a woodcutting detail. Oddly enough, last-minute volunteers who begged to go along gave Fetterman the eighty men he had always said he needed to defeat the Sioux.

Just as Fetterman had predicted, the Sioux warriors fled before his eighty—until the eighty entered the trap set for them and encountered the rest of the war party, some two thousand of them, waiting just out of sight. It took less than an hour for Fetterman and his eighty men to die.

It took a few weeks for news of the massacre to arrive in the East where Abner Marsh read and reread the account, barely able to contain the rage he felt when he read the graphic descriptions of what a Sioux warrior did to his enemy to make certain that in the next life his spirit would be both helpless and disfigured. But in the face of his wife's growing friendship with the Indian women on the next section, Abner was forced to contain that rage. In the interest of maintaining peace at home, he concealed his unchanged opinion of Indians. He sent Sally to quilting at the Grants'. He nodded when Sally mentioned how nice Genevieve was. He echoed his wife's hopes that Nancy Lawrence's baby would arrive healthy. He even let Pris and Polly go along to help watch the Grant twins.

When Sally expressed surprise at his open-mindedness, Abner shrugged his shoulders. "Don't see as any harm can come from a quiltin' bee. No call for my girls to be left out." But every time "his girls" were gone to quilting, Abner headed for the barn. He threw open the doors to let in more light and he made his plans.

"Goliath!" he called to a massive black-and-brown dog waiting expectantly at the door of a cage. When his master released him, Goliath raised up and put his paws on Abner's shoulders, offering his master a slobbery kiss. Abner accepted the affection and then, pushing the dog off, he released Pilate and Thor, Goliath's littermates and partners in training.

Wrapping his arm in burlap, Abner held it up above his head for a moment. He made a clicking sound against the roof of his mouth and called for Pilate. Holding his arm down, he baited the dog. A bit too enthusiastic about his job, Pilate slashed the back of Abner's hand. When Abner roared with pain, the dog cowered and sneaked back into its cage.

"Pilate, come," Abner said briskly. When the animal obeyed, Abner reached in his pocket and gave the animal a piece of dried liver and an inordinate amount of praise before letting the animal go back to its cage. The rest of the time while his wife and daughters were at the Grants', Abner trained Thor and Goliath.

When Jeb brought his wife and girls back from quilting,

Abner Marsh smiled and shook Jeb's hand. "Long winter," he said. "Thank your missus for including my girls in the bee."

"I'll do that," Jeb said. "Marjorie's hoping this can be the start of better relations between us all." While Abner didn't say anything, he nodded. Jeb decided he would be content with that. It was at least a beginning.

～

"Can't you look a little more . . . *Indian?*" the photographer asked, pulling his head out of the black drape that surrounded the rear of his camera. He peered doubtfully at Ecetukiya, otherwise known as Big Amos, who sat before a painted backdrop dressed in a suit and tie, a black felt hat poised on his knee.

The Dakota brave contemplated the question, not sure the photographer was serious. When he realized the youth wasn't kidding, Big Amos couldn't resist. Without a hint of a smile he replied, "Sorry. Me leave warbonnet and tomahawk in tepee on reservation. Not want to frighten white women in Great White Father's house."

"Well," the boy asked, smoothing his oiled hair self-consciously. "Didn't you bring *anything* Indian with you to Washington? Don't you at least have some beads or a bear-claw necklace or something?"

With an amused glance towards the back wall of the studio where Elliot Leighton and young Aaron Dane were waiting, Big Amos shook his head, clearly enjoying the game. He winked at Aaron before drawling, "Me no great hunter. Me afraid of bears."

The photographer sighed. "All right, then." He directed Big Amos to shift his position. "We'll do a profile. That looks more . . . noble." He disappeared back beneath the black drape. His bank of lights flashed and he was finished. "Bring him back at the end of the week," he said to Elliot. "I can have this ready then." He lowered his voice and stepped closer. "Are you certain he doesn't have any of his native dress? We could discuss an interesting marketing opportunity if he could pose again. As the western tribes are subdued, I predict the market for this kind of thing," he said, holding out a small print of a Teton warrior in full battle regalia, "will enjoy quite a surge in demand."

Elliot Leighton stood up abruptly. He straightened his shoulders and assumed what his wife and Aaron had come to recognize as his "marching orders" pose. "Young man," he said, putting his hand on the photographer's shoulder, "Mr. Dane will call for the photograph tomorrow afternoon." Applying pressure to the shoulder he added, "And before you photograph any more of the Dakota delegation, I would remind you, sir, that they are *men*. Not *commodities* to be marketed." Gently, Elliot pushed the photograph away.

When Big Amos and his white friends had exited the studio into the light of day, Elliot sighed. The streets of Washington were a sea of mud. It caked the men's boots, splattered their clothing, and, on occasion, sucked a shoe right off some unsuspecting pedestrian's foot.

Aaron spoke up. "I promised Aunt Jane I'd watch Meg and Hope for her while she goes to some tea with the senators' wives. Guess I'd better be getting back to the hotel." He held out his hand to Big Amos and, after a firm handshake, headed off up the street towards the hotel.

Elliot stood on the street corner, eyeing the abandoned stump of a proposed Washington Monument rising next to the Potomac River marshes not far away. "What haven't you seen, my friend? What would you like to do?"

"Get on the train and go home," was the reply. "Help Two Stars and Robert plow up a new field. Take Rosalie to see Nancy's new baby."

Elliot looked up at his friend, mindful of the curious glances of passersby. Although an entire delegation of Dakota had been in Washington since February, people still stared at the white-haired officer and the towering Dakota Indian wherever they went. Big Amos and his friends had been taken to every possible place of interest from the Ford Theatre to the Smithsonian. They had even heard the renowned former slave Frederick Douglass speak. Big Amos had commented to Elliot that he hoped the Great White Father would be kinder to his Dakota children than his friends were to the thousands of freed slaves roaming the streets of the nation's capital.

Elliot was indignant after the group was taken to the navy yard, then seated in a makeshift bandstand at the arsenal and treated to a display of military arms in action. He said as much to his former classmate, Senator Avery Lance. "You are preaching to the wrong audience, Avery. These men already know they have no power. The agent at Crow Creek reported last winter they were living on bark with an occasional meal from a horse or cow dead of starvation or disease. I'd say their humiliation is complete. The warriors you want to impress with the power of the United States military are at this moment wandering west of the Missouri. A few of them likely participated in the Fetterman debacle. Your efforts are wasted on Big Amos and the rest of the peace delegation. They only want the government's promise that they will be allowed to stay in Nebraska Territory where they can actually grow crops and feed their families. You needn't make a point about the great American military. Most of these men don't even own working rifles." Elliot snorted. "The truth is, half of them are more afraid of the hostile Sioux than you are. Big Amos has already decided he's not going back to the reservation because it's too close to the hostiles. He wants to join my friends in Minnesota."

The Senator was unimpressed. "I know *these* men aren't dangerous. But you can't know that some of these very men will, next year, while they are quietly living on their government-granted farms, be visited by old friends. It's been rumored that Sitting Bull himself was at Crow Creek three winters ago."

"We'd better hope that rumor was wrong," Elliot muttered.

"Why?"

"Because," Aaron had interjected, "if a man of Sitting Bull's reputation saw what's been done to the Santees, he and his warriors would never trust a white man again."

Elliot nodded his head. "And the battle will rage long and hard."

"The battle may rage a bit longer than we had hoped. But we will win it," the senator said firmly. "And these Dakota men will be sure to testify of that to anyone who cares to ask what they saw in Washington."

That had been weeks ago. Since then, the Dakota had been wined and dined and impressed but had accomplished nothing for their people. They wanted a permanent home. They got fried oysters, steak and onions, and *pâté de foie gras* in such copious amounts they frequently became ill. They wanted farming tools and oxen. They got a view of guns and military power they never intended to challenge. They wanted funds to recover some of the thousands of dollars lost when their Minnesota lands were taken. They got an indelible impression that the Great White Father and his friends were completely indifferent to the fate of the Dakota.

Even their missionary, Dr. Stephen Riggs, was discouraged. He confided to Elliot late one night that he hated lobbying the ignorant and powerful on behalf of what he considered to be the most intelligent and best-educated Indians of the West. "Just when our labors of the last twenty-five years are bearing fruit, all of Congress seems united in a vast conspiracy of deliberate ignorance," Riggs said. He sighed.

"We won't give up," Elliot said firmly. "My family needs to get home to New York, but I won't leave until we have a distinct promise of the new reservation on the Niobrara. And Senator

Lance has promised the farms in Minnesota for the scouts. We have made some progress."

"The promise of land and the actual ability to live on it are not the same things, I fear," Dr. Riggs replied sadly. "I hope you can secure a home for Daniel and Genevieve and the Lawrences." He shook his head. "Heaven knows I've been powerless to do it."

He left Washington half-sick, having secured nothing for the Dakota beyond vague promises of help at some indeterminate point in the future.

Elliot sent Jane and the younger children home, allowing Aaron to stay only after the boy presented a convincing argument that it might benefit the Indians someday if he had experience in Washington. But in spite of Elliot's connections and Aaron's innocent appeals, they made little progress on behalf of their friends. With post war reconstruction ongoing in the South, and Red Cloud causing trouble in the West, Congress had little money and almost no interest in helping a few defeated Dakota Indians in Nebraska and Minnesota.

Elliot put his hand on Big Amos's shoulder. "I, too, wish we could head west, my friend. Mrs. Leighton and I promised Daniel and Genevieve we would be out to visit this spring. The children are counting on it." He sighed. "And all I can seem to accomplish here are more delays and fruitless meetings."

The two men ambled off toward 14th and Pennsylvania streets. When the Willard Hotel came into view, Elliot asked Big Amos, "Are you hungry? We could get some lunch."

Big Amos forced a smile. "What I would really like at this moment is a chance to rip open a fresh kill and—" he stopped abruptly. Looking down at Elliot, whose blue-gray eyes were filled with empathy, Big Amos smiled. "But I will settle for beef steak instead of buffalo liver. And a cherry pie." He turned to go inside. Elliot followed, smiling to himself at the memory of the first time

Big Amos had tasted pie. Since that moment, whenever pie was on a menu, Big Amos ordered—and ate—pie. Usually an entire pie. Men like Avery Lance had meant to impress the Dakota with military displays. What Big Amos would remember most about Washington was the taste of the Willard Hotel's cherry pie.

❧

"I thought it might help," Nancy said, blushing furiously as she held the oddly shaped cushion between Violet and the hard-backed chair. Violet leaned back stiffly.

"Wait," Nancy said. "Lean forward." She shifted the cushion. "Now try."

Violet leaned back, surprised at how comfortable Nancy's creation made the chair. Reaching behind her, she examined the cushion to see how Nancy had adjusted the thickness of the filling to allow for Violet's crooked spine, creating channels in the fabric and then varying the amount of stuffing in each channel. There was just a slight cushion in the center and then successively more and more until, at the outer rim, the cushion was nearly as fat as a down bed pillow. Violet leaned back with a sigh. "It's—it's wonderful," she whispered, squeezing Nancy's hand. "Thank you."

Violet's sister Lydia looked up at Nancy. "No one's ever done anything so nice for my sister, Nancy. God bless you."

Nancy shrugged. "It's only chicken feathers." She lifted her eyes to where Marjorie was standing at the stove frying chicken. "Marjorie says if we could find someone with geese, the down would be even softer."

"I'm hoping to get some geese brought in in the spring," Sally Marsh offered. "If the wolves don't get 'em before they're growed, you can have all the down you want."

❧

"Oh, hush, Earl," Harriet Baxter snapped impatiently. "I don't want to hear another word of that 'Sioux Uprising' nonsense." She snapped her dish towel for emphasis.

From where he sat smoking his pipe beside the fireplace, Earl Baxter shot his wife of nearly thirty years a look of surprise.

"I mean it," Harriet said, drying out her mixing bowl. "That trouble was years ago. Long before we came to Minnesota. And that Fetterman thing happened halfway across the continent from us. It's got nothing to do with us, and I won't have you stirring up more trouble for everyone just because Abner Marsh has a bee in his bonnet about a stolen horse that came home the same day it was stolen. That man's got a temper that's going to get him in trouble someday. There's no reason for you to be part of it."

"Now, listen here, Harriet—" Earl made the mistake of pausing to draw through the pipe.

"—No, *you* listen, Earl Baxter. You're all riled up and the fact is you don't know beans about Daniel Two Stars or Robert Lawrence. I don't know 'em either, but I know their wives and I can tell you there's no two nicer women in the county."

Earl stopped rocking. He leaned forward. "And just how would you know that?"

Harriet felt the blush coming up the back of her neck, and so she turned away so Earl wouldn't see. She hadn't intended for Earl to know Marjorie Grant's quilting bees included the Indians. Not yet. But, Harriet thought, what was done was done. Harriet always recovered quickly. So now, she turned to face her husband, red-faced and defensive. "They been comin' to Marjorie's for quilting."

Earl snorted and sat back.

Harriet put her hands on her ample hips and stalked towards her husband. "Marjorie just up and invited 'em. What was I supposed to do? Make Jeb hitch up the sleigh and bring me back home?" She smoothed her graying hair nervously and walked back to the sink to retrieve the towel. While she dried dishes, she talked. "I didn't like it at first. None of us wanted 'em. But they're good quilters, and it just made sense to get our work done faster." Harriet whirled around, blustering defensively. "You got no idea what it takes to make enough bedding to keep a family warm, Earl Baxter. If you won't get me a sewing machine like Jeb got his wife—"

"Now, Harriet, I told you," Earl said, raising his hands in the air, "I just can't justify spending nearly twenty dollars on a machine that does little more than help a woman with her house-keeping." The minute he said the words, Earl Baxter knew he was in trouble. He saw the tears gathering in Harriet's eyes and knew he had stepped over her line of tolerance. Knowing he was in for it, anyway, he decided to try to avert disaster and get back on the topic of Indians. "But if I would have known going to a *quiltin' bee* would turn my wife into a gol-durned *Injun lover*, I'd have ordered one right up!"

If he expected a fight, Earl Baxter was disappointed. Harriet glared at him for a moment and then she turned away and returned to drying her dishes. While Earl sat beside the fireplace, she worked. When she finished with the dishes, she disappeared into the bedroom. She emerged with a threadbare blanket and one pillow, which she tossed at her husband. "Genevieve Two Stars and Nancy Lawrence are my friends, Mr. Baxter. And if you do anything to harm them or their husbands, you will be sleeping alone for a very, very long time." At the doorway to the bedroom she paused. "And the next time you want breakfast, or dinner, or supper, or a shirt mended, or a warm bed, or a clean house, or fried chicken, or greens, or gooseberry pie, or the garden weeded, or a new pair of pants—" she paused and bit her lip to keep from bursting into tears. "I been a good wife to you, Earl Baxter. I worked side by side with you for nearly thirty years. Now I guess I know exactly what all that was worth. Maybe you should've hired someone to do what I done for free. Then you wouldn't have some fool woman thinking she earned the right to a little easing of her burden."

After a nearly sleepless night stretched out on the kitchen table, Earl Baxter rose early and saddled his old mare and headed for New Ulm. On the way, he rode by Abner Marsh's place where he found Abner in the barn feeding his three dogs. With a deep breath and a gulp, he told Marsh he didn't want to stir up any more trouble with the neighbors and he guessed Jeb Grant had a right to hire whoever he wanted to work his place. And then Earl rode on into New Ulm to Ludlow's Variety Store, searched a catalog, and paid the ridiculous sum of twenty-three dollars for a sewing machine to be delivered as a surprise from her beloved husband to Mrs. Harriet Baxter.

≈

"I don't *care* what Abner Marsh thinks, Thomas." Lydia Quinn raised up on her right elbow and looked across the bed at where her husband lay staring up at the ceiling. "I don't want you involved in any trouble." She swallowed hard and lay back down. "There's something I haven't told you." She paused, drew a deep breath, and plunged ahead. "Marjorie Grant invited those Indian women to quilting a few weeks ago. At first I didn't want to say anything because—well, Violet gets so little chance to socialize, what with her feeling so conscious about her hump and all. I just didn't want to disappoint her and she seems to enjoy Marjorie's boys so." When her husband did not speak, Lydia dared a sideways glance. "Now, Thomas, I know what you're thinking and I'm sorry. But I just couldn't tell Violet we couldn't go back. I didn't think it would do any harm. We never saw their husbands at all. It was just the women. At first we hardly even talked."

Thomas snorted, but said nothing.

"It's true. We just weren't comfortable. But even Harriet Baxter stayed. And Marjorie would read the Scriptures." Lydia stopped again, trying to collect her thoughts. "I don't know how to tell you, Thomas. But something just happened over that quilt. I don't expect you to understand what it means to a woman here on the frontier to have friendship—to work together to make something beautiful. Men don't seem to need that kind of thing. But women do, and it just feeds our souls to work together like that." Lydia paused. "Don't you laugh at me, Thomas."

"I'm not laughing, Lydia," Thomas said gently. "I know you and Violet have been lonely. Especially this winter, being cooped up in the cabin so much." He cleared his throat. "And I know how hard life has been for Violet. I don't say much, but I'm not as thickheaded as I act sometimes."

"Well, then, Thomas," Lydia said, blurting the rest of it out. "Then I guess I can just go ahead and tell you that I kind of like Genevieve and Nancy. Yesterday at quiltin' Nancy had a special cushion she made for Violet's back, and you should have seen the look on Vi's face when she leaned back against that chair and it—it—didn't *hurt* her. All I could think was I should'a done something like that years ago. And here these women who were nothing but *savages* . . ." Much to her embarrassment, Lydia began to cry. She blinked rapidly and tried to wipe the tears away, but the dam was burst and she couldn't hold the tears back.

"Why, Lyddi," Thomas whispered. "Don't cry, Lyddi . . . it's all right." He pulled her to him. "I won't do anything to interfere. Not if it means that much to you. Please, Lyddi, please . . ."

Lydia looked up at her husband. "You—you haven't called me Lyddi in a long time, Thomas."

He kissed her forehead. "I haven't made you cry in a long time."

She smiled shyly. "I—I—like it when you call me Lyddi." She kissed his cheek.

She kissed the place just next to his mouth where his beard didn't quite fill in. And somewhere in the next few moments Thomas Quinn realized that he really didn't care if four harmless Dakota Indians lived in his county in Minnesota. Not one bit.

Five

"Trust in the LORD with all thine heart; and lean
not unto thine own understanding. In all thy ways
acknowledge him, and he shall direct thy paths."

—PROVERBS 3:5–6

"BUT *WHY* DO WE HAVE TO GO?" HOPE PROTESTED, JUMPING
onto the edge of Meg's bed and bouncing up and down angrily.

In her most practiced grown-up-be-patient-with-the-children
voice, from where she sat at her writing desk, Meg answered "We
don't *have* to go." She arranged several preserved white roses on a
plain sheet of paper. Some she lay in profile, their leaves intact.
Two she snipped as close to the head of the blossom as possible
and opened them full out. "We *want* to go," she said, surveying
the rose-filled shadowbox she was making for Genevieve Two
Stars. "Gen has been our friend since Aaron and I were little. And
she was our *mother* for nearly two years. We love her."

Meg inhaled the faint aroma still clinging to the roses. Finally satisfied with her creation, she laid aside the glass top and went to sit down beside Hope. She caressed the child's long blonde hair. "Don't you remember her at all, Hope—not even a little? She's only been gone a little more than a year. She taught you to walk. Your first word was when you called her *Ma*."

Hope sighed. Closing her eyes, she tilted her face towards the ceiling, thinking. "I remember blue eyes," she said slowly, "and something—something ugly." Hope brushed her hands across both forearms and then hugged them to herself.

"Do you remember the story of how Genevieve got those scars on her arms?" Meg questioned, patting Hope's shoulder.

"You told me a million times," Hope said impatiently. "It was when you were with the bad Indians and they made you walk through the brambles and she put her arms like this," Hope slapped her arms to her sides, "and covered you up so you wouldn't get hurt. And she got all cut by the stickers." She jumped down off the bed and peered at the shadowbox on Meg's dresser. "But I *still* don't want to go to Minnesota."

"Well," Meg said, standing up, "we're going as soon as Uncle Elliot and Aaron get back from Washington." She frowned and pressed her palm against her forehead, wishing the headache that had been plaguing her all day would subside. "It'll be fun. An adventure." She smiled at Hope. "Gen is going to be so surprised to hear how well you talk. I guess Aunt Jane was right. Being the baby in a house full of grown-ups makes a difference."

"I'm not a baby!" Hope protested. "I'm all growed up."

"You're only four years old," Meg said quickly. "Just because you can talk so well doesn't mean you aren't still my baby sister."

"I'm not a baby!" Hope hollered.

Meg winced. "Don't yell, Hope. You make my head hurt even worse. Only babies cry when they don't get their way."

"Amanda don't want us to go either," Hope said. "She cried about it. And she's all growed up."

Ignoring Hope's reference to Amanda Whitrock, Meg said, "We're going to camp. In a tent. And Two Stars will take us fishing. Maybe you'll catch your own dinner!"

Hope made a face. "I don't like fishing. You have to touch worms to fish." She shuddered. "I wanna stay with Gran-ma."

"Grandmother Leighton is too old to take care of a nearly-five-year-old troublemaker," Meg teased, tousling Hope's blonde hair. "Now go find Bess so she'll be right here when we pack tomorrow."

"You can't pack Bess. She won't be able to breathe!" Hope retorted.

"She's a doll, Hope. She doesn't need to breathe." Meg pressed her palm against her forehead again.

"I'm carrying her."

"You won't want to carry her all the way to Minnesota."

"Then I'll put her in the bag when she needs to sleep," Hope insisted. "But until then, I'll carry her."

"Oh, all right," Meg blustered. "Have it your way. But don't be asking me to hold your doll when you don't want to be bothered. And don't be thinking Aunt Jane will do it for you, either."

"Will we see lots of Indians?" Hope wanted to know. "Amanda says Indians aren't nice. She says—"

"Amanda Whitrock doesn't know the first thing about Indians," Meg snapped. "When did she say that, anyway?"

"When Aaron said he wanted to be a soldier and go West and help the Indians."

Meg sat down on the edge of her bed. "Were you eavesdropping on Amanda and Aaron?"

Hope frowned and shook her head. "I was in the kitchen and Betsy gave me some cocoa and then we heard Amanda and Aaron arguing on the back porch."

"You shouldn't repeat what others say when they don't know you are listening."

"I won't tell anyone else," Hope murmured. "But Amanda said—"

"You let Aaron worry about Amanda Whitrock and her notions about the West," Meg said firmly, "and you worry about finding Bess."

Hope started for the door, pausing just outside in the hallway. "She's on the swing in the garden."

"Then go get her," Meg said. She lay down on her back and closed her eyes.

"What's the matter, Meg?" Hope hesitated at the doorway.

"Nothing. I'm just going to lie here a minute while you get Bess and see if my headache won't go away."

When Hope didn't come right back inside, Meg got up and went downstairs. She made some tea to settle her stomach and then went outside, where Hope sat in the garden swing, cradling Bess. When Meg approached, Hope looked up and demanded the rose story again. Meg sat down beside her. "I don't feel like telling a story right now, Hope. How about you tell me the rose story?"

Hope hopped down and went to the corner of the garden. Stepping carefully over the rock border, she smoothed her pink calico dress and took on the role of instructor and center of attention. She gestured dramatically towards the smallest rose bush in the L-shaped flowerbed. "This one's for your Mama named Ellen, the one I didn't know. It's red 'cause that was her favorite. I got her name in the middle and that's why I'm Hope *Ellen*." She pointed to another bush with red blossoms. "And this one is for Papa Simon Dane. And all the pink ones are for you an' me and Aaron," Hope said, twirling around as she spoke.

"That's right," Meg said. She took a deep breath, wishing her stomach would settle. "Do you remember helping us put the rocks around the edge?"

"I was too little," Hope protested, shaking her head.

Meg agreed. "You could hardly talk at all. And you carried off more rocks than you put in place." She smiled weakly. "When we see Gen, you'll be able to tell her how big her white rosebush is, and how every time we see it we think of her."

"Why don't we have a rosebush for Daniel?" Hope asked abruptly.

"Because we made this rose garden to remember our family," Meg explained for the hundredth time. "And when we planted the bushes we thought our friend Daniel was dead."

"He's the one that founded me," Hope said as she fingered a pink rose.

"He did," Meg replied.

"Tell me," Hope said.

"I'll tell you when we're on the train," Meg said. She stood up abruptly. "I'm going to go lie down." Suddenly, she covered her mouth with her hand and ran for the house.

❧

Elliot Leighton and Aaron Dane stood, carpetbags in hand, staring in disbelief at the sign on Leighton Hall's front door.

QUARANTINE. MEASLES.

"*Measles?!*" Aaron could barely pronounce the dreaded word. He knew all about measles. The disease had struck an Indian village near the mission when he was a little boy. He could still hear the women keening their losses as tepee after tepee were emptied of their dead.

Before Elliot could say anything, Jane appeared at the parlor window. She opened the window, but when Elliot stepped forward she waved him away. "Stay back, dear. We can't take any chances." She took a deep breath. "It's Meg. Only Meg for now, thank God. But we aren't allowed out of the house. Dr. Voss's assistant has been delivering food every day." Jane laughed sadly. "I thought cabin fever was only something we experienced in the West when the snow piled up." She forced a smile. "But it appears even mansions can breed cases of cabin fever. We're rather at one another from time to time." She passed a trembling hand over her forehead and blinked back tears.

"What about Meg?"

"Oh, I don't know," Jane said miserably. "Her fever has come down a bit and Dr. Voss says that's a hopeful sign, but—" her voice cracked, "she's very ill. We just don't know."

"We?" Elliot asked. "Who exactly is we?"

"Hope, Betsy, Mother Leighton, and I. That's all. Cook was on holiday when Meg got sick."

"So you and Betsy are caring for the entire household as well as nursing Meg around the clock?" Elliot frowned.

"Oh, we're all right," Jane protested. When she looked at Elliot, her eyes filled with tears. "I'm so glad you're home." She wiped the tears away and sighed. "You'll have to put up at the hotel. We can't let you in. I seem to have some natural immunity to measles. Dr. Voss was quite amazed when I told him I'd nursed many patients back in my mission days." She forced another smile. "So you see you don't have to worry over me. And I really do think the worst is over. If we can just keep Mother Leighton and Betsy and Hope from catching it—" Jane sighed and closed her eyes. "I'm making them stay in their rooms. Hope wanders from one to the other. They all hate me." She changed the subject. "You'll have to wire Daniel and Gen. We can't possibly go now." Her voice wavered a little. "And I don't quite know what to tell them about Meg."

Hope appeared at an upstairs window. When Betsy opened the window, the child called down to her uncle, demanding to go with him. Jane told her she must stay inside and insisted that she could not go to Uncle Elliot or Aaron. Hope began to wail.

"I'm sorry, Captain Leighton," Betsy said as she pulled Hope away from the window and pulled down the sash.

"I have to go, too" Jane said wearily. "I just wanted to—" she held in a sob, "I had to see you."

"We'll be back as soon as we've made arrangements," Elliot said.

As the men made their way through the village, they noticed more quarantine signs in windows. At the hotel, they were questioned so vigorously about their health that Elliot stormed away.

"Where are we going?" Aaron asked.

"We are going home to Leighton Hall where we belong," Elliot said firmly. "We'll drag the old tent out of the carriage house and you can stay there. I'm going to help Jane. I don't care what the doctor says."

"But, Uncle Elliot, you could—"

"I cannot," Elliot said. He pressed his lips into a fine line. "The disease hasn't been created yet that can fell an old soldier like me. I've been exposed to everything there is, including a cannonball. And all that managed to do was blow my hand off. I'm too stubborn to let measles get me. And I'm not going to let my wife spend another day alone in that house."

"Then I want to help, too," Aaron said.

"And you shall," Elliot said. "We'll put the tent up in the garden before I go in. You can live there."

And so he did. Aaron camped in the garden. He ran to the apothecary, ran for the doctor, and did the marketing. At the doctor's behest he set up a huge iron pot near the carriage house, daily washing linen with lye soap and then dipping everything into boiling water before hanging it out to dry. He waved at Hope when she appeared at the window and did everything possible to make her laugh, including dancing and strutting like a rooster. Every morning he put a fresh white rose beside the back door to be taken up to Meg's room, and on the day when Meg herself finally appeared at the window, Aaron shouted for joy.

Measles had finally left Leighton Hall. It took no one's life and spared everyone but Meg. But for Meg, life would never be the same, for when measles left Leighton Hall, it took Margaret Marie Dane's sight with it.

❦

"I'll write," Aaron whispered, touching Amanda's arm. "Will you—will you answer?" They were seated together on the swing in Leighton Hall's garden, so close to one another Aaron could just catch the faint aroma of lavender that seemed to follow Amanda Whitrock everywhere she went.

Amanda snatched her arm away and studied the rose garden a few feet away. "I don't imagine they will have mail delivery off in *Indian* territory," she sulked.

"Why, of course they do, Amanda," Aaron said, eager to explain. "Even when I was a little boy we got regular mail. They brought it up from Fort Ridgely every week. Now there's a railroad all the way to St. Anthony and beyond. We get Gen's letters the same month she writes them. Sometimes within just a week or so." He dared to touch the back of Amanda's hand, thrilling at the softness of her skin. "Please say you'll answer me. Please."

After a prolonged sigh, Amanda turned her clear-blue eyes upon him, studying him for a moment before looking to one side. She bit her lower lip to dramatize how very hard it was for her to decide before grimacing slightly and shrugging. "All right. I guess I'll answer. But don't think I'm not still angry about you missing my birthday party!

The notion that Amanda Whitrock, the prettiest girl in school, had set her attentions upon him thrilled Aaron right down to the thin leather soles of his best shoes. He studied the small, white hand, positioned tantalizingly atop the folds of her royal blue silk skirt. With his heart pounding, he reached out quickly, covered that hand with his own and then gave a little squeeze before withdrawing and jumping to his feet. "Let's—let's go back inside," he said quickly, hoping Amanda could not see the blush on his cheeks.

To Aaron's dismay, because he blushed even more furiously when it happened, Amanda slipped her hand into his. He led her around the side of the house, up the wide stairs leading to the veranda at Leighton Hall.

"Meg will be so excited to have company," Aaron said. "The other girls seem to be avoiding her since—well, you know. It's been hard on her, knowing she can't go with me to see Daniel and Genevieve. But I promised her that next year when her strength is back and she's learned how to manage better, I'll take her West." He shrugged. "We're not going to let a little thing like this ruin her life. We aren't."

Amanda suddenly withdrew her hand. "I'll visit Meg soon, Aaron. Honestly I will. But right now I must be getting home."

He could read the message in her brilliant blue eyes, and with a sudden burst of maturity, decided against being ruled by them. To Amanda's dismay, Aaron did not beg her not to go. Instead, he nodded and guided her down the front path to the gate and across the street to her own front door. Before they parted, he asked, "You'll come to the station to see me off tomorrow?"

Amanda pouted, but not for too long. "Of course I will." And then, just to put him in his place and to remind him, she added, "I'm sure Stephen Bannister will want to come, too. He can bring me."

Stephen Bannister. Inwardly Aaron blanched. Stephen Bannister was all the things Aaron was not. Elegant and wealthy, with parents who doted on him and bought him the finest of everything, from a fine pair of matched standardbreds to pull his carriage to the best in tailored suits and leather boots. And, unlike Aaron, Stephen Bannister was going nowhere for this summer. He would be right here in New York, calling on Amanda at every opportunity. *Why*, Aaron thought, *Stephen will probably be sitting next to Amanda in the family pew at church by the third Sunday I'm gone.*

All of this and more flashed through Aaron's mind as he stood looking down at Amanda. But something else took precedence, and that something was an intangible yearning Aaron felt every time he thought about the West. It was an indiscernible tug, as if he could still hear warriors' chants around the campfires, still see the faces of the native children, still hear the cries of hopelessness as squaws mourned their dead. That something, Aunt Jane had often told Aaron, was a *call*. And, Aunt Jane had said, he had best answer it or be haunted for the rest of his life by a sense of failure.

He was not certain if Aunt Jane was right. But one thing was certain, and that was that he must go West now, this year, and give God the opportunity to speak to him more distinctly about what he, Aaron Riggs Dane, was supposed to do with his life. He had promised God to make himself available, and that promise stood apart from and above everything else in his young life— including, *please God*, Miss Amanda Whitrock.

"If she's the one for you," Uncle Elliot had said once, "then she will share your dream. And if she cannot share your dream, then trust me, son, you don't want her." Uncle Elliot had gone on to say that Amanda was young and spoiled, and that in time Aaron would see what she was made of and know. In the meantime, he had said, Aaron should be about his duty.

Duty. Aaron was not certain what all his duty included, but he was certain that part of it was to journey West to visit Genevieve and Daniel Two Stars, who had risked their lives more than once to save his. Something in Gen's letters of late had made Aaron uneasy. They might be leaving Minnesota, she said . . . but they still longed to see the children. Oh, how he hated being included in that oft-spoken phrase. *The Children.* Within him, Aaron knew he had not been a child for a very long time. He had ceased being a child the night Daniel Two Stars appeared just in time to save Genevieve from being attacked by his drunken friend Otter. No one knew Aaron understood exactly what had happened that night—what had nearly happened to Gen—but he did. And understanding what could have happened, and knowing he was absolutely powerless to do anything about it, had caused Aaron Dane to grow up in a matter of minutes.

Now, as he stood looking down into the innocent blue eyes that betrayed the inner workings of Miss Amanda Whitrock, hearing her taunt him with the name Stephen Bannister, Aaron rediscovered his maturity. "Well then," he said, "that'll be great. I was worried we might not have room for you in Grandmother Leighton's old carriage. Meg wants to go, but she'll have to lie down on one of the seats. She isn't strong enough to sit up for that long yet. If Stephen can bring you, that's great." He stepped away from Amanda and tipped his hat. "I'll see you tomorrow."

Aaron was not certain, but he thought he felt two brilliant blue eyes boring holes into the back of his best jacket as he walked back across the street, through the massive ornamental iron gate, up the path, and into Leighton Hall. When he closed the door behind him, he peeked through the lace panel just in time to see Amanda spin around and flounce up to her own front door. With a contented smile, Aaron climbed the winding staircase to the second floor where he soon had Meg howling with laughter as he described an imaginary encounter between Stephen Bannister and a Dakota Indian.

❧

"Look at that," Elliot Leighton said, nudging Jane and nodding to where Amanda and Aaron stood on the platform saying their good-byes before Aaron headed west. "Already an expert at feminine wiles."

Amanda stood looking up at Aaron with an expression of devotion . . . but all the while her hand was on Stephen Bannister's arm. She nodded her head and gave Aaron a brilliant smile. She even gave Aaron her hand long enough for him to squeeze it. But the minute he let go she clung to Stephen and let herself be led away.

Aaron watched while Stephen helped Amanda into his carriage. He was rewarded when Amanda blew a kiss. But she did not protest when Stephen whipped his magnificent team of matched bays into a prancing, dancing display of elegant gaits as they pulled away. Remembering the team of oxen that had pulled his wagon at Lac Qui Parle Mission, Aaron slouched and headed back to where the Leighton's carriage waited.

"I'll miss you, sis," Aaron said, gently kissing Meg on the cheek.

"You won't forget to give Gen my gift," Meg prodded.

"It's right here in my carpetbag where I can keep it safe," Aaron said gently. He reached for Meg's hand and poised his bag on the edge of the carriage. "There. Feel that bump? That's it."

Meg smiled bravely. "Tell them—"

"Yes," Aaron interrupted. "I'll tell them you'll be coming next summer." He lowered his voice. "And you see that you work hard for your tutor so you are ready."

Meg ducked her head and swallowed hard. "I will. I promise."

The train whistle blew and she lifted her head. "I guess that means you'd better go."

Aaron kissed her cheek. "I'll write."

"I'll answer," Meg said. "Betsy promised she would help."

After a flurry of hugs from Hope and Jane, Aaron mounted the steps to the train. Elliot followed. He sat down beside the boy and pounded his knee. "Cheer up," he said, "Meg's going to be fine. She's weak, but she still has the same spirit. She'll adapt. And you'll be back long before anything serious can happen between those two." He nodded towards the carriage bearing Amanda Whitrock towards Stephen Bannister's home where, she had told Aaron, she would be dining that evening to take her mind off Aaron's departure.

Aaron looked out the window. "You think so?" he said hopefully.

"Of course," Elliot said. "Miss Whitrock will do the same thing with Stephen she'd be doing with you."

"What's that?"

"She'll dangle every letter you write under his nose and probably squeeze out a real tear or two just to convince him how she really feels about you. And he'll spend the summer tied up in knots. Just like you." He slapped Aaron on the back. After a moment of silence, he grew serious. "Tell Daniel and Robert I'm sorry I haven't been able to accomplish more for them. But I won't stop trying. I've an appointment with Senator Lance in two weeks, and I'm going to do everything I can to get assigned to the commission visiting Niobrara this summer."

Aaron nodded. The conductor shouted his final warning and Elliot stood up to go. "Jane and I are very proud of you, Aaron, as would your father be. Write those letters you promised. Be yourself. And let the good Lord handle Miss Whitrock's heart." He squeezed the boy's shoulder and was gone.

Uncle Elliot was right, Aaron knew. As the trained pulled out of the station, he determined to follow his uncle's advice. He would write faithfully. He would pray for Amanda. But most of all, he would get about doing his duty, because only if he was doing God's will would he ever be truly happy. He had learned that from his father and he believed it with all his heart.

Pulling his hat down over his eyes, Aaron sighed. *The problem was*, he thought, *believing something didn't always make it easy to live it.*

"He that hideth hatred with lying lips,
and he that uttereth a slander, is a fool."
—PROVERBS 10:18

ON A SUNNY MORNING IN MARCH, WHEN SNOWMELT
was swelling the streams and converting roads to seas of mud,
Daniel Two Stars sat outside the lean-to that served as a barn
mending harness. Looking up the road towards the Grants'
house, he could see Gen and Nancy hurrying home.

"Robert," Daniel called to his friend, who was carving a new
handle for a broken plow. When Robert looked up, Daniel nodded towards the women. At sight of his wife in such a hurry,
Robert dropped the piece of wood and hurried towards her.

"It is time?" he asked, taking Nancy's arm.

Breathless with the effort of walking the quarter-mile from

the Grants', Nancy shook her head. "No, no—still too early—" she giggled. "Relax, husband. Everything is fine. Everything is wonderful! Mrs. Marsh—was here—yesterday. She said she has been admiring the railing you made around the Grants' porch all winter." Nancy gasped and hiccuped, finally shaking her head and motioning to Gen. "You tell them."

"Mrs. Marsh was admiring the porch railing you made." Gen's eyes glowed with enthusiasm. "And Marjorie began to tell her what a good carpenter you are. She showed her all the other things you made for the house, Robert. The shutters, and those pretty decorations high up on the—" she held her hands over her head, fingertips touching, searching for the word.

"On the gables?" Robert asked.

"Yes," Gen nodded, "those fancy carvings on the gables. Mrs. Marsh loves them. And she said she's sending her husband to talk to you, to see if you would do the same thing for them. For their new house." She laughed. "Marjorie was wonderful. She hesitated, said she didn't know if Jeb could spare you to do the work. And Mrs. Marsh just kept insisting until she said you could charge whatever you wanted."

"Doesn't Mrs. Marsh know I'm one of the Indians her husband thinks is going to murder his family in their sleep?" Robert said doubtfully.

"She just wants her house to be as pretty as the Grants'," Nancy giggled. "After she left, Marjorie asked me to make you promise you won't make anything quite so fancy for the Marshes as you did for her."

Daniel patted Robert on the shoulder. "Beware, brother. Being trapped between two women is not a good place for a man to be."

"And what would you know about *that*?" Gen teased.

Daniel grinned at her and winked. "I can only imagine, little wife."

"You're supposed to wait until Saturday and then drive to the Marshes'. I think she needs that long to convince her husband." Gen added, "And Marjorie said to tell you Jeb would go along to make certain you get paid what the work is worth. In *cash*." Chattering happily, the two women headed inside to begin supper. After they had left, Daniel and Robert unhitched Robert's team and led them to the corral the two families shared. While he was pumping fresh water for the team, Daniel said hopefully, "Maybe things are changing."

Robert shrugged. "I've lived long enough to know there is no time limit on hatred in the hearts of men. So have you. And men with such a deep hatred as Abner Marsh are not easily won. What happened back in '62 changed our lives forever. We did nothing wrong, but we will suffer alongside those who did."

Daniel sighed. "I know I must trust God, but sometimes I do not understand what He is doing."

"We have good homes and good wives," Robert said. "God kept us safe through a terrible winter. Genevieve and Nancy have found friendship with the women. For these things and more, we can give thanks." He smiled. "I have heard Jeb speak of the Marshes and their house. It is very large. I will need help with this work. Perhaps we will both be able to afford good horses by harvest."

❧

Nothing in his recent past could have equaled the horror Daniel Two Stars felt when Abner Marsh came out to greet Robert the day he was to begin work on the "gee-gaws" Mrs. Marsh insisted adorn her expansive new home overlooking New Ulm. As soon as he recognized the man, Daniel jumped down off the wagon and walked to the well where he began to draw water for Robert's team. He pulled his old army hat down as far over his brow as possible, and stuffed his long braid inside his shirt. And he prayed, how he prayed.

But Abner Marsh was not a man to miss an opportunity to assert his superior position in the universe. Having introduced himself to Robert, the brawny farmer strode to where Daniel stood, half-hidden behind Robert's team. Thrusting a huge paw at Daniel he said gruffly, "Abner Marsh."

Daniel muttered a greeting and shook the man's hand without looking up.

"Don't take to workin' with a man what can't look me in the eye," he said abruptly. Daniel tipped his head back and peered up into the man's eyes for an eternal moment, thinking surely this would be the end of life as he knew it. But Marsh only nodded and turned towards Robert. "Don't take to Injuns as a rule," he said. "Had a run-in with 'em before. But Grant says you're all right. Says you worked as scouts for the army against your own. That right?"

Robert nodded.

When neither of the men offered any more comment on their lives as Indian scouts, Marsh grunted. "My missus thinks she'll die if'n she don't have those fancy railings and such like you carved for Marjorie Grant." He reached into his pocket and, withdrawing a wad of tobacco leaves, took a pinch and shoved it in his mouth before asking, "Where'd you learn to carpenter?"

"Hope Station," Robert replied. "By the Upper Agency. And I helped build Dr. Wakefield's home at the Lower Agency."

"You one of them mission Indians?" Marsh said. "One of them that got religion?"

"We are both Christians," Robert said quietly.

Marsh snorted. "Only mission Indians I ever saw was the day I caught three of 'em tryin' to steal my horses."

Robert remained silent, eyeing Marsh carefully.

Motioning for the men to follow him, Marsh led them to the

barn. "Now what I got to show you here is just to get things straight in all our minds," he said. He led the men inside the barn to a back stall. Inside the stall were three wire cages, each one housing a massive dog. All three were predominantly black, with powerful builds and sleek coats. One had pale gray eyes. At the sight of Daniel and Robert, the one with pale eyes lifted its upper lip, showing huge teeth in a silent snarl. Marsh uttered a strange word and the dogs instantly transformed into raging beasts, furious to escape their cages.

When he saw both Daniel and Robert take a couple of involuntary steps backward, Marsh smiled. "Now these boys usually have the run of my place. They take good care of things. I taught 'em only to eat what comes from my hand." He glared at Daniel. "Had me a bulldog once that was a good dog—until one night an Injun got hold of him by offering him some jerky. Broke that dog's neck like it was a piece of stick candy." He grimaced. "Learned my lesson with that one. Used a pair of moccasins from a trader friend to teach these boys to attack anything that smells of Injun. Attack and ask questions later." He sent a long stream of tobacco juice into the dirt. "I'll see they get shut up in here right after sunrise on the mornings I know you're comin' to work on the place." He glared at Daniel. "Just see that you don't surprise me and we'll all get along fine." He led the way out of the barn and back to the plain, two-story house.

Stepping up on the porch, Marsh opened the front door and shouted, "Sally! Come on out and tell these men what you want."

Two young girls' faces appeared at a window.

"Them's my girls," Marsh said abruptly. "Don't reckon you'll have need to talk to them at all."

Mrs. Marsh came out on the porch. She was rail thin and so pale as to look ill, but when she extended her bony hand to greet Robert, her grasp was firm. "Now, Abner," she said in the voice of a woman not often denied her will, "there's no reason for you to waste good daylight listening to a woman's plans for fancyin' up the place. You just go on about your business, and I'll go on about mine with the carpenters."

After making his displeasure known by clearing his throat and spitting another stream of tobacco in disgust, Abner hopped down off the railless porch and headed for the barn. It wasn't long before he emerged behind a team of mules. "I'll just be up plowing the new field, then," he called up to his wife, who dismissed him with a wave of her hand. Marsh made another attempt at appearing in control of his woman. "See you let the dogs out after these boys are gone," he said.

The moment Abner was out of sight, his two daughters appeared at the doorway, tittering like two nervous sparrows. They were pale like their mother, with dull brown hair pulled back into tight buns at the base of their thin necks and hazel eyes that were never still as they glanced nervously from Robert to Daniel and back to Robert.

"Girls!" Mrs. Marsh said impatiently. "Stop acting like you were raised in a cabbage patch." She looked down at Robert. "Mr. Lawrence, this is our youngest, Priscilla, and her sister Polly." She turned to the girls. "Girls, this is Mr. Lawrence's helper, Mr. Two Stars."

Priscilla and Polly offered limp hands to the two men and dipped into exaggerated curtsies, giggling all the while.

"You must excuse my girls," Mrs. Marsh said quickly. "Neither of them seems to have ever seen an Indian before."

"Oh, Mama!" the girls said in chorus, blushing.

"Well, then," Mrs. Marsh said stiffly, "since perhaps you *have* seen an Indian or two before, it would seem you could stop acting as if you have just discovered the seventh wonder of the ancient world and get some chores done."

"Yes, ma'am," Polly murmured.

"Yes, ma'am," Pris echoed.

While the girls shuffled back inside, Robert explained why he wanted to use oak instead of pine for the railing, why just the opposite would work better for the decorations high up on the gables, and how long the work was likely to take.

While Robert and Mrs. Marsh talked, Daniel watched Abner plowing the field in the distance. His heart slowed down and he relaxed a bit. Presently he found himself thanking God that Abner Marsh had not recognized the only surviving member of the trio of thieves who had once plotted to steal the man's three best horses.

Seven

"Hatred stirreth up strifes . . ."

—PROVERBS 10:12

Leighton Hall
May 5, 1867
Dearest Genevieve and Daniel,

There is no easy way to say this: measles is making the rounds in New York and has stopped at Leighton Hall. Meg has been very ill. She has recovered but has a long convalescence ahead of her. God spared everyone else. But we cannot come to Minnesota, dear ones.

Elliot sends his love and has departed once again for Washington where he feels he can do more good than in coming to you. He is determined to be a member of the new commission visiting Niobrara this summer and, if God wills, may come in the fall to gather up Aaron for the return to New York. That is the good news in this letter. Aaron is coming to Minnesota. We have just returned from sending him off at the railway station. And now a word from Meg.

Looking at the child-like scrawl that slanted awkwardly across the page, Genevieve frowned. She read:

Dear Mama-Gen and Daniel,

I am so sorry not to be coming with Aaron, but he promises that if I work hard this summer and through the year to adjust, that he will certainly bring me to see you next year. I have asked Aunt Jane to let me tell you myself. My eyesight was affected by the measles. But I can still see light and dark and I am learning to get around the house very well. Grandmother is getting a tutor who works with the blind and he will be teaching me to do all kinds of things, even making my own tea. It is very hard, but when I remember all that you have suffered and how brave you have been, it helps me to be brave, too. I have seen roses and the sunset, and I know how eyes change when a person looks at you in love. I think that is quite a lot to have seen, don't you? I love you both very much. Meg

At the bottom of the letter, in inch-high letters, Gen read,

Hello Ma. I am five. I can write my name see? HOPE.

Daniel and Gen had come to their favorite place on the farm to read the letter, a rock ledge that jutted out from the ground behind Jeb Grant's barn where a spring bubbled out of the earth. More than once they had removed their shoes and dangled their feet in the cool water while they talked at the end of a hot summer day. But this spring evening their attentions were drawn more to the graves beneath the cottonwood tree that shaded the rock than to the music of the bubbling spring. Death had nearly taken Meg. And although defeated, death had left its mark and Meg was blind. And so, Daniel Two Stars gathered his wife into his arms while she wept.

"Why?" Gen sobbed. "Why would God do that to Meg? I don't understand."

Daniel sighed. "More and more I don't understand the God we serve, Blue Eyes," he paused, "but I trust Him."

"It hurts," Gen sobbed.

"I love you, little wife," Daniel said, "I don't know what else to say. I am here. God is here. We both love you."

"It doesn't seem fair. For Meg to have to—suffer."

"It is not fair," Daniel said gently. "But it is, and God will work it for good. He loves Meg more than we do."

"How did you get to know so much?" Gen muttered grudgingly.

"I tried doubting His love. It didn't work very well," Daniel said, hugging her fiercely. "He just kept on pulling me back."

Gen sighed and kissed his cheek. "I'm glad He did," she said. "I needed to hear those things. And I need you."

Daniel returned her kiss. "See that you remember my wise words for the times when *you* must remind *me* of the things I know."

"Do you think it's all right for Aaron to come? I mean—with all the trouble here."

Daniel thought for a moment. "Jeb says things are better with the Quinns and the Baxters. If Aaron is anything like Elliot or Simon, he will be all right even if there is some trouble. He's nearly a man now anyway."

"Pray for Meg," Gen said.

Daniel leaned back against the tree. Gen moved so that she was facing him, seated inside the circle of his legs. And they prayed.

Abner Marsh crouched down behind his plow and, taking a handful of the freshly turned black earth, inhaled deeply. *Nothin' smells better than fresh plowed dirt.* And this was his dirt. His farm. He stood back up, admiring the color and texture of the soil before dropping it and wiping his palm on his soiled overalls. Taking off his hat, he wiped his brow with his forearm before standing a moment and looking across the field towards the house. His house. His wife. His girls.

Girls. Abner sighed. He loved his girls but wished to the gods almighty that Sally could give him at least one boy. She'd have done it, too, if it hadn't been for the murdering Sioux. Sally had lost their baby boy right after they hightailed it off their old place up by Acton. She hadn't wanted to go. Said she was feeling poorly and afraid what a long wagon ride would do. But Abner had insisted and, as it turned out, their place was burned to the ground the night after they left—at least that was what the neighbors told them a few weeks later. And nothing had been the same since. Sally lost the baby, and in the ensuing months she became thin and pale and hard. She didn't complain and Abner never saw her cry, but she was nothing like the woman he had married. He'd come to accept that neither of them was anything like the doe-eyed couple in their wedding picture. Probably never would be again. As for Sally, all the quilting bees and understanding women in the world couldn't change what had happened to her inside. Her religion, weak as it was, hadn't been much comfort either.

Plopping his crumpled hat back on his head, Abner shrugged the sadness off his shoulders by lifting the reins he'd draped over the plow handles and hollering to his mules to "gid-ap." Walking the long, straight furrow revitalized him. When he turned the corner and headed back towards the house, he got a glimpse of the two men he'd hired to give Sally her railing and the other useless stuff she wanted on the house. He'd fought her on it, but not much. Sally hadn't showed much interest in anything new in years. If it gave her pleasure to think on fancying up the house, Abner didn't mind. He could afford it. Maybe granting Sally's wish would give him a glimpse of the girl in the wedding picture. He wouldn't mind seeing her again. He'd tell her all this was for her, that he was born to farm and he loved the land, but it wouldn't mean much without someone to share it with. He'd tell her he was glad she stuck by him all these years. If the old Sally reappeared, that's just what he would—

The mules turned up a larger-than-usual rock. Something about its color or shape made Abner holler "Whoa!" Loosely tying the reins over one plow handle, Abner reached around and picked it up. It was a human skull. Catching his breath, he stared at it for a long time before noticing other, smaller bones scattered along the freshly turned split in the earth. Walking to the end of the furrow, he emptied his water bucket and returned to the plow, collecting bones and thinking: *Red Cloud. Little Crow. Wabasha. Fetterman. Shakopee. Uprising. Massacre.*

When he had finished collecting all the bones he could find, Abner set the skull atop the pile in the bucket. He walked back to the edge of his field and set the bucket under a tree. Crouching down, he stared at it, shuddering when he realized that he might have just dug up all that was left of some little girl like his Polly or Pris. He was clutching the last thing he found— a tomahawk. Looking towards the farm, he saw the two Indians working on Sally's porch railing. His grip on the tomahawk tightened until his knuckles were white.

~∞~

"That's terrible, Abner," Thomas Quinn said. He shuddered as he looked down at the bucket sitting at his feet. "I'll help you bury them."

"I didn't bring 'em here to get your help buryin' 'em," Marsh snarled. "I brung 'em to bring you to your senses. Both of you." He looked from Quinn to Baxter and back again.

Quinn scratched his beard. "I don't want to make any more trouble for Jeb Grant, Abner. I already told you that."

"So did I," Baxter interjected. "What's done is done." He looked down at the bones. "Poor little thing."

"I'm not trying to make trouble for Jeb Grant," Marsh insisted. "I'm trying to save his thick, Injun-lovin' hide. Can't you fellers see that?" Marsh reached into his back pocket and withdrew his final piece of evidence. He thrust the tomahawk at Quinn. "Found that with the bones. Guess that says it all."

Quinn pushed the tomahawk away. "Look, Abner, I read the same newspaper you do. I read all about Fetterman. I been readin' all the news about Red Cloud and all. But, Abner, those things are happenin' a thousand miles away. They got nothin' to do with me. Nancy Lawrence has been real nice to Violet and my Lydia."

"Harriet don't say nothing bad about them women. Says they're real hard workers," Earl offered, adding as a last thought, "and one of 'em's about to have a baby."

"Nits make lice," Marsh said, "birthin' another warrior right under our noses." He swore. "And you're both too stupid to stop it."

Quinn scratched his beard. Smoothing it, his finger landed on the open spot next to his bottom lip—the spot Lydia liked to kiss. He cleared his throat. "Look Abner. I'm sorry if it makes you mad to hear this, but the truth is, even if Daniel Two Stars and Richard Lawrence *did* do something bad during the outbreak, I got to think they've paid ten times over. Two Stars was nearly hung and the both of them spent months in prison. We got to move on, Abner. It isn't healthy, brooding on something that happened years ago. It just isn't healthy and it doesn't do anybody any good."

Baxter, a man of few words, climbed aboard his wagon. "I agree with Tom," he said quickly. He nodded down at the bucket.

"You want me to take them into town and see to the buryin'? I got to pick up Harriet's new sewing machine at Ludlow's."

Marsh bent down and snatched up the bucket. "I'll see to it," he grunted, and headed inside his barn.

Quinn mounted his mule and trotted after Baxter. "That man's gone a little off in his head. We better keep an eye on him."

Baxter shrugged. "Oh, Abner's all right. He's just bullheaded. He won't do anybody any real harm."

Quinn clucked to his mule and headed off towards home, lifting his hand and waving to Baxter as he disappeared over a rise in the distance.

❧

Having faced his demons, both literal and imaginary, having won against challenges to his new Christian faith, having followed the example of his biblical name-bearer Daniel and lived among the lions without being devoured, Daniel Two Stars was finally to be beaten by a threadbare shirt. He was seated on an upended tree stump sanding one of the rungs for Mrs. Abner Marsh's new porch railing when a horsefly began to torment him. Slapping at the horsefly, Daniel dropped the porch rail. Bending over to retrieve the porch rail, he felt the shoulder seam of his worn red shirt give way. He trotted behind the barn to inspect the damage. When he took off the shirt, he let out a sigh of frustration. It was beyond repair. He pulled it back on and returned to work.

"Two Stars!" Abner bellowed when he and Robert drove in later that day. "Lend a hand here."

Daniel followed the wagon behind the barn. While he and Robert unloaded the lumber, Abner clomped up to the house and disappeared inside. By the time he came back, Daniel and Robert had nearly finished unloading the wood.

"Had the missus get this for you," Abner grunted, tossing a shirt at Daniel. "Won't do to have my girls watchin' a half-dressed Indian work on the place." At Daniel's look of surprise, Abner shrugged. "Fool girls seem to think you two men are a subject to be studied."

Daniel was shirtless for only a brief second, but it was long enough for Abner to notice the scars. He grabbed Daniel's left hand and inspected the old wounds across Daniel's left shoulder and down his forearm. "Didn't think the scouts did much fightin'," he said, peering into Daniel's eyes. "Thought you boys said you were on the peace-keepin' side of things back in '62. Jeb Grant vouched for you." He pointed at Daniel's shoulder. "But that's a bullet hole if I ever saw one."

Daniel pulled his hand away. While he buttoned Abner's gigantic shirt he said quietly, "I owe my earthly life to a white woman who took care of a foolish boy who got hurt. I owe my eternal life to white missionaries who told that same fool about God." He stared up at Marsh. "I am no longer a fool, Mr. Marsh. I only want a peaceful life."

"*Abner! Abner!*"

Marsh spat tobacco juice and looked away. "You want a peaceful life, boys, don't marry a woman with a voice like a coyote howlin' at the moon." He sent another stream of brown liquid at the barn wall and stomped away. "You boys go on home. There's not enough daylight left to accomplish much." He paused and looked back at Daniel. "That shirt makes you look like a scarecrow flappin' in the wind. If your missus can make it fit, you can have it. Otherwise bring 'er back tomorrow." With a nod at Robert, Abner headed for the house.

"I can't come back here," Daniel said. "He's going to recognize me sooner or later."

"I'll tell him Jeb Grant needed you to plow a new field," Robert said, slapping the reins against his team's rumps and heading them up the road towards home. "That's the truth. Jeb is trying to help us by letting us work for Marsh, but he's measuring new fields in his head all the time we're here. I heard him tell Mrs. Grant he about has Quinn talked into selling him some more land." He paused. "Don't worry about it. It's been five years since you were a horse thief." He forced himself to laugh. "Come to think of it, you never actually *were* a horse thief. Didn't you tell me Marsh got all three animals back?"

Daniel nodded. "But if he decides I was the one who tried to take them, I don't think that will matter very much." He gripped the side of the wagon seat. "Tell me again what you know about the new reservation in Nebraska."

❧

Sally Marsh was dreaming of inviting Marjorie Grant to tea in a brick house with a carved mahogany staircase when her husband Abner sat straight up in bed and began to curse. The string of epithets flying around the darkened bedroom was like nothing Sally had ever heard before. So vile were the things Abner was saying that Sally was momentarily silenced—until Abner jumped out of bed and his oaths were slowed as he clutched his foot in a vain attempt to make his stubbed toe stop hurting.

"Abner Marsh!" Sally hissed. "What on earth is the matter with you?"

"I can't believe it," Abner muttered. "I can't believe I was so stupid." He pulled on his pants. "When I get finished with them—"

"With who, Abner? When you get finished with who?"

"Robert Lawrence. Daniel Two Stars. Jeb Grant. He was probably in on it, too. Probably laughing his beard off thinking how he put one over on Abner Marsh."

Sally slipped out of bed and pulled on her duster. "What's this about Robert and Daniel? What have they done? Their work is beautiful. The porch is coming along fine. I certainly don't have any complaints. Why, Eulalie Gibbons was up today while you were in town, and she is just green with envy to see how the place is coming along."

Abner appeared not to have heard his wife. "I knew I'd seen 'im somewhere before," he muttered. "I knew it." He pulled on his shirt. "Those scars." He snorted angrily. "And all he could say was how much he loves white people." Abner swore again. "I'll show him love!"

Sally shook her husband by the shoulder. "If you don't tell me what you're talking about, Abner Marsh, I'm going to assume you're having a nightmare and wake you up with one of my iron skillets!"

Marsh stood up and pulled his suspenders over his broad shoulders. Finally, he answered his wife. "Daniel Two Stars is one of the young bucks that stole our horses up at Acton. Maybe Robert Lawrence, too, although I don't think so."

"Don't be ridiculous, Abner," Sally retorted. "That was years ago. Whoever did that is either dead or out West with the other hostiles." She shook her head. "Let it go, Abner. All these years you've never let it go. It eats at you all the time."

Abner stood up. "When I think what might have happened to you and the girls . . ." Abner clenched his fists and stared down at his wife, suddenly more precious to him than she had been in months.

"They were after the horses, Abner. That's all," Sally said sensibly. "If they had been after us we wouldn't be standing here having this ridiculous conversation. And maybe Two Stars looks like one of them, but you can't prove he *is* one of them. And besides," her voice dropped, "they both do wonderful work."

"Wonderful work," Abner repeated. He grasped his wife's shoulder. "Can't you see, Sally, what they're doin'? Just gainin' our trust. All of us. Waitin' until we think they are law-abidin' citizens like the rest of us and they can call their friends from the West to come back home and do it all over again. And when they do, you know what they'll do to the Abner Marshes and the Jeb Grants?"

"Stop it," Sally said, twisting away from him. "You're frightening me."

"Good," Abner said. "We been too complacent, lettin' them live right here among us." He charged out of the bedroom with Sally following close behind. Snatching up the rifle stored over the back door, he ordered Sally to "stay put" and headed outside. By dawn he had rounded up several of his neighbors, terrifying them with prophecies of midnight attacks and scalpings.

Eight

"Blessed are the peacemakers . . ."
—MATTHEW 5:9

THE SCRAWNY MAN BEHIND THE COUNTER AT LUDLOW'S Variety Store in New Ulm, Minnesota, chewed on his cigar while he eyed the newcomer suspiciously. Things had been slow all day. Here was news. There wasn't a man in town who wouldn't be interested to know about a white boy from the East looking for the Injuns down on Jeb Grant's place.

The front door creaked, a bell rang, and a lanky man with a thick black beard ducked inside. "Quinn," the clerk nodded.

"Maybe you can help me, sir," Aaron said, abandoning the clerk. He offered a handshake to the man named Quinn. "I'm trying to locate Jeb Grant's farm. Actually," Aaron said quickly,

"I'm trying to locate Daniel and Genevieve Two Stars. They live on the Grant place."

Thomas Quinn grasped Aaron's hand. "And just how do you know them—if you don't mind my asking?"

"Genevieve Two Stars is my stepmother," Aaron said, "and Daniel is a good friend."

The clerk behind the counter nearly swallowed his cigar.

"Your stepmother?" Quinn said. He looked Aaron up and down. Then, with a sideways glance at the clerk, he thrust out his hand and smiled warmly. "Then you'd be Aaron Dane."

Aaron's blue eyes smiled. "Yes." He grabbed Quinn's hand and shook it again. "Yes. You know them?"

Quinn nodded, then shrugged. "Can't say as I know them real well, but my missus has been quiltin' with Mrs. Two Stars and Mrs. Lawrence, and we've tried to be neighborly." Quinn smiled. "My Lydia says, Mrs. Two Stars talks about you and your sisters a lot. She said you'd be comin' to visit." He cleared his throat. "We were right sorry to hear about your sister. I hope she's doing better."

"Thank you," Aaron said, "she is. Just not ready to travel. I promised her we'd come again next summer when she's stronger."

"You don't mind waiting while I do a little shopping, I'll take you out to their place. I go right by it on my way home." He nodded towards the door. "My team's dapple gray."

"Great," Aaron said, "that's great. Thank you." He headed for the door.

Quinn handed the clerk his list.

Reaching behind him to retrieve a spool of thread, the clerk said, "Ain't that somethin'. A white boy calling a squaw his mama. Bet his real mama don't like that one bit."

Quinn turned away. Walking to the back of the store, he rummaged for a box of nails. When the clerk made another reference to Aaron's blond hair and Genevieve Two Stars's blue eyes, Quinn cleared his throat. "Just fill the order, Harley," he said abruptly. "I got to get home."

❧

"Now calm down, Abner," Jeb pleaded. He rubbed the back of his neck, looking nervously at the half-dozen men gathered on his front porch, rifles in hand. "Let me set my coffee cup down," he said. "I'll be out. We'll talk things over."

"Nothin' to talk about," Abner said loudly. "You're getting rid of those thievin' field hands of yours today—or we're doing it for you." He raised his rifle in the air and was only prevented from firing by Jeb's grabbing the barrel.

"No reason to be scaring my boys, is there?"

"All right then," one of the other farmers answered. "But get out here quick. We got business."

Jeb backed inside and closed the door in his neighbors' faces with a trembling hand. He took a deep breath and headed upstairs where Marjorie was putting the twins down for a nap. "There's trouble," he said. "Bad trouble, I'm afraid. Abner's convinced himself Daniel is some kind of horse thief."

Marjorie snorted indignantly. "What nonsense." She started to laugh. "I'll make them all my special coffee cake. They'll settle down soon enough."

Jeb shook his head. "I don't know, Ma. They're awful riled up about this." He took his wife's hand. "I'm going to herd them all into the barn for a meetin'. The minute we're all inside, you run down and warn Daniel and Robert. I hate to say it, but it might be good for them to make use of the trader's place up near the old Redwood Agency. Tell 'em I'll come for 'em soon as it's safe."

Marjorie's chin trembled and her eyes filled with tears. "But

Nancy's about to have the baby, Jeb. They can't just be running off somewhere. Not now."

Jeb paused at the doorway and looked back over his shoulder. "You get down there as soon as you see we're all in the barn, you hear?" With a glance towards the other bedroom he said, "We'll just have to hope the boys sleep through it." He hurried down the stairs.

❧

"But Abner," Jeb Grant protested, "be reasonable. That Fetterman thing happened way out West. And we don't even know how much of what you read is true. The only thing published in our papers is what the Indian does to the white man. We rarely hear what the white man does to the Indian." He looked at the half-dozen men gathered in the barn and vaguely registered the absence of Thomas Quinn and Ed Baxter. Then he plunged ahead. "You don't even know those bones you found are white. It could just as easy be some Chippewa killed a long time ago. Or some trader that got lost in a blizzard. It could be anything. Anybody." Jeb pleaded, "I trust Daniel and Robert like they was kin."

"We trusted some of them back in '62, and you know what happened," one of the farmers retorted.

A young man with flaming red hair and a hint of a moustache spoke up. "Look, Jeb. We're not saying they're all bad. There's exceptions to every rule. What we are saying is we should learn from experience. We didn't come to Minnesota to live near Indians. They're getting a good reservation in Nebraska. They should go there."

"Government's givin' 'em everything they need. They even drove a herd of horses up from Kansas so's they could all have one. Can't see why they don't just move on," another one said.

"Because this is their home," Jeb said. He swallowed hard. "Listen. This is the exact homestead these two men had before the uprising." While he waited for the men to absorb the news, Jeb paused. When they were quiet, he continued. "Fact is, after what happened last spring when those hostiles broke through the border and killed those homesteaders, I sleep better knowing Robert and Daniel are on the place. It never hurts to have an extra pair of eyes keeping a lookout, and they've proved themselves to me."

"Fool," Abner muttered.

Jeb drew himself up and challenged Abner. "You think I'm such a fool I'd let them stay on if I thought my boys and my wife were in danger?"

"I didn't say that," Marsh said quickly.

"Well, fact is, Abner, you did," Jeb said. Sensing a glimmer of weakening in the onlookers, he hammered his argument. "I know most of you feel nothing but hatred for everything in the form of an Indian," Jeb said. He eyed the faces in the small gathering, once more relieved that Quinn and Baxter were absent. He cleared his throat. "But I've known Daniel and Robert for nigh on two years now. I've seem them work hard and look the other way when they was called names and their women was treated poorly. You have any doubts about Daniel Two Stars and Robert Lawrence, you just take yourself on up to Fort Ridgely and ask Captain John Willets what he thinks of his two Indian scouts. He'll tell you a thing or two about those men." Jeb thrust his chin out and stared into the eyes of the six men surrounding him. "And I'll tell you this. The day hasn't dawned yet when somebody can ride onto the place I'm sweating to build and pouring my lifeblood into and tell me I got to tell two families I count as friends to git."

"Never picked you for a Injun-lover, Jeb," Abner Marsh said. He added a few other choice terms to the moniker, stopping only when Marjorie appeared at the barn door.

"I'll have fresh coffee and cake for you men directly," she called out cheerily. "You'll all stay, won't you?"

"Got no time for socializin' today," Marsh replied.

"I didn't say anything about socializing, Mr. Marsh," Marjorie teased. "I just don't want you going home hungry, that's all. My reputation's at stake." She looked at her husband. "I checked in with the Lawrences for you, Jeb. Robert said to tell you he'd get to plowing that new field today." She glanced over the crowd of men. "Now you men don't forget to stop up at the house for coffee when your meeting's done."

When Marjorie had disappeared inside the house, Jeb took a deep breath and glared up at Abner. "We don't see things the same, Abner. But I always respected you. I know you've had some run-ins with the Dakota. I don't blame you for being suspicious. But I take it personal when you don't believe what I know to be true." Jeb eyed the other men, who looked away nervously.

"I won't have Injuns livin' nearby," Abner said stubbornly.

"Well then," Jeb said with a wicked smile. "I guess your place'll be for sale. I'll pay you a fair price."

When the other men snickered, Marsh's face reddened and he let out another stream of profanities. He snatched up his rifle and headed outside. "You keep yer Injuns if ya like, Jeb. Just see they stay close to home."

Jeb followed him. "What's your Sally going to say when she finds out her porch railing's not going to get finished?"

"I'll handle Sally," Abner shot back. Snatching up his horse's reins, he mounted up. Looking past Jeb to where the other men stood watching he said loudly, "Just see they stay close to home. A man never knows when some varmint'll come out of the dark and blow him away. Be a shame if your blood brothers or their women got kilt by accident." He wheeled his horse around and with a savage kick to its ribs, charged off towards home.

⌇

"Uh-oh." Thomas Quinn turned to watch Abner Marsh retreat into the distance. Marsh had come flying towards them at such a furious pace, Thomas had pulled his team over on the side of the dirt road to let him pass. Now Abner was gone, but neither Quinn nor Aaron had missed the rage on the man's face as he whipped his horse past them.

"Who was that?" Aaron asked.

"Marsh. Abner Marsh." Quinn guided his team back onto the road. "Guess we'd better see what's going on." He urged the team to a trot. They had gone nearly a quarter of a mile before Quinn said, "Guess I ought to tell you that Marsh doesn't take to the idea of Daniel and Mrs. Two Stars and the Lawrences living so close."

He pulled his team into a narrow lane leading to an attractive two-story house. From his vantage point on the wagon seat, Aaron looked away from the house into the valley below. Two log cabins were visible in the distance, but there was no sign of activity near either one, and no smoke rose from the chimneys. He wanted to jump down and tear off down the hill, but hesitated when a crowd of men emerged from the barn. A woman appeared on the front porch of the house. She rested her hand on the ornate railing and called out, "Now who wants coffee before they head home?" When no one answered, she said, "Coffee cake's just about done, too."

One by one, the men declined the woman's invitation, tipping their hats and thanking her in a tone of voice at once polite and, Aaron thought, a little embarrassed.

Quinn approached a short man with a grizzled beard and extended his hand. They exchanged a few words before the man limped over to where Aaron waited. He reached up to shake hands. "Jeb Grant," he said. "Glad to meet you, Aaron. Call me Jeb." He called up to the woman on the porch, "Marjorie, this here's Aaron Dane."

At mention of Aaron's name, Marjorie hurried down off the porch. "Aaron! Praise the Lord, it's good to see you—Genevieve has just been—" she broke off, looking down the hill and then at her husband.

Jeb took his hat off and swiped his forehead with his sleeve. He put it back on and raised his hand to the driver of the last wagon to leave the farmyard.

"Where is Gen?" Aaron asked abruptly. He looked past Jeb down the hill to the cabins.

Jeb grasped his arm and pulled him along. "She's safe. They all are." Quickly, he explained the neighbor's uneasiness about having Indian neighbors. "But after this winter, I thought that was all part of the past."

"What changed things?" Aaron asked.

Jeb grinned at Marjorie. "Quilting," he said.

Quinn nodded. "That's right. Mrs. Grant invited my missus and a couple others to quilting." He looked to Jeb and then back to Aaron. "Putting a face on things you think you hate can change your mind. Your stepma and her friend Nancy Lawrence are good women. If it's up to me, they can live wherever they want."

Aaron said, "But from what we saw when we rode in, that's not how most of the rest of the neighbors feel."

"It's changin'," Jeb said. "Just takes time."

"Where are Gen and Daniel now?"

Jeb cleared his throat. "When this crowd come ridin' in, they were pretty riled up. I got 'em all in the barn where they could say their piece. While we was in there, Marjorie ran down and warned 'em. Far as I know they went to an old traders place up by the Redwood. I told 'em we'd come for 'em when it was safe."

"Do you think it's safe?"

Jeb nodded. "Most of 'em wasn't that set on causing trouble anyway." He ran his hand through his hair. "If I could just get Abner Marsh to settle down, there wouldn't be any more trouble. But he won't let it go. He's convinced Daniel was one of the three Dakota that stole some horses from him years ago."

Aaron inhaled sharply. "A bay gelding and two others?" When Jeb nodded, Aaron continued. "Only the bay was worth anything. Otter let him go when Daniel got shot. The farmer got all his horses back."

"You know about that?!"

Aaron nodded. "When we were in the captive camp back during the outbreak, Daniel used to tell us stories. One night he told us how he almost got killed for a horse." Aaron sighed. "He was talking about how God had changed him. And how sin can haunt you for years after you've done it." He was quiet for a moment. Then he looked at Quinn and Grant. "It sounds like Abner Marsh could be a dangerous man."

"Well, he's angry. He plowed up some bones in a field the other day and he's convinced it's a victim of the uprising. It got him pretty stirred up."

"Do you think he'd talk to me?" Aaron asked. "Do you think he'd listen if I told him about the Daniel I know?"

"I don't know," Jeb said. "Maybe. After he has a few days to calm down. He didn't get much support today—in spite of what it looked like when you rode in."

"If I can borrow a horse, I'd like to go get Ma and Daniel and the Lawrences and tell them they can come home now," Aaron said quietly.

"I'll take you," Quinn said.

"If it's all the same to you," Aaron replied, "I'd rather go alone." He looked at Jeb. "I know about the trader's cabin." He cleared his throat. "Fact is, Daniel stopped there during the outbreak to warn some newcomers to get away. He was trying to get some supplies to help Robert." He leaned forward. "Robert Lawrence had gone into the agency to get a horse shod the day the trouble started. He got shot in the belly. Daniel went after him. Carried him out of the worst of things and then helped Nancy get him to safety." He stopped abruptly. Looking at Jeb he said, "You get Abner Marsh and anyone else you can to come to a meeting. I'll tell them a few things about Daniel Two Stars and Robert Lawrence!"

"We just might do that, son," Jeb said. "But first let's get 'em back home. How well can you ride?" When Aaron looked surprised by the question, Jeb explained, "Don't take it personal, son. I've heard Captain Willets up at Fort Ridgely moan about the city boys that sign up for the army and never sat a horse before. Happens all the time."

"My Uncle Elliot started teaching me to ride as soon as I began talking about going into the military," Aaron said.

"Well then. We'll just saddle up Bones and send you on your way. He don't look like much, but he loves to run."

As the men headed for the barn, Thomas Quinn said, "I'll drop your bag off down at the Two Starses', Aaron," adding, "and if you organize that meeting, let me know and I'll be there. I don't need any stories to convince me about Robert and Daniel, but it can't hurt to have somebody on your side in the crowd."

"Thank you," Aaron said warmly. "And thank you for the ride out from town."

Aaron and Jeb headed for the barn. Quinn murmured, "That might be a boy in years, but there's a man inside."

Marjorie nodded. "Maybe the good Lord is going to solve this mess after all."

Nine

"Entreat me not to leave thee, or to return from
following after thee: for whither thou goest,
I will go; and where thou lodgest,
I will lodge . . ."

—RUTH 1:16

"DON'T *TELL* ME IT DOESN'T MATTER!" DANIEL SLAMMED
his hand down on the table with such force the coffee in Gen's
cup sloshed over the rim. Seated opposite Gen on Daniel's left,
Aaron took a sudden interest in the oatmeal left in his bowl.

The force of Daniel's words made Genevieve flinch. He had
never shouted at her before. She put her spoon down and, clasping her hands in her lap, watched a drop of coffee slide down the
side of her cup and pool in the chipped saucer.

"I'm sorry," Daniel said quickly. He ran his hands through his
hair in frustration. Gripping the edge of the table he said, "I'm

not angry at you, Blue Eyes. I just—" he stopped abruptly and, pushing himself away from the table, stalked outside.

Aaron finally broke the uncomfortable silence in the cabin. "I shouldn't have been the one to come find you and tell you it was safe to come out of hiding. I should have let Mr. Grant do that."

Gen picked up a knife and pried a wedge of cornbread out of the pie tin in the center of the table. Sliding it onto the small plate beside Aaron's cereal bowl she said, "I'm glad you came." She stood up and walked around to his side of the table and patted him on the shoulder.

"I'm glad I came too, Ma. But I'm thinking about the last time he saw me. I was a young boy looking up to him like a hero. And this time—"

"This time you find him hiding out instead of defending himself," Gen murmured.

"That would be hard on a man's pride," Aaron said. "Awfully hard."

"Yes," Gen sighed. "I suppose it would. And that would matter, wouldn't it. A lot. I hadn't quite thought of it that way." She nudged the plate of cornbread towards his cereal bowl. "Finish your supper. We'll be back directly." She headed for the door. Just outside she hesitated. There was no lamplight spilling through the Lawrence's window. She'd hoped to procrastinate by checking on Nancy.

"He went up towards Grants'." Robert's voice sounded from across the road, just barely loud enough to be heard.

"I thought you were asleep," Gen said, making her way across the road. When she got close enough to see Robert sitting in the doorway, his rifle leaning up against the cabin, she shivered involuntarily.

"Is Nancy all right?" she asked.

"She sleeps," he said.

"I can't believe she managed what we—what we did today."

"Not many women could." Robert's voice was so filled with pride Gen wanted to cry.

"At least she had Bones to ride on the way back," she said weakly. "At least she didn't have to walk all those miles twice."

Robert stood up and pulled the door of his cabin closed behind him. "You shouldn't be walking alone tonight. Where is Aaron?"

"He's finishing his supper," Gen said. "He thought—well, he thought maybe it embarrassed Daniel to have him be the one who came to get us."

Robert considered this. Finally, he nodded. "I'll walk you up the hill. Aaron can finish eating."

Robert reached for his rifle. Gen tucked her hand under his arm. When they were halfway to the Grants', Robert stopped abruptly and peered into the darkness towards the Grants' barn. The moon came out from behind a bank of low clouds, illuminating the landscape just enough to reveal the outline of someone sitting on the rock ledge below the burial ground. Raising one hand to his mouth, Robert mimicked the hooting of an owl. When the call was returned, he nodded. He watched Gen climb the hill towards the ledge. Only when he saw Daniel reach out to her did he turn away and trot down the hill towards his cabin.

They sat in silence for a long time just listening to the gurgling spring and feeling the night breeze blowing across their skin. Presently Gen got up and, walking around behind him, began to rub Daniel's shoulders. After a few moments, she reached around to unbutton his shirt and slid her hands beneath the soft flannel, continuing to massage his shoulders and the back of his neck until she could feel the tension begin to flow out of him.

"I didn't know it would be so hard," she finally said. And then, as if she had read his thoughts, she corrected them. "I don't mean this trouble with Mr. Marsh. I mean—" she draped her arms around his shoulders and rested her chin atop his head. "I didn't think it would be so hard to understand you."

For a moment he was still and then he reached up to catch her hands in his own and pull her down beside him. He laughed quietly and put his arm around her.

"Why is that funny?"

"We are sent running for our lives into the nearest ravine. Aaron arrives at the worst possible moment. Just down the hill our friend Robert is standing guard with a rifle. And instead of hiding in the house trembling with fear, my little wife worries because it is hard to understand her husband." He paused. "Does that not seem—unusual—to you?"

Gen sighed, resting her elbows on her knees, her chin atop her hands. "Of course I care about all those other things. And things you don't even mention. I was worried for Nancy and the baby today. But Nancy is safe in her bed tonight." Her voice wavered. "What might have happened to you, and what has happened—inside you—those are the things I worry most about."

He grunted softly. "Today only proved what I already knew to be true, Blue Eyes. I knew it in my heart, but I wanted to be like the warriors of old—the ones who decided where they would live and fought for the right to make it happen." He leaned back against the cottonwood tree. "I wanted this to be home. Home where the railroad brings the children. Home where you can have quiltings with the other women. Home where our children and our children's children grow strong and live good lives."

"That can still happen," Gen whispered gently. "Aaron wants to have a meeting with those men who made the trouble today."

"Aaron is a good boy, but I don't think anything he can say will make a difference to those men. Certainly not to Abner Marsh."

"Are you upset with him?" Gen asked.

"Who?"

"Aaron."

"Why would I be upset with Aaron?"

"He said he shouldn't have been the one to come find us and bring us back home. He thinks he should have let Jeb do that." She studied Daniel's profile in the moonlight. "I was so happy to see Aaron, I didn't think about it. About how it made you feel." She paused before saying, "It *does* matter to you. I should have understood that. I'm sorry."

Daniel shrugged. "Everything has come to be just as I thought it would. Aaron has come and found, not the warrior he remembers saving his life, but a weak man who cannot even protect his own wife."

"Stop that." Gen said quickly. She put her hand on his knee. "That's not who you are at all. I know it. So do the rest of us—Aaron included."

Daniel squeezed her hand. "It's not just about what happened today, Blue Eyes. It's everything about our lives now. It hurts me to see how far down you have come to be my wife. When you were Mrs. Dane, you lived on an estate in New York. Now we beg for the government to give us a little piece of land . . ." He traced the frayed edge of her shirt cuff. "Genevieve *Dane* wore fine clothing. Now you mend the rags you call dresses over and over again because I have no money—even for a few yards of calico." He paused. "And now Aaron sees all of these things . . . and more. He sees Daniel Two Stars, the man who runs and hides instead of fighting for what should be his." He anticipated her response and gently pressed his fingers against her lips. "I know, Blue Eyes. It doesn't matter to you." He sighed wearily and muttered, "But it matters to *me.*"

"We have each other," she said. "We have the friendship of some. And at least respect from the others. God has been good to us, Daniel. I am content."

"And will you still be content when Abner Marsh and his

friends throw rocks at you and call you a sow or spit on you the way they did on Nancy the last time she was in town?"

"I didn't come back to Minnesota expecting life would be easy."

"Robert and Nancy want to go to the reservation in Nebraska. I am thinking you and Aaron can stay with the Grants while I ride up to Fort Ridgely to see if Captain Willets still needs scouts. Or maybe Aaron will want to go with me. If Captain Willets takes me on as a scout, you can go back to New York with Aaron for a while. You'll be safe there."

"You—you want me to—go away?" Gen stammered. "But if you think we should go—why can't we go to Nebraska with Robert and Nancy?"

"Nebraska means a reservation and another farm. I hate farming, Blue Eyes. And I'll never be very good at it."

"It would be different if it was *yours*," she said.

Releasing her hand, Daniel leaned forward. His words were laced with emotion as he said, "I don't want to live waiting for the government to give me something. That's what they do on the reservation. Wait for seed, wait for plows, wait for horses, wait for annuities." He shook his head. "Captain Willets depended on me. He respected me; so did the other soldiers. Even the ones who hated Indians in general learned that I could be trusted." He paused. "That was a good feeling."

"I'll go with you," Gen said abruptly.

He shook his head. "No. I won't have you living at a fort. You don't know how soldiers treat Dakota women. Anything could happen."

"Scouting can't be the only answer," Gen pleaded. "It's too dangerous. There has to be something else."

He got up wearily. "Don't be a child, Genevieve. This is not one of those fairy tales you used to tell the children where the prince and his princess live happily-ever-after."

"Don't call me a child!" Gen ignored her husband's extended hand and leaped up.

"Are you going to stomp your foot now?"

The bitter sarcasm in her husband's voice fed Gen's anger and frustration. An inner warning flashed, but she was too upset to heed it. Instead, she gave herself to the drama of the moment and unleashed the tide of emotions broiling just beneath the surface. She backed away from him. "Fine. Send me away. All this time I thought I had brought you happiness. Now I see I'm just the thing that keeps you from doing what really makes you happy. I didn't know you hated farming. I didn't know you wanted to go back to scouting, to wandering around the territory on horseback. I didn't realize—" Her voice trembled with desperation. "I didn't realize I was the reason for so much unhappiness."

Daniel had been prepared for anger, for the now-familiar stomping of a foot. Confronted by brokenness and the quiet desperation in his wife's voice, he wished his mocking challenge back, but it was too late. In the moonlight he could see tears gathering in the great blue eyes he adored. When they spilled down her cheeks, he reached for her. "I didn't mean it that way. Don't cry, little wife. Please—don't—cry." He meant to gather her into his arms, but she pushed him away.

"Leave me alone," she said. Resignation and weariness sounded in her next words. "We'll do what you want. I'll tell Aaron tonight. We can leave whenever you say." Her voice wavered again. "Then you can do something that makes you happy."

Covering her face with her hands, she turned and ran down the path away from him. She could hear Daniel calling her name, but she kept running, down the hill, past the cabin, into the woods beyond. Her chest began to burn and she was gasping for breath when she tripped in a hole and fell. Daniel caught up with her, ignoring her struggle to push him away. Helpless, she became even more furious and renewed her efforts to break free, kicking and scratching at him until, exhausted, she fell back against him while he whispered her name in Dakota and covered her face with kisses.

"We'll find a way, Blue Eyes," he said, choking back his own tears. "I didn't mean to hurt you. We'll find a way." He took her face in his hands and covered her mouth with his to silence her anger, murmuring promises until there was no more need for words.

∞

Later that night, after Gen gave Aaron his quilt, after Aaron and Daniel had discussed their plans for the summer, after Aaron insisted he would sleep in the barn, after Daniel and Gen made love, Gen laced her fingers through her husband's and said quietly, "There's something about New York you don't understand. You have this mental image of how wonderful it must have been, but the truth is—" She paused, then said slowly, "The truth is I was always *that Indian*. No one ever thought about the part of me that spoke French or could recite Shakespeare. Everyone was nice because Mother Leighton and the children loved me. But I never really belonged. When I thought you were dead and Simon wanted me as his wife, I told God I would do whatever He asked. And I was happy enough. But New York was never *home*." She raised her head to look into his eyes. "*This* is home." She patted his chest. "Wherever you lodge, wherever you go. We just have to trust God to take care of us. Please, best beloved. Don't send me away."

He covered her hand with his and squeezed it. "All right, Blue Eyes. I will learn to trust God to care for you at the fort while I am scouting . . . and you will learn to trust Him to care for me when I am gone."

"Where will we go?" she wanted to know.

"Probably Fort Wadsworth in Dakota."

"Tell me about it."

He told her what he could remember about the fort, built only a few years ago to defend the border of the civilized settlements against hostile Sioux from the West. "There was talk among some of the Christian scouts of starting a church two years ago. But Dakota is a hard place to live. And the fort—well, the fort can be terrible. There is always the call to drinking and wild living, and many of the men will answer it."

"You won't," Gen said quickly.

"By God's grace, I will not," he agreed. "But everything there is different from what we have known." He took a deep breath. "Dakota is a barren land compared to Minnesota, Blue Eyes. I have ridden for days at a time and never seen a tree. Can you imagine what that will be like after living all your life near the Big Woods?"

"I shall plant trees," Gen said.

"What if it means you don't get to see Meg or Hope next year? I don't know if Elliot and Jane will want to bring them to such a wild place. Especially if there is trouble with the hostile Sioux out there."

"We will write letters and they will understand." She kissed his cheek. "And when they do finally come, I'll pray they have a little brother or sister to meet." She snuggled next to him, singing softly, "Cling fast to me, you'll ever have a plenty, cling fast to me, and you'll ever have a plenty, cling fast to me."

Daniel nuzzled her ear. "Where did you learn that, little wife? Dakota men sing that when they are courting."

"My father used to sing it to my mother when I was little," she said. "I used to dream of a tall, handsome stranger carrying me away on a white horse while he sang that song."

Daniel sang back to her, "Wherever we choose, together we'll dwell . . . mother so says." Then he changed the words, laughing softly. "Wherever we choose, together we'll dwell, Blue Eyes so says." He teased her. "And all the time I thought the Scriptures told the wife to be submissive to the husband."

"They do," Gen said. "But God also told Abraham to listen to his wife Sarah on occasion."

"Once," Daniel said. "He said that *once*."

"Then this will be our 'once,'" was the answer. "The one time you listen to me will be now, when I say you must not send me away." She raised her head off his shoulder. "Do you think we could convince Robert and Nancy to come with us to Fort Wadsworth instead of going to Nebraska?"

"I think, little wife," Daniel said quietly, "that you have done quite enough plotting for one night." He kissed her fiercely, and for a few moments in the night neither threats from neighbors, nor barren lands, nor Robert, nor Nancy, mattered in the least.

Ten

"The wicked in his pride doth persecute the poor . . . "
—PSALM 10:2

"I'M SORRY, PAPA," POLLY MARSH PLEADED, COWERING away from her father. "I won't say it again."

"See that you don't," Abner snapped. Releasing his hold on Polly's upper arm he shoved her away. "I don't want to hear any more about Aaron Dane! I put up with it long enough and now I'm puttin' my foot down." He glared at his wife. "The Marshes don't have nothin' to do with Injun lovers. Let Marjorie Grant take care of her own brats. And tell that boy if he comes snooping around my daughter again I'll set my dogs on him!"

"Oh, Abner," Sally said, clucking her tongue. "Mrs. Grant just wanted the girls to watch the twins for the afternoon. She didn't want to burden Genevieve and Nancy, what with Nancy's baby coming any day now. Aaron's driving her by on their way into New Ulm. You let the girls go to the Grants' before. What's wrong with—?"

Before Sally could finish the sentence, Abner slapped her. "I'll not have my own wife disrespecting me in front of my own daughters!" he growled.

Sally lifted her hand to her cheek and stared at her husband in terrified silence. When Polly began to cry, Abner turned towards her in fury. Sally grabbed her daughter and pulled her close. "I'm all right, Polly. Papa didn't mean it."

"I did mean it!" Abner leered at them both. "And you'll get worse if you don't learn to respect me and do as I say!" He bolted from the house and disappeared behind the barn.

Trembling, Sally Marsh sank into a chair. Polly pumped cold water onto a rag and handed it to her mother, who lay it over her cheek where a purplish hue was already beginning to color the swollen place just above her left cheekbone.

"What's wrong with Papa?" Polly croaked, handing her mother a glass of water and sinking into the chair beside her. "He—he's been letting you go to quilting with those women. And he let Mr. Lawrence finish the railing. I thought he *liked* Aaron. What's wrong now?"

"I don't know," Sally managed before tears spilled down her cheeks. She closed her eyes. "Just do as Papa says, Polly. Don't argue with him. Things will be better if we just do as he says." She stood up. "Get your sister and the two of you go on out and feed the chickens. When you come back in, if I'm not up, come and get me. I'm just going to go lie down for a minute and collect myself."

Without waiting for her daughter to answer, Sally wobbled up the stairs and collapsed on her bed, terrified. It was coming true. Everything her parents had warned her about was happening. They had told her of Abner's father's dark moods, of his raging temper. *But Abner isn't like that,* Sally had insisted. *He's the sweet-est, gentlest boy. He never gets angry.* And by the end of the month Sally had run off with Abner. That had been well over a dozen years ago. As she lay in bed trembling, Sally Marsh closed her eyes against the truth.

Out in the barn, Abner once again emptied the contents of the bucket. It had become almost a ritual for him, this counting of bones, the arranging of them in just the right position on the floor before his dogs' cages. He always placed the skull last, in the center, with the hollowed-out eye cavities facing him. He backed away and crouched down on his haunches, thinking. He'd fooled everyone into believing he'd come to terms with the neighbors. Letting Sally go to quilting and having the older buck finish their railing had all been part of his plan. He'd even let Polly flirt with Aaron Dane. He congratulated himself on his brilliance. He pictured the Injuns worrying over headless chickens and dead raccoons, knowing he hadn't once left a trail and that everything he did in the open made it appear he was a converted Injun-lover. Yep, Abner thought, when he made his move, everyone would be surprised.

He stared at the bones, thinking. His dogs watched him, their ears alert, their noses resting on their front paws. Finally, the last piece of the puzzle fell into place. He knew exactly what to do. It would work, too. And they wouldn't be able to come back at him with any kind of law. But when it was all said and done, the Injuns would be gone and the county would be safe again.

He must move quickly, though. He wished the youngster from New York would leave, but Polly had already said—with a much-too happy expression on her face—that Aaron was going to stay the summer. Too bad. On the other hand, maybe he'd learn the real meaning of choosing sides with the thieving Sioux.

Abner looked at the dogs and smiled so broadly his tobacco-stained teeth shone in the fading light. Slowly, he picked up the bones. He hung the bucket high on a hook and left the barn. At supper, he teased his girls, confused by their subdued manner.

When Sally got up to clear the table, he looked at her with a scowl. "What'd you do to yourself, Sal?" he asked.

Sally looked down at him with surprise. He touched her cheek. "I got to fix that loose board on the porch. I'm sorry, Sal. That must have been a hard fall."

Sally raised her hand to her cheek. She didn't speak, and while the girls busied themselves clearing the table, Abner got up from the table and headed outside. They could hear him hammering late into the night.

❦

"Finally!" Nancy panted, leaning over to peer at the puddle of water on the earth. She extended her hand to Gen. "We'll just go on inside," she said between contractions. When Gen expressed concern that the men had gone up to Fort Ridgely to talk to Captain Willets again, Nancy smiled. "He'll be back soon enough. He'd only make a fuss right now, and it will surely be—a—while." As a contraction gripped her, she struggled to manage the last few words, stopping just inside the cabin door and breathing deeply. "I'm fine," she encouraged Gen. "Remember I've done this twice before. You get some water to heating. I'm going—to —lie—down."

"Marjorie wanted to be here," Gen reminded her as she grabbed a bucket and headed outside to get water.

"You go," Nancy called from the bedroom. "Things seem to be calming down a little. I'll be fine. Just hurry." There was still plenty of time for Robert to get back before his baby entered the world. Nancy settled back on the bed, willing herself to breathe deeply, thanking God for the new life, surprised by the stab of grief she felt behind all the anticipation and joy. She had become accustomed to the ever-present absence of her two lost children.

The army had said they were protecting them back in '62 when they crowded women and children inside a stockade just outside Fort Snelling. Perhaps they were. The enraged citizens of Minnesota threatened to break through the stockade often enough that awful winter. But in protecting them, the soldiers also killed them. Disease spread quickly in the camp. Being underfed and half-frozen most of the time took its toll first on the very young and the very old. It took Nancy and Robert's children.

As contraction after contraction wracked her body, Nancy began to think perhaps she had not impressed Gen with enough of a need to hurry. After all, she scolded herself, she had already given birth twice. This third child might come more quickly. Having been so stubborn about entering the world, having resisted so long, perhaps it had finally decided to hurry into the world. Certainly it had begun to feel that way. She wished Gen would come. She could birth a baby alone if need be, but she didn't want to.

In one short burst, things became serious. Nancy reached over her head and gripped the tree limb forming the headboard of their handmade bed. Her ability to reason or think was obliterated by the intense pressure as the baby sought its way into the world. Being alone no longer mattered. Nothing mattered but herself and the child and the wonderful, horrible thing that was happening. She prayed for strength, she yelled, she pushed, and finally, she felt her child slip from her body.

Panting and crying, Nancy reached for what appeared to be a lifeless body. But he was not lifeless. The moment she lifted him into her arms he wailed lustily. She lay him across her abdomen and wrestled with the pillow next to her, removing the pillowcase, cleaning him as best she could. When her body expelled the placenta, she lay the baby down. Slipping to her knees beside the bed, she whispered a prayer before rising to her feet and wobbling across to the kitchen where she found a knife. Returning to the bed, she cut through the cord that had once carried life from her body to her son. She made her way back to the bed, to the clean side. Climbing beneath the muslin sheet she lay her head back on Robert's striped pillow. She managed to wrap the baby more securely in Robert's pillowcase. Then, cradling him in her arms, Nancy brought him to her breast. He latched on willingly, raising a tiny fist to his mother's flesh, a diminutive symbol of ownership and life. Looking down at the scrunched-up face, stroking the silken black hair, Nancy wept.

❦

It was nearly dark when Robert and Daniel and Aaron returned from another visit to Fort Ridgely and Captain John Willets. This one had borne fruit. Things were heating up in the West. Willets expected to receive his orders to head West any day. If Robert and Daniel wanted to sign on as scouts, they'd not only be welcome, they would have immediate and pressing duties. And their wives could certainly go as far as Fort Wadsworth in Dakota. Both men were pleased to learn that, with the help of the fort physician, the Christian Dakota had founded a thriving church. Captain Willets had heard the missionaries were planning their summer camp meetings not far from Fort Wadsworth. Mrs. Lawrence and Mrs. Two Stars might even be able to get reacquainted with some of the mission teachers they had known before the uprising. The news convinced Robert that he could grant Nancy's wish to stay close to Genevieve. All in all, Daniel and Robert were satisfied. They would both sign on as scouts.

Captain Willets even hinted that if Aaron wanted to ride west as a civilian aide, something might be arranged.

"Edward Pope always likes having help in the kitchen," Willets had said, smiling at Aaron. "If you don't think taking orders from a cook is beneath you."

"I'll do anything," Aaron replied. "Anything at all."

"I like your attitude, young man," Willets had said. And he had taken Aaron to meet Pope.

It had been a good day for the men, and they rode back to the Grant farm rejoicing. When no light shone from their cabin windows and no smoke rose from their chimneys to welcome them home, neither man was worried. Robert glanced up the hill towards the Grants' and muttered something about women and quilting. "Late supper, I suppose," he said. "Might as well bed down the horses before we go get the women." They rode by the Lawrences' on their way to the small shed that served them both for a barn.

"Robert! Robert! Is that you?" Nancy's weak voice called out from inside the cabin.

Robert and Daniel dismounted and hurried inside. Still, neither one thought anything was terribly amiss. While Daniel lighted a lamp and Aaron fired up the stove, Robert lifted his son from Nancy's arms and nuzzled the baby's cheek, his face streaming with happy tears.

"Tell Gen and Marjorie to come in," Nancy finally said.

The men looked at one another with raised eyebrows.

"Aren't they with you?" Nancy said. She laughed softly. "I told Gen I didn't think it would be long." She shrugged. "Obviously I was wrong."

"Stay," Daniel said to Robert. "Enjoy your new son." He motioned for Aaron to follow him outside. "We'll see about Blue Eyes and Marjorie."

He tried to ignore the sensation in his belly. He told Aaron not to worry. Still, he broke into a lope only a few feet from the Lawrences' cabin, and a few strides later he was running.

Somehow, he knew what Marjorie would say.

"Genevieve? Nancy's had her baby? But Genevieve hasn't been here, Daniel," Marjorie said. She recovered quickly. "Jeb rode into town. If Aaron can watch the boys, I'll get down the hill to Nancy right away. You see about Genevieve, Daniel." She hurried towards the stairs. "I'll just collect a few things and be right down."

The words were barely out of her mouth when they heard a horse tear into the farmyard. "Barn's on fire!" Jeb screamed at the top of his lungs. "Barn's on fire!"

The mystery of Genevieve's absence was lost in the fury of the next half hour.

Marjorie ordered the twins to stay on the porch while she ran for the well and began pumping water into the horse trough. Robert tore up the hill and joined the men who had disappeared into the smoke pouring out the barn door.

A few buckets and farm tools and the plow were dragged outside. They had just managed to get Jeb's team and harness out when the roof fell in, sending a shower of sparks high in the darkening sky. The men staggered towards the well, coughing and sputtering, plunging their hands into the horse trough and scrubbing their faces. While they recovered, information was shared in short bursts. No one had seen any trace of Genevieve. Nancy was all right. Marjorie would take the twins and go down to stay with her. Jeb would stand guard over them with his rifle while the rest of them looked for Genevieve.

While Robert and Aaron saddled the horses, Daniel headed down the hill to retrieve their bed rolls. When his friends caught up with him, he was on his knees just inside his front door, clutching a piece of paper in his hands.

Aaron pulled the piece of paper from his hand and read aloud: THE ONLY GOOD INDIAN IS A DEAD INDIAN.

Eleven

"Recompense to no man evil for evil . . .
dearly beloved, avenge not yourselves . . ."

—ROMANS 12:17, 19

"PLEASE," GEN BEGGED. "I CAN'T—I CAN'T BREATHE."
She struggled to sit up, but in one savage move her captor slammed
her back onto her side. She could smell damp earth beneath her,
and something else. Oh, yes. The dogs. They were quiet now, but
the dogs were here. A blast of cool air made her shiver. She lay still,
waiting. *How long,* she wondered, *how long have I been here?* She
tried to make herself think back, hoping it would help her breathe
more evenly and gain more control over the sense of desperation.
She turned her head, struggling to shift the foul-smelling cloth tied
so tightly around her face so she could fill her lungs with air, but
when she moved again he shoved her harder.

She didn't know how long she had been in this place. One moment, she was hurrying along the road towards the Grants' to summon Marjorie for the birth of Nancy's baby. The next, something dropped out of a tree behind her and everything went black.

"I'll be back," a man's voice grunted, "don't move or my dogs will eat you alive."

At the sound of the man's steps retreating, she listened carefully and in the ensuing silence thought she could discern the presence of two, perhaps three, animals. She could hear them panting. She tested the man's warning by wiggling her foot. Immediately, there was a low growl. She spoke and the growl stopped. But when she moved her foot again, the growl came back, forcefully punctuated by snarls.

One of the dogs came to where she lay. She tried to lie still, praying desperately while the animal went over the entire length of her body sniffing her, all the while sounding a low rumble in his throat. Moisture from what she could only think was the dog's mouth salivating at the thought of chewing her flesh wet her bare arms.

After what seemed like hours, footsteps sounded and the man returned. He tossed something behind him and she could hear the dogs tear into it. He grabbed her and made her sit up, then slammed her against something hard. He pulled the blindfold off. She blinked and tried to focus. In the darkness her attention was drawn to his eyes, so filled with hatred Gen shrank back against what she now realized was the wall of a cave.

She couldn't see the entrance. He had built a small fire or it would have been completely dark. She almost wished it were. If it were dark, she wouldn't have those eyes peering at her. The fire produced just enough light to send the dogs' shadows dancing on the cave walls. Still, she couldn't make out enough of the man's outline to discern much about him.

He sat opposite her, staring at her. When he finally got up,

Gen realized he was a giant of a man. It was all she could do to keep from flinching when he crouched next to her and lifted her chin to inspect her face. She closed her eyes, afraid to look at him.

He swore and called her a vile name. "Look at me!" When she opened her eyes, he smiled wickedly. "Good. At least you're not pretending you don't speak English." He sat back down opposite her. "I know a lot about you. Do you know who I am?"

She shook her head.

He jerked the gag off her mouth. "Answer me."

Blinking back tears, Gen stammered, "N-n-no. I d-d-don't know y-you." She swallowed.

"Well, you will before this is over. You'll never forget me, either. I'll guarantee you that."

When this is over . . . she would remember. He didn't mean to kill her. The surge of joy Gen felt was immediately replaced with a shudder of dread, for there were worse things than dying and the way this man was staring at her made her wonder if he had a few of those things planned.

"I suppose you're wonderin' why?" he asked abruptly, throwing a log onto the fire.

"Y-y-yes," was all Gen could manage.

"I'll tell you. But first you have to tell me somethin'. You have to tell me what makes an Indian so stupid he don't know when he ain't wanted. What makes him think he can put down roots and farm land filled with the bones of people he's killed." The man didn't wait for Gen to speak. Instead, he reached behind him and dragged a bucket out of the shadows and shoved it at Gen, who flinched when she saw the human skull atop what must be a pile of bones.

When Gen didn't say anything, the man picked up the skull. He inspected it for a moment, then turned it in his hands and held it so that it appeared to be looking at her. When she tried to look away, he grabbed her chin and forced her to look at it.

"That's what they done," he said. "Killed and killed and killed again. Emptied the whole territory. And now they think we're going to let them back in to farm like nothin' ever happened."

"Daniel and Robert didn't do any of it." She held back tears, begging, "Please let me go. We only want to live in peace. To be left alone."

"You want to live in peace and be left alone, you get that buck of yours and his friends to pack up and get out of this county."

"Is that why you brought me here? To frighten us into leaving?" She spoke quickly. "But we're going. As soon as Daniel's reward money comes. And Nancy's baby. That's all. We're just waiting for the money to buy good horses . . . and the baby."

Afraid to meet his gaze, Gen looked past him. "Please," she begged softly, "just let me go. There won't be any trouble if you just let me go before anyone gets hurt."

He laughed roughly. "Now who you think's gonna get hurt? Not me. Not my family." He stood up. "Ain't nobody goin' to care much about one little squaw no bigger'n a schoolgirl."

"My husband was a scout for the army," Gen said. "He'll find us."

The man laughed again. "He ain't gonna be lookin' for you yet. Not when there's a barn fire to fight. And beside that, I made plans. We ain't anyplace he's goin' to think to look."

A barn fire? Whose barn had he burned? Surely not Jeb's. Gen tried to think what to say. Finally, she said, "He'll follow your trail."

"I didn't leave no trail," the man said.

"Everyone leaves a trail. Daniel can follow anything."

"You think I'm stupid?!" The man slammed the skull back into the bucket and called the dogs to him. With a wicked smile on his lips he whispered something low and the dogs went wild, snarling and snapping at Gen. She put her hands over her head and pulled her knees up to her chin, cowering against the wall, barely managing to keep from screaming.

As suddenly as the dogs had begun to bark, they stopped. Gen hadn't heard the man give them the order, but they just curled up in a pile against the opposite wall, watching her. One by one, the man slipped a rope over their necks and tethered them to pegs he drove into the floor of the cave. He turned towards her again. When he pulled a huge knife from his pocket and opened it, she shrank away.

"I ain't gonna' hurt you," he said. He bent over and freed her hands. Then he handed her a sack. "Eat. I got things to tell you."

Gen pulled a stale half-loaf of bread from the sack and began to gnaw on it while he talked.

"I had me a good place up by Acton back in '62," he said. "Everything was goin' good. Then one mornin' early I wake up to find three young Dakota bucks in my barn about to make off with my horses."

Abner Marsh. Dear God, it's Abner Marsh, and he knows it was Daniel.

Marsh stopped midsentence. He stirred the fire and peered at Gen. "Seems like maybe you know this story." He sat back, nodding. "Guess you can see how I don't think too much of all those sad stories about how the poor Injun's been mistreated. Me and my missus and the two girls got away just in time to see our place go up in flames." He stared at the fire. "My Sally's never been the same since."

"I know about—" Gen swallowed hard. When Abner looked at her, she tried to soften her voice. "She told the women about your baby boy. At quilting one day. I'm very sorry."

"I'm not a bad man," Abner said. "I want peace, too. And as soon as every last Injun is out of Minnesota, I'll have it." He stood up slowly. "I'm goin' to let you go tomorrow mornin'—if you promise that soon as you get there, you and your friends will pack up and get out of my part of the country." He paused. "If you don't, the next time somethin' burns down, it just might be Jeb Grant's house instead of his barn."

"They'll know you did it," Gen said. "They'll know and they'll come for you."

Abner roared with laughter. "Who'll come for me? You think the sheriff in New Ulm is gonna take action to help Injuns? You think my neighbors are gonna come against me on your account? Fact is most of 'em agree with me. They don't want your kind anywhere near their families." He spat on the ground. "They're just too lily-livered to do anything about it."

"Nancy's had the baby. Today." Gen tried to make her voice sound conciliatory. "You don't have to do anything more. We were just waiting for Nancy's baby. Captain Willets up at Fort Ridgely is waiting for Daniel and Robert to come."

Abner stooped down before her. His eyes were dark slits. He rubbed his thumb across Gen's chin, down her throat and across the front of her dress, then down her arm and across the back of her hand. There was no pressure, but the suggestion made Gen's skin crawl. "Well now," he said, "that's good news. Guess we'll just look on this little incident as insurance. Something that will make it clear in our minds. Keep your men from changing their minds." He looked at her and licked his lips. "Anyone talks about changing their mind and staying on, you'll be able to set 'em straight."

Gen nodded and Abner stood up. "I'm going now." He nodded towards the dogs. "But they know what to do if you try anything, so save us both the trouble. There's a storm brewin'. I'll be back when it's over."

He ambled out of sight, leaving Gen in the shadows of the dying fire.

※

"You do what you want," Daniel said. "I'm going to find my wife." He swallowed hard. "And if she's hurt—" He gestured towards where Abner's trail led off into a field. "He leaves a trail as wide as an entire village."

"We need help," Jeb said. "The law."

"You get whatever law you think will help a Dakota brave against a white man," Daniel said. He motioned to Aaron to follow him. "I'm going to get my wife."

"But, Daniel," Jeb called.

Robert grabbed his arm. "Let him go. Can you ride up to Fort Ridgely and get Captain Willets?"

"I don't see no call to get the military involved," Jeb said uncertainly.

"You're a good man, Jeb. But if there's going to be trouble, I'd like to have more than one white man in Minnesota on my side. You tell Captain Willets what's happened. He'll come. I pray to God we won't need him. But I want him."

In less than an hour Jeb had headed for Fort Ridgely and Robert had joined Daniel and Aaron, following the trail left by Abner Marsh.

"Someone should have gone to the Marsh farm," Robert said quietly. "Just to make certain it is him."

"It's him," Daniel said tersely from where he knelt on the ground studying the shadow of a track. Clouds moving in from the West caused the wind to pick up. He got up abruptly and began to run along the creek bank.

Robert went to the opposite side of the creek bank. After a few moments when nothing had turned up, he called across to Daniel, "He's not as careless as we thought."

It began to drizzle. The men pushed ahead, frantic to find some trace. In the gathering dark Daniel finally found the imprint of a shoe. He tore up the creek bank and headed north just as it began to rain. At the top of the hill Aaron found a fragment of cloth clinging to a bramble.

"It's Gen's," Daniel said and climbed back into the saddle. "But where is he taking her?"

Just as Daniel asked the question, the skies opened, drenching all three men in a matter of moments. Lightning flashed and the horses began to dance nervously.

"Let's find shelter," Robert shouted above the rain. "We'll start again as soon as the storm passes." No one mentioned what they all knew—that the storm was obliterating Abner Marsh's trail and when the rain ceased they would be standing helpless in the middle of a field with no inkling of where to go or what to do.

An hour later, the men were still hunkered beneath a rocky ledge, wet and miserable. Robert spoke up. "If he meant to harm her, Daniel, he wouldn't have had to take her so far away. I don't know what he has in mind, but I don't think he means to harm her. For some reason he's just hiding."

Daniel was quiet so long that Robert began to think he had fallen asleep. When he acknowledged what Robert said, it was only to croak, "I can't think God would have given her back to me only to let evil take her again."

"Neither can I," Robert said. He put his hand on Daniel's shoulder. "We'll find her."

"God loves her more than we do," Aaron said suddenly. "We should pray."

Daniel stared at the boy. "Then pray, Aaron. I know I should. But I can't."

Aaron gulped and looked guiltily at Robert. He meant to help, but in the face of desperation, his call to prayer felt like a meaningless cliché. Embarrassed, he bowed his head and said nothing.

"Father God," Robert said, "Daniel has no words. Aaron has no words. I have none, except to say that we give You Genevieve. We give You ourselves. And we ask You to show us what to do." He paused, sighed, and then looked down, muttering, "I am sorry, my friend. That is all I know to say."

Daniel scrubbed his face in a vain attempt to hold back the emotions raging inside him. He was doing his best to serve God and to trust Him. It certainly seemed to him that both he and Blue Eyes had suffered enough for one lifetime. He had resisted anger at God and a dozen other feelings threatening to overwhelm. The one emotion he could not seem to beat back was fear. He was afraid of losing the trail. Afraid of never finding Blue Eyes. Or worse, of finding her and learning that she had been harmed in some horrible way that neither of them would ever be able to reclaim. He was afraid, too, that he would find her . . . and with her, Abner Marsh. The thought terrified him, because if Abner Marsh had harmed his Blue Eyes, then he would not turn the other cheek, and he would be guilty of an act that might prove a permanent denial of his faith in Christ. And that was the greatest fear of all.

Twelve

"Save us, O God of our salvation,
and gather us together, and deliver us from the heathen,
that we may give thanks to thy holy name,
and glory in thy praise."

—I CHRONICLES 16:35

ABNER HAD SAID A STORM WAS BREWING, AND ALTHOUGH Gen couldn't see outside, she could sense a change as if the air were charged with something new. The dogs sensed it, too. They grew restless, alternating between lying down and sitting, their ears always alert as they turned their attention first towards Gen, then towards the entrance of the cave and back again. Once the storm began, they grew even more restless, straining against the ropes that bound them, sniffing at one another, whining and pacing back and forth. One fierce flash of lightning followed by a clap of thunder caused a frenzy of yelping and straining against the ropes that tied them to the floor of the cave.

When the storm increased its fury and thunder echoed through the cave, they seemed to forget about Gen. They yelped and cried out, paced and jerked at their tethers in a frenzy of fear.

They're afraid. With the realization, Gen sensed a flicker of hope. Taking a deep breath, she inched away from the wall behind her. One of the dogs, the one with pale eyes, noticed. Gen paused, willing herself to stare back into the animal's eyes. When a loud burst of thunder sounded through the cave, the dog looked away from Gen, straining and pulling against the stake for all he was worth. The stake began to loosen in the soft earth of the cave floor and while the storm outside raged, Gen pulled and pushed at the splintered piece of wood, never taking her eyes off the dogs.

Once, when the storm seemed to quiet, all three animals turned to watch her. With her heart in her throat, Gen rolled out of harm's way. Only when she was once again pressed against the cave wall did she realize the dogs had not tried to attack her. They watched her with a kind of curiosity, looking from her towards the doorway and back again, almost as if in their desperation they begged her to release them. Carefully, slowly, she inched back towards the stakes, never taking her eyes off the animals, praying her hands would not shake, begging God to keep any scent of fear from setting them at her. As if in answer to her prayer, the storm picked up again, hurling flashes of light into the cave and once again setting the dogs into a frenzied pattern of pacing and yelping and struggling against the ropes.

"If you'd let me touch you," Gen said, more to herself than to the animals, "I could untie you and you'd be free."

But they only continued their pacing and struggling while Gen knelt beside a stake and, grasping it with her hands, began rocking back and forth with all her might. Finally, the wood gave way and the dog at the other end of the rope leaped away.

Their partner's absence sent the two remaining dogs into a

heightened frenzy. They lunged again and again away from Gen while she worked at the second stake. When it gave way and the second dog tore away, the remaining animal seemed to forget all about Gen in its desperate attempt to get free. Emboldened by the ferocity of the storm and the animal's obvious terror, Gen reached for its collar. The creature lashed out at her more out of mindless fear than any intent to harm, opening a deep gash across one forearm, but at the moment the dog's teeth found flesh, Gen managed to release the rope from around its neck and the animal tore away.

With shaking hands, Gen began to work at the ropes binding her ankles together. When lightning illuminated the cave, she realized the gash on her forearm was oozing blood so freely it ran down her arm and was dripping all over her feet. Impatient to be free, she ripped a strip of white cloth from her petticoat and wrapped her forearm, then returned to working at the knot securing the rope around her ankles. The storm began to quiet and with the cessation of the lightning, it was nearly impossible to see. She scooted across the floor of the cave towards the opening. The sky was clearing.

Oh, God, Gen prayed. *Don't let the dogs find their way home too soon . . . don't bring him back. Not yet. Help me, Lord.* She prayed continually while she worked at the ropes around her ankles and at last she was free. Springing up to run away she stumbled, surprised at how stiff her legs had become in the hours she had been bound. She landed hard against a rock and for a moment lay staring up at the brilliant night sky gasping for breath. When she finally managed to get back up, her head was throbbing. She winced and raised her hand to feel a huge welt rising near her left cheekbone. A noise in the underbrush near the cave sent her staggering ahead blindly. She held her arms before her face and made her way through a thicket of trees and up and up until, finally, she came out of the brush atop a hill.

She paused, blinking stupidly, looking about her, dismayed that she saw nothing familiar and had no idea which way to run. *Which way, Father? I don't know where I am . . . which way?* The only answer was the sounds of the night creatures recovering from the storm and beginning to creak and squeak their way through another few hours of darkness before dawn.

At last she thought she saw a glimmer of light off in the distance. With a shudder, she wondered if it might be Marsh's campfire. No, she reasoned, no one could have kept a fire going through the storm. A cabin, then? Her heart racing, she stared into the distance and, breathing another prayer, she headed for the light.

∞

She is Mine. I love her far more than even you. Give her to Me.

Hunkered under a rock in the driving storm, Daniel tried to ignore the inner voice. He had been trying to ignore it for what seemed like hours, and yet as he watched the violence of the storm that would wash away all trace of any trail that might lead him to Blue Eyes, as he fought the rising desperation that clutched at his midsection, Daniel knew what he must do. He had asked Robert to pray because he did not have it in him to say what he must. Even now, when he allowed the conscious thought, he didn't think he could do it. *How can I do that?* he argued with himself—or with God, although he preferred to think of the raging thoughts in his head as being only the human rantings of a man beside himself with worry. *How can I simply open my hand and give her over?*

You might as well give her to Me. I know where she is. Even at this moment I can see her. She is Mine, and I do as I please with what is Mine . . . and if you are Mine, you must learn to trust Me. I do only what is best for time and all eternity. But My ways are not your ways.

Daniel begged, *Don't let her be hurt, God. Please. I couldn't stand it if she were—if another man—*

I made a man out of the dust, My son, and I make beauty out of ashes all the time. I will do it again. Give Genevieve to Me.

I can't, Daniel begged. *I can't.*

You can do all things, Daniel Two Stars, for I will give you strength.

Even as the Scriptures sounded in his heart, Daniel rebelled. He did not want strength to do nothing and trust God. He wanted strength to find Blue Eyes and to make whoever had taken her suffer.

As if he had heard Daniel's inner struggle, Robert said gently, "The heavenly Father loves her far more than you ever will, Daniel. You must believe that. Think back to all that He has done for you and trust Him. He makes beauty from ashes."

Hearing Robert speak some of the very words Daniel had been thinking sent a shiver running down his spine. He ran his hands through his hair. "I know it in my head. It is a very different thing to believe it on a night when she has been taken—when someone might be—" His voice wavered. He took a deep breath. "When I think what could be happening—she's so little," he gulped. "She couldn't defend herself, not if—"

Robert read his friend's fears and began suddenly to pray, "Dear Father, we beg a miracle. Keep Gen from harm." He paused. "Please, Lord, show Yourself to my friend in a way that he will never forget. We believe, Lord. Forgive our unbelief." Robert grasped his friend's shoulder. "The rains stop. Let's go."

"We don't know where to go," Daniel muttered miserably, even as he stood up and stretched his stiff legs and mounted his horse. He sat with his head bowed for a moment, then looked up at the clear night sky. Far off in the distance he thought he could hear dogs barking.

"Marsh has dogs," he said quickly and nudged his horse to a

trot. A lump rose in his throat as he and Robert and Aaron urged their horses into a deep valley and across a swiftly running creek newly filled with rainwater. Slowed by mud and wet grass, the men plodded towards the sound of barking dogs.

He should have known he couldn't trust those fool dogs. Not in a storm like the one last night. Abner Marsh slipped on the muddy slope leading up to the cave, but not before he saw the signs of escape. Scrambling up the path and charging inside the cave, he grabbed up first one wooden stake and then another, shouting a string of epithets aimed at small Injun women and big dogs. He went back to the mouth of the cave and then to the top of the hill outside where he stood as the sun rose, staring around him at the countryside, immune to the beauty of a world washed clean.

Somewhere far in the distance he thought he could hear something. Abner cocked his head and squinted, listening carefully. Then, with a smile, he descended the hill into the swirling early morning fog, mounted his horse, and with a savage kick to the animal's sides, set off in the direction of what he thought just might be his dogs barking at a treed animal.

It was going to be a beautiful day. Dawn illuminated clear azure skies. The scent of freshly washed grass and damp earth filled the morning air as Gen closed her eyes and inhaled. In the predawn light she had headed towards a glimmer in the distance. She could no longer see it, but she kept in the general direction anyway. In spite of the thick morning fog, there was something oddly familiar about the landscape and she began to think she might be near either the old Redwood Agency, or even perhaps Fort Ridgely.

She hurried along, ignoring her aching head and the throbbing in her arm where one of the dogs had bitten her. Coming upon a violently rushing stream, she hesitated only a moment before plunging across it only to emerge shivering on the opposite bank. It was then she thought she heard something in the distance behind her. She hurried on, trying to ignore the sound until she could no longer deny the fact that somewhere behind her dogs were barking.

Gen had just leaped across another stream when she turned just in time to see Abner Marsh's dogs break into view out of the fog and tear across the valley towards her. She began to run, aware that the dogs were closing fast. Instinct sent her to a tree just ahead. She leaped once, twice, a third time, managing to clutch a low branch and scramble up just as the first dog reached her. With one leap the animal caught the hem of her dress. She could feel the tug and hear the fabric rip as the dog landed beneath her, a strip of her dress dangling from its mouth. She climbed higher, crouching on a limb, looking down at the dogs as they snarled and leaped high in the air in a vain attempt to reach her.

Please, God, Gen thought desperately, *send help!*

The prayer had scarcely formed in her mind when Abner Marsh came into view astride a tall bay horse.

Gen pulled her legs up beneath her and wrapped her arms around her knees in a vain attempt to become invisible. Trembling with terror, she began to cry. Inwardly she was screaming, *God . . . send help!*

Marsh pulled his horse to a walk and approached slowly, enjoying the sight of his dogs doing as they had been trained. Still dragging a piece of the rope that had tied it in place in the cave, one of the dogs was shredding a portion of the little squaw's dress. The other two alternately jumped high against the tree and spun in circles in a frenzied attempt to get at her. She was there, perched high in the tree, her legs drawn up beneath her, her dark skin paler than usual. As he got closer, he realized she was look-

ing at him. He pulled his horse up and stared back at her, hoping
the hatred he felt for her and her kind showed on his face. When
he nudged his horse closer, he could see the tears streaming down
her face. Still, he thought, there was something in those blue eyes
that was neither surrender nor fear. There was something else. In
another setting, he would have thought the expression was one of
pity. He could see her lips move. But she wasn't calling out for
mercy. It occurred to him that the fool woman was praying.

And as Abner looked up at the treed Indian woman, something
happened. She was so small, he thought. Hardly big enough to be a
grown woman. More the size of Pris and Polly back at home. And
the dogs. The dogs were doing their job. Having treed their prey they
were still trying to get at it, waiting for their master to shoot it out of
the tree, ready to tear it to pieces. He looked at the woman again.
Sally had said something about her one night at supper, something
about her going to Marjorie Grant's and helping the women with
their quilting. When Sally said Harriet Baxter and Lydia Quinn
thought Genevieve Two Stars was a nice woman, he'd slapped her
and reminded her what she was to think about Indians. But now,
looking up at the Indian perched on the tree branch, shivering and
staring at him with those brilliant blue eyes, he had to look away. No
one had told him Genevieve Two Stars was a half-breed. It didn't
really matter, he supposed, but if she was part white . . . Abner
blinked. He wished she would do anything but just sit there quietly looking at him with her lips moving like that. Her hair covered
half her face, but he could see the bruise anyway. He saw the bloodstained rag wrapped around her forearm, the white petticoat showing from beneath the skirt Goliath had ripped.

"Goliath!" he shouted. "Pilate! Thor! Off!" Immediately the
dogs moved away from the tree. They trotted over to Abner's
horse and waited.

Gen braced herself, thinking Marsh would either shoot her
now or order her down. She had decided she would not get

down, not of her own free will. Her heart pounded as she stared back at him. *God help me*, she prayed.

Abner Marsh's face changed. The twisted hatred shining in his eyes faded and was replaced with something. Gen could not call it kindness. Perhaps it was shame, she would think later. Whatever it was, it signaled the end. He looked down at his dogs. He pulled back on his horse's reins and the animal backed away. When the dogs hesitated, Abner stopped. He did not look back at Gen. Instead, he yelled for his dogs, urged his animal into a trot, and rode out of sight.

❧

Daniel pulled his horse up. Behind him, Aaron and Robert followed suit. "What does it mean when they are silent like that?" he asked. He didn't expect an answer and he didn't wait for one. The men urged their horses ahead, descending into the morning fog as they picked up the pace. Ahead of Robert and Aaron and on a faster horse, Daniel disappeared into the swirling mists.

His legs and feet soaked with moisture from the tall grasses, Daniel forged ahead, forcing himself to pray, but fearing God would not give what he asked. When the fog grew thicker, he had to pull up. Behind him he could hear Aaron and Robert's horses plodding towards him. He listened for the dogs somewhere up ahead, but all he could hear was the sound of some large animal breaking through the underbrush. Reaching behind him for his rifle, Daniel climbed down off his horse and waited for Robert and Daniel to catch up. When they did, he motioned for them to dismount. Both men slid off their horses, using them as a shield against whatever was approaching.

There was a barely perceptible flash of color in the fog ahead. Daniel dropped his rifle and charged toward it. It only took a few strides for him to reach his Blue Eyes, to pull her into his arms and lift her up. His eyes closed, he held her to himself, thanking God at the feeling of her arms around his neck, listening to her sob out love both to him and their God.

When he finally set her back to the earth and brushed her hair back from her face, his fingers traced the lump at her temple and touched the bruises. He touched the bloodstained bandage around her forearm and his dark eyes filled with rage. When he noticed her ripped skirt something else appeared on his face— hurt, and disbelief, and desperation.

Aaron and Robert, who had been about to join the celebration, took one look at Gen and turned away. "Give them time alone," Robert muttered. Together he and Aaron headed off to wait beneath a tree just coming visible as the morning sun cleared the fog away.

Daniel gathered his wife in his arms and began to weep.

"It's not what you think, best beloved." Gen reached up to touch his face. "Look at me," she lay her open palm against his cheek and met his gaze. "He didn't hurt me." She touched the bruises and the lump on her face. "I slipped and fell this morning and hit my head." Her eyes filled with tears. "It's a miracle, Daniel. Just for you and me. Abner Marsh didn't hurt me."

Holding her close, Daniel stroked her hair. "I believe you," he whispered. "It's just—I didn't think—I didn't think God would answer the way I wanted Him to." He sighed. "I doubted Him. Again." He waved Robert and Aaron over. "She's all right," he said as they approached.

"He had me tied up in some cave," Gen explained. "And this morning when I got out, my legs were so stiff, I slipped in the mud and hit my head. And then," she looked down at her ripped skirt, "then when the dogs had me up in a tree one of them managed to grab hold and tear—"

Daniel almost growled, "Abner Marsh had his dogs tree you like some animal being hunted?"

Gen looked up and saw something new in her husband's face that frightened her.

The emotion was echoed in Robert's and Aaron's faces as well. She hurried on. "The dogs couldn't get at me. They just paced around below."

"We heard them," Aaron said bluntly. "That's what brought us this way."

Gen nodded. "Yes. Well, Mr. Marsh must have been a good ways ahead of you. He could have done anything. Anything at all." She stopped and swallowed hard. "I was up on a branch looking down at him. All I could think of was to pray." She shuddered. "If you could have seen his face—" She paused. "But I was praying, and suddenly he just stopped and looked at me and then—oh," she put her hand on Aaron's arm, "I couldn't believe it, he called the dogs to come to him. And they left."

"Just like that?"

Gen nodded. "Yes." She looked at each of them. "Just like that. I know he didn't hear you. The only sounds were the dogs. I don't know what happened. One minute he was riding towards the tree with that evil smile on his face and the next he was calling his dogs and leaving. He never even looked back. He just disappeared into the fog."

The men stood looking at one another. Daniel put his arms around her shoulders. The sun came up, bright and shining on the morning dew. Everywhere around them it looked like God had scattered jewels on the grasses and trees. Gen sighed and leaned against her husband. Everything that had happened to her seemed to wash over her at once and she began to shake. Once again, Daniel swept her off her feet and into his arms. Lifting her up onto his horse, he leaped up behind her. When he reached around her for the reins, she leaned back against him and kissed his cheek. And together, they went home.

Thirteen

"But I say unto you, Love your enemies,
bless them that curse you, do good to them
that hate you, and pray for them which
despitefully use you, and persecute you."

—MATTHEW 5:44

CAPTAIN JOHN WILLETS SET HIS COFFEE MUG DOWN AND leaned back in his chair. He was sitting across from Daniel and Genevieve Two Stars at the rough-hewn table in their tiny cabin. To his left sat Aaron Dane. Footsteps sounded behind him and Willets turned around just in time to see Robert and Nancy Lawrence duck inside. Willets shook his head and swiped his hand over his blond goatee. "Glad to see you Robert," he said abruptly. "Maybe you can translate what I just heard, because, Daniel," he peered across the table at Daniel, "I can't believe what I just thought I heard is what you really said."

Daniel took Gen's hand. "We said to let it be, Captain. We don't want to cause any more trouble."

"That man said the next time something burns it might be Jeb and Marjorie's house," Willets said firmly. "Am I right, Mrs. Two Stars? Isn't that what the man said?"

Gen nodded. "Yes. But he won't do anything. Because we're leaving. There's no need to cause any more trouble."

"He threatened Jeb and Marjorie?" Robert asked. "When?"

"In the cave," Gen said quietly. She smiled and reached out to stroke Nancy's baby's hair. "But he won't do it. We don't have to worry about that."

"You can't just let this go!" Aaron spoke up. His was shaking with rage. "You can't just let someone like that mistreat you and do nothing."

"I agree with the boy," Captain Willets said. "I can't act on official jurisdiction, of course, but there's a few men up at the fort who would be happy to pay an unofficial visit to the Abner Marsh farm. And he wouldn't have to know the visit was unofficial."

"No." Gen said firmly. She pressed her lips together and shook her head. "No."

"Don't let him do this to you," Aaron urged. He leaned forward, pleading with Daniel and Robert. "This isn't like you. You don't just run away and do nothing."

"We are not doing *nothing*," Gen said gently. She looked at each of the men in turn. "We are deciding to forgive him."

"He won't care! The only thing a man like that understands is the kind of thing Captain Willets can do." Aaron's blue eyes flashed angrily. Something in the way he held his head, the way he tensed his jaw, reminded Gen of his father.

"Aaron," Gen said. "Neither your heavenly father nor your earthly one would want you to take vengeance out of anger. You know Simon would never approve."

Aaron shoved his chair back and stood up. "Daniel," he

begged. "Don't let her—don't let her tell you what to do! It isn't right! We have to do something. He should have to pay—"

"And he will," Daniel said, looking up at the furious boy. "But not because of something I did back to him."

"Are you sure about this?" Captain Willets spoke up. He looked from Daniel to Robert.

Robert nodded. "He might blame Jeb and keep the threat to start another fire. The Grants have two boys. We can't risk it. And I don't want to be the cause of any more pain."

Daniel was gripping his coffee mug so tightly Willets thought it might break. Still, he looked at his wife and nodded. "Blue Eyes insists she wasn't really hurt. We will thank God for that. And we will move on." He looked up at his friend. "Can we still come to Fort Ridgely?"

"You know you can," Willets said. "I'll be proud to ride with you two again." He stared at the two men. Family or none, friends or not, he knew without a doubt that only a few years ago either one of them would have taken bloody vengeance on Abner Marsh and his family and relished hanging their scalps from their tepee poles. He had fought alongside Daniel. The man was a merciless warrior in battle, someone Willets would gladly entrust with his life, knowing it was in good hands. Willets had never seen either of these men express a shred of weakness or fear. And yet, here they were, practicing something Willets could not fathom . . . something that was inherently against their traditions. They were talking about forgiving Abner Marsh, a man who didn't think he needed forgiveness and who would likely never know it had been granted by his victims. What galled Willets even more was the knowledge that Marsh would likely boast for the rest of his life about the time he took action and rid the county of the last of the savages threatening his family.

"You sure about this thing with Marsh?" he asked again. "I know enough about the Dakota to know how you usually handle this kind of thing. Someone hurts one of yours, you hurt them. An eye for an eye. I'm not saying we'd hurt Marsh. But I'd take singular delight in putting the fear of God in him. And I'd let him know that if anything suspicious ever happens to the Grants, he'd likely be held responsible."

Gen spoke up. "No. There's more to it than just us and the Grants, Captain Willets. That man is sick. Sick with hatred and anger. I can't imagine what it must be like for his wife and his two daughters living with a man like that. It could only get worse for Sally and the girls if we seek revenge."

At mention of the Marsh girls, Aaron blanched. He hadn't thought of that. Of what things might be like for Polly. She was a nice girl, too. Maybe not as pretty as Amanda Whitrock, but she had her good points.

Daniel said firmly, "Let it be."

Willets stared at his friend for a moment before finally shrugging. "All right. If that's what you want."

"What I want," Daniel said quickly, "is to torture Abner Marsh for a few hours before I tear his head off and feed it to his dogs." The force of his words made everyone uncomfortable. It grew so quiet in the room they could all hear the infant in Nancy's arms snoring softly.

Daniel sat back in his chair and took a deep breath. "But God wants me to forgive."

"Marsh won't ever even know he's been forgiven," Willets said abruptly. "He doesn't comprehend there's anything to forgive."

"I can't control Abner Marsh," Daniel said. "All I can do is try to keep the hatred out of my own heart. I can't say I have forgiven him yet. But I can ride away without seeking vengeance. That's a beginning."

Willets pondered what his friend had said. He shook his head. "I don't understand it. But I'll tell you one thing: I can appreciate that doing it probably takes more strength than what I proposed."

Daniel took in a deep breath. "You have no idea," he said. Then, he turned towards Nancy. "I haven't gotten to hold him yet."

Nancy smiled and willingly gave the infant up. Daniel pulled the bundle to him and sat down abruptly, managing the baby with all the grace of a two-year-old trying to tote a ripe watermelon.

"Here," Gen said, laughing and taking the baby to cuddle. "You look ridiculous."

"His name?" Daniel asked.

"Comes Out Alone," Nancy teased.

Robert grinned. "Last night we read in the Scriptures together about a man who was taken to a foreign place. Others meant to do him harm and sent him away. But God turned it to good so that many were blessed. We will name our son Joseph. And we will hope that what Abner Marsh has meant for evil, God will use for good." He nodded at Daniel. "Beauty for ashes."

"You'll come to Fort Ridgely then?" Captain Willets said quietly. When everyone around the table nodded, he said, "You can camp across the parade ground where you did last time. As long as you want. Pick a spot and I'll send some men over with tents." He grinned. "I'll venture a guess Edward Pope will be around with a pot of soup as soon as you get there." He made a loose fist and pounded Aaron on the shoulder. "And if you come with them, I'll see to it you get a taste of army life if you want it." He teased, "Real army life, son. Not what you'll hear about at some fancy military academy with a bunch of boys who haven't ever been West."

Aaron's eyes widened with anticipation.

Gen smiled at him. "We'll write Jane and Elliot tomorrow and let them know you're staying a while longer." Then she added, "But don't think for a minute I'm going to let you go any farther West than Fort Wadsworth. When Daniel and Robert leave with Captain Willets, you'll be on your way back to New York on the first boat that heads downriver."

"Oh, Marjorie," Gen said, blinking back tears. "We can't take Goldie. We just can't." She sat on the wagon seat next to Daniel choking back tears.

"You surely can," Marjorie said firmly. She tied the cow to the back of Gen and Daniel's wagon.

Gen protested. "But she's your best milk cow."

"And you been my best friend since Jeb and me been here in Minnesota." Marjorie patted Gen's hand but didn't look up. Instead, she turned to where Nancy was riding in the wagon box, nestled into fresh hay in one corner, her baby in her arms. "At least you won't have to worry if yer milk don't hold up," Marjorie said to Nancy. As she spoke, she reached out to stroke the baby's cheek. "Never saw such a head of hair," she muttered. Surveying the small collection of household goods packed behind Nancy, Marjorie shook her head. "Wish we could do more." She bit her lip. "Wish you didn't have to go."

"It's for the best," Nancy said gently.

A familiar clatter in the distance turned everyone's attention towards the horizon and presently two wagons followed by about half a dozen men on horseback appeared on the road from New Ulm. To everyone's surprise, the cortege turned in at the Grants'. Thomas Quinn and Earl Baxter were driving the wagons. The mounted men had been to Jeb's before—with Abner Marsh one morning a few weeks ago.

Jumping down from his wagon and striding over to Jeb, Quinn said, "Earl and me and some of the neighbors are starting a new barn today. You be thinking where you want it while we unload." Walking to the back of his wagon, Quinn pulled aside the canvas cover to reveal a rooster and hen inside a homemade cage. There were two stoneware crocks and a side of dried beef.

Quinn grabbed one of the crocks and walked up to Daniel

and Robert. "Thought we'd just bring a few things to help you on your way," he said, and set the crock in the back of Daniel's wagon.

Earl Baxter followed suit, contributing a huge piece of salt pork, a basket full of dried beans, a hundred-pound sack of flour, and a small crock he said was dried apples. "Harriet says it'll do to make you a pie come Christmas." Tipping his hat to Nancy and Gen, Baxter joined the group of men unloading lumber.

The Lawrences and the Two Starses would never forget the kindness of their Minnesota neighbors. But what happened next gave not only the Lawrences and the Two Starses, but everyone present, something to wonder over for the rest of their lives. A light carriage with a solitary driver turned in at the farm. Sally Marsh pulled her horse up and climbed down. Pulling a bundle wrapped in brown paper from beneath the carriage seat, she approached Gen. "You want to throw this back in my face, you got every right," she said nervously. She did not look into Gen's eyes, but when she reached out to thrust the package at Gen, her bonnet fell back from her face. Gen and Nancy and Marjorie let out a collective gasp at sight of the dark bruises encircling Sally's right eye. She snatched the bonnet back up in place and ducked her head. "Abner don't know I come."

Gen untied the package. When the brown wrapper fell away, it revealed a small quilt made of hundreds of fragments of fabric, each one no bigger than a thumbnail. "Oh, Sally," Gen said, and reached out to put her hand on Sally's arm. "It's—it's just beautiful."

Sally whispered hoarsely, "I made that for my boy. The one that died. I never could stand to look at it after that. Took it out more'n once to burn it. But I couldn't. Had it all these years just put away in my trunk." She finally summoned the courage to look at Gen. "I worked hard on it, and it's a beauty. If you'll take it, maybe you can give it a happy meaning. Use it for your own child someday." Her chest heaved and she let out a ragged breath.

"I'm so s-s-s-orry for what happened." She seemed to want to say more, but instead she turned to go.

"It isn't your fault," Gen said gently. She touched Sally's hand, but Sally withdrew it and clutched both her hands to her midsection. Gen repeated, "It isn't your fault, Mrs. Marsh. None of it." She ran her hand across the surface of the little quilt. "It's beautiful. And when I look at it, I'll always remember your kindness."

Sally glanced up at Gen. The women's eyes met for only a second before she turned away. "Thank you for talking to me," she said. She straightened her shoulders a little, as if a small burden had been lifted. Wearily, she climbed back up onto her seat and, without looking back, turned the carriage around and headed back up the road.

As soon as Sally Marsh's carriage was out of sight, Daniel and Genevieve said good-bye and climbed up onto the wagon seat. Robert and Aaron mounted up—Robert on the horse they had bought with Abner Marsh's cash payment for his carpentry and Aaron on Bones, accepted by Daniel as payment for the spring plowing he'd done. "And I won't take no for an answer," Jeb had said. "You take him now or I'll have to follow you up to Fort Ridgely and tie him to your tent stake some night."

"You'll let us know where you end up." Jeb said. He picked up one of the twins. Marjorie followed suit. They stood watching and waving until Daniel's wagon topped the hill and dipped out of sight.

"Are you all right, little wife?" Daniel said after a few moments.

Gen moved closer to him. She put her hand on his knee and began to hum a familiar tune. *Cling to me and you'll ever have a plenty . . .*

Fourteen

"Hast thou given the horse strength?
Hast thou clothed his neck with thunder? . . .
He paweth in the valley, and rejoiceth in his strength:
he goeth on to meet the armed men. He mocketh
at fear, and is not affrighted."

—JOB 39:19, 21–22

EDWARD POPE CAME TEARING INTO FORT RIDGELY. "THEY
got him!" he shouted to anyone who would listen, waving his hat
in the air and beating his mule's flanks in a futile attempt to get
the creature to move faster. "Chrisman and Buford got the white
stallion!"

Heads emerged from tents just in time to see Pope's mule
dump its rider in the dust. "It's true," Pope insisted, lifting one
hand as if taking a vow and dusting off his backside with the
other. "I seen him myself. A rope on all fours. They got him
nearly spread-eagled up that way," Pope pointed towards the
north. "Nearly spread-eagled and he's still fightin' like a demon."

He ran towards where the scouts were camped and yelled at Daniel and Robert. "Come on! You got to see this."

Daniel and Robert were only too willing to mount up and follow Edward Pope for a chance to see the horse everyone was talking about. Their life at Fort Ridgely had been happily boring for the past two weeks since Captain Willets received news that he would be heading West soon and could he please recruit some new scouts. He assured Daniel and Robert their wives could accompany them at least as far as Fort Wadsworth, where they could settle with the other Dakota families. And young Aaron Dane could get a taste of army life.

Daniel and Robert got reacquainted with some of the men they had known before, not the least of which was Edward Pope, who blushed furiously when he was introduced to Genevieve and quickly won the women's hearts by buying trinkets for Nancy's baby Joseph at the sutler's. "Got nothing else to spend it on," Pope said when Nancy protested his generosity. "Ain't likely I'll ever have a boy of my own. Not many women care for a man that looks like he was put together with spare parts from God's ugly bucket."

Except for the tales of a legendary wild horse roaming the hills far to the west, there was little excitement at Fort Ridgely. Aaron had grumbled that he wasn't learning very much about the Army.

"On the contrary," Captain Willets said. "You're learning a lot. If you can't handle a little boredom, you won't do very well in the Army." He gave a knowing look to Robert. "Ask anyone you know who has good character and they'll tell you one of the worst things they meet up with is the temptations that surround camp life when there's no campaigns. There aren't many things worse in this world than a bored soldier."

Aaron saw plenty of evidence to uphold Willets's opinion in his first couple of days at Fort Ridgely. There was gambling at almost every hour of the day. The men told stories and fished. A few played battered musical instruments. And Captain Willets's best attempts at keeping the men busy with dress parades and inspections could not eradicate the pursuit of entertainment of the female variety in a well-sequestered cabin the location of which the men kept secret.

Pope's announcement was the biggest news most of the men had heard in weeks. In minutes, a column of nearly two dozen soldiers mounted up and headed out to see the newly captured horse.

"He's gathered up quite a little herd of mares," Pope explained to Daniel and Robert as they rode along. "Strays from a few years ago, I guess," he said. "There wasn't exactly an organized effort to round up all the livestock wandering free."

"Have you seen him?" Daniel wanted to know.

Pope shook his head. "Nope. Only heard stories." He smiled. "There's been kind of a contest to see who could catch and ride him. Guess he's somethin' to look at."

They heard him before they saw him. Unearthly squeals punctuated by human shouts carried on the clear morning air. Daniel's army-issue bay sidestepped and tossed its head nervously as they grew closer to the source of the awful noise. Finally, they rounded a massive pile of rock left from some long-ago rockslide. Daniel caught his breath when he saw the horse. It was a magnificent creature even in its worst moment. Chrisman and Buford had, indeed, managed to lasso each foot separately and completely immobilize the stallion by pounding stakes into the ground and tying the ropes in place. Now they had lassoed his head as well.

But even though the animal could barely stand and had no hope of escape, it would not be beaten. It had struggled against the tethers until blood coursed down one of its fetlocks, darkening the earth around it. And the eyes—the animal's eyes showed murderous intent as it stood, nostrils flaring with the effort to suck in air and continue the defiant screams, even though it could barely raise its head.

"Who's gonna ride 'im?" someone hollered.

"You mean who's gonna' get kilt?" came the reply.

"You scared?"

"You bet I am. I never sat a horse before I joined up, and I'm not about to risk my life on that devil. Army issue is good enough for me."

"Two bits says even the Injuns can't ride him," someone shouted.

"I'll take that bet," Edward Pope said quickly. He had seen Daniel and Robert slip to the side of a horse galloping at full speed and had no doubt one of them could stay aboard the stallion for at least a few minutes.

Someone else spoke up and before long the entire group of men were harassing Robert and Daniel.

Robert grinned at his friend. "Just don't break your neck."

Chrisman produced a halter, and while two other men held the stallion's head still, he slipped it over the velvet-soft muzzle and up over the ears. The horse screamed in protest and managed to leave an imprint on Chrisman's left forearm with huge teeth. But after a few moments, the halter was on, the rope attached to form a primitive kind of reins.

Daniel approached the animal cautiously. It was when he began to circle around to inspect the creature that he saw something unbelievable. Plainly visible in the gleaming white coat along the withers were a series of wicked scars. Frowning, Daniel walked around the back of the animal and inspected the other side, and then he knew. And when he realized whose the horse had been, he also realized that however formidable the creature seemed, it was no longer a young animal. And contrary to legend and what these soldiers believed, the creature had been ridden—often and for long distances.

Completing his inspection, Daniel crouched down before it, inches from its muzzle. He began to talk to the horse in a low voice.

"What's he doin'?" one of the soldiers said. "Tryin' some Dakota medicine to cast a spell?"

"He's telling the horse his name," Pope said matter-of-factly. "And—" Pope, who was usually more than happy to boast of his knowledge of the Dakota language, saw the scars across the stallion's withers and suddenly shut up.

"Well?" the soldier demanded.

Pope shook his head. "Can't say."

And it was true. He couldn't, because then Daniel's successful ride would seem less miraculous.

"You remember me, great one," Daniel was saying. "You were a great war horse to my friend Otter. When he died, you stayed in my friend's barn for a while." Daniel reached out to touch the horse's muzzle. The animal flared its nostrils wide and snorted, but it smelled Daniel's hand and did not bite. "And then I came to get you. And I took you to freedom." Gently, ever so slowly, Daniel worked his way up to the horse's forehead. When the creature deigned to let Daniel scratch its forehead, Daniel slowly stood up, all the while talking. "Only the night before I let you go, the great cat attacked you. I was able to kill the cat. I still have its skin. I am sorry that I was unable to make your wounds better that night, but I see they have healed well." By this time, Daniel was at the horse's side. When he reached out to touch the scars, the horse shivered. But Daniel continued talking, running his hand down the topline from the withers to the flank while the horse turned its head to look at him. "And now you have a lodge of mares. You should have taken them farther towards the setting sun. I will set you free again, great one, if you will only let me ride you so these foolish white men will leave you alone. You can stay with me until we are ready to move on. And once we are farther west I will set you free again and you can collect a new band of wives."

Slowly, Daniel slipped up onto the stallion's back. The horse didn't move, but his nostrils flared and he made a strange sound of protest deep in his throat.

"Four of you," Daniel said quietly in English, "get ready. And be certain you roll out of the way the instant you let the ropes go."

Four men sidled up to the four stakes. They lay on the ground and reached towards the ropes. Chrisman spoke up. "On four."

Daniel gathered up the halter's rope and nodded that he was ready.

"One . . . two . . . three . . . FOUR!" At the same moment as Chrisman and Buford pulled their lassos off the stallion's head, each man yanked the knot free binding the horse to the stakes, covered their heads with their arms, and rolled across the earth away from where the stallion stood.

The horse stood. Still.

The men gaped at the picture in disbelief.

The horse took a step forward, then sideways. It twisted its head around and everyone waited for him to take a chunk out of Daniel's leg, but instead he rolled his eyes and looked first to the right, then to the left.

"Thank you, great one," Daniel said in Dakota. "You are showing these white men how sensible a good pony can be." The horse snorted and tossed its head, and the group of men watching backed up.

When Daniel nudged the animal in the sides it began to buck.

"Here we go!" someone shouted, and in one voice the men let out a whoop.

The stallion took off as if shot from a piece of field artillery, streaking out of the canyon and onto the open prairie. Daniel leaned against the animal's neck, his eyes tearing up from wind and mane in his eyes—and from emotion, for almost it was as if he were a boy again, astride his favorite pony, chasing after the buffalo that must be just over the next rise.

But just beyond the next rise there was only a cluster of about two dozen mares. The soldiers riding in pursuit of Daniel and the white stallion made a wide circle around and stampeded the mares back in the direction of Fort Ridgeley. The stallion needed no guidance to turn and follow, and after a mad dash that lasted for several miles, the mares settled down and permitted themselves to be herded over the hills and down into the valleys until, late in the afternoon, they were circling nervously inside a corral at Fort Ridgely.

"And so Daniel, here, takes up the reins, and—"

"Give it a rest, Pope," Chrisman said wearily. "Everybody's heard it."

"I ain't heard it," Pope's audience, a blond-haired youth who helped Edward with the company's camp kitchen, said.

"Well wait 'til I'm out of earshot before you hear it," Chrisman shot back testily.

He slurped up the rest of his stew before standing up and retreating to his tent. Bringing in the stallion and his small herd had been a good start to an otherwise boring day, but as he looked across the compound to where the white stallion now grazed peacefully alongside the Dakota scouts' worn-out team of mules, Chrisman realized for the tenth time that day that he had been suckered into a losing bet. Obviously Daniel Two Stars knew some kind of Indian magic that put horses in a trance. He had heard of people who could do that. Just his luck, Chrisman thought, for him to run into one of them.

He plopped onto his bunk. Through the open tent flap he could see Edward Pope crouched beside the dying fire, his face intent as he told Timothy Fields what had happened that day. At least, he thought, Captain Willets had been pleased when they brought in the small group of mares, sleek from grazing on abundant grass and, Captain Willets surmised, most of them likely with foal.

Tomorrow they would have an old-fashioned rodeo and see to it that the mares were branded as property of the U.S. Army. As for the white stallion, no one seemed to mind that Daniel Two Stars had taken possession of the creature. No one else seemed willing to take it on, and as far as he, Chrisman, was concerned, if a fool Indian wanted to risk his neck with a half-wild horse, who was he to protest. Besides, he had his eye on one of those mares—a leggy buckskin with one blue eye. Edward Pope had pointed her out with a mind to claim her the next day. They would see about that.

Fifteen

"A man that hath friends must show himself friendly."
—Proverbs 18:24

"Stop that!" Daniel shoved the white stallion away and returned to untangling its long mane. But the horse reached out again, taking just enough of Daniel's sleeve between his teeth to prevent Daniel's arm from moving. When Daniel jerked his arm away and bopped the horse on the muzzle, the creature curled its lips away from its teeth in protest. Stretching its neck, it bobbed its head up and down and danced away, spinning sideways around the tether anchored in the soft soil beneath an oak tree.

"If you can't control that animal," a voice called out, "you'd better requisition another mount. You'll need something dependable in the next few days."

Daniel turned around to find Captain Willets leaning against the tree trunk, his arms folded, a grin on his face.

"A few days?"

Willets nodded. "Yep. Orders came in today." He walked over to the horse and began to stroke its muzzle while he talked. "There's a change, though. I thought sure we'd be headed for Fort Wadsworth. Seems now we're providing a small detachment to go with a special commissioner making the rounds to all the tribes of the Missouri. Meeting him at Fort Randall. He'll have a wagon and supplies and his own interpreter. We're just supposed to give him an escort to make sure he doesn't get himself killed."

"*Another* special commission?" Daniel snorted and shook his head.

Willets shrugged. "From Fort Randall we head up the Niobrara west through Nebraska. We'll drop south along the border and head to Fort Laramie. Then on up to Powder River country and Fort Phil Kearney. After that it depends on the commissioner. There's another powwow planned for September at Fort Laramie." He nodded with satisfaction. "Join the army and tour the West. See real live hostile Indians."

Daniel thought for a moment. "It's time for Aaron to go home to New York."

Willets nodded. "Thought you'd say that."

"You don't agree?"

"Well . . . " Willets adjusted his hat.

"Let's hear it."

"Younger men than him enlist all the time." He cleared his throat. "I was just thinking if he really thinks he wants a military career, I can't think of a better way for him to start one than with you and Robert scouting—and me in command." He grinned. "And I say that with all due humility, of course."

Daniel leaned on the stallion, his arms across the animal's

back. The horse lowered his head and sighed. "Blue Eyes would never agree to that."

"What if she could come, too?" Willets said quietly. At Daniel's look of surprise he said, "Carrington took entire families with him last winter when he went north to Fort Phil Kearney. 'Course it didn't turn out very well. But I'm not cocky like Fetterman, and I'd like to think I understand Indians a little better than Carrington. At least I've been in the West for a while and I've weathered some action. And we're not going to run into any trouble this side of Fort Laramie. Mrs. Two Stars could help Edward cook."

"She might like that."

"Like it? She'll jump at the chance and you know it," Willets teased. "I think she'd offer to be the company blacksmith if it meant she got to stay with you." He was suddenly serious. "I don't think I've ever seen a woman look at man the way she does you, Two Stars. It's enough to make a man almost wish he was married."

Daniel studied his curry comb for a moment and then began to brush his horse again. "We waited a long time for each other," he said. Then he looked at his friend. "God has blessed us."

"Hmph," Willets shook his head. "It's always God with you, Two Stars. Did God pick those wildflowers I saw you bringing her yesterday?"

Daniel shifted his weight uncomfortably and tried to change the subject. "Robert won't want Nancy coming with the new baby. We were counting on Aaron taking them to the reservation on the Niobrara next week. Two of the teachers from the old mission are working there. Blue Eyes and Nancy would be welcome." He brushed his hand down the stallion's dusty spine.

"Robert can take a detour to see his wife and baby settled at Santee and catch up with us later at Fort Randall. And Mrs. Two Stars can wait for us at Fort Laramie if we end up going into hostile country. We can work it out."

"I don't know about leaving Blue Eyes at Fort Laramie alone. You know how Indian women are treated around the forts."

Willets interrupted him. "I know the doctor at Fort Laramie. He's an old friend and his wife is your kind of Christian. She'd see to Mrs. Two Stars if it came to that. "

"My kind of Christian?"

"You know what I mean. Most of the men around here are just the go-to-church-on-Sunday kind. Then there's your kind. The do-what-the-Good-Book-says-every-day kind. That's Mrs. Beaumont. Mrs. Two Stars will like her. Trust me." He grinned again. "I haven't told you the best part of all this yet. The special commissioner is some old soldier from 'the recent unpleasantness.' Got his hand blown off at Antietam and took to diplomacy. Name's Elliot Leighton."

❧

"Genevieve!" Elliot Leighton gripped her around the waist, lifted her off her feet, and spun her around. He pounded Daniel on the shoulder. "Living with this renegade obviously agrees with you," he said lifting her chin, thoroughly enjoying the blush rising on her cheeks. "Daniel." Elliot grasped Daniel's hand and held on. For the moment, neither of them said anything. Then, Elliot broke the spell. "Where's the boy?"

"Here, Uncle Elliot." Aaron stepped forward.

"No!" Elliot exclaimed, taking Aaron's outstretched hand and pulling the youth into a hug. "It can't be. You've grown another foot." He turned his head sideways and squinted. "And you're growing a *beard?!*"

Aaron smiled shyly and brushed his cheek with his hand. "Trying." He laughed self-consciously.

Behind the group, laborers began hauling trunks and bundles down the gangplank from the steamboat to shore. When a small black trunk came into view, Elliot yelled, "Here! Bring that right here!" He grinned at Aaron. "There you go, muscle-man. Load that on that wagon over there. I'll watch for the other provisions. They should bring the horses down soon." He talked while watching crates and boxes being carried off the steamship. "I couldn't believe it when I got Captain Willets's letter about who my escort was going to be!" He frowned slightly. "Obviously there's a lot that I haven't been told. We got your letter about leaving New Ulm. But you seemed to be thinking you'd just be going north to farm near the old agency. What happened?"

"Abner Marsh is what happened," Aaron said abruptly.

"Who?"

Daniel sent a warning glance to Aaron. "Abner Marsh," he said quietly. "He was one of the neighbors. We can talk of that later."

Gen interrupted. "Tell us about Meg." Her eyes filled with tears.

"Here!" Elliot called out, waving towards another crate.

"I'll get that one," Daniel said and headed off.

"Meg's doing well, Gen," Elliot said while they watched Daniel retrieve a crate and hoist it into the wagon. "A letter from Jane arrived just before I left St. Louis." He patted his coat. "It's right here, and as soon as we've settled in camp—never mind. No need for you to have to wait." He pulled out a thick stack of papers out of his coat. "Here it is. Take it with you." He held out another, thinner envelope. "And one for you, Aaron. From a Miss Whitrock."

Aaron reached out for the envelope and tucked it in his coat pocket. Gen clutched her packet and headed for Elliot's wagon, oblivious to the crowd. Presently there were more boxes to load, and then there was another surprise when Big Amos was seen leading Elliot's team and an extra horse down off the steamship.

"Three Dakota scouts," Elliot said. "I hope Captain Willets won't mind."

"Mind?" Willets said, hurrying up and pumping Big Amos's hand up and down.

That evening around the campfire, Big Amos regaled the group with his version of Washington, D.C., which included an emphasis on the Willard Hotel's cherry pie. When he learned that Robert had left to take Nancy to the reservation, he nodded. "We have a good church and the land is much better than Crow Creek." He went on to explain that Rosalie was helping the Mission teachers teach in one of the schools. "We are going to have a baby. Scouting this summer will help us get a better team for next year's plowing." Leaning back against a tree, Big Amos put his hands behind his head and smiled. "I promised Rosalie this is my last time to be a wild Indian."

❧

Elliot's interpreter and guide, Zephyr Picotte, wore his hair in two greasy braids and chewed tobacco constantly. He could have been middle-aged or he could have been ancient. His face was so lined with deep creases that no one would venture a guess at the man's age. But his experience was unchallenged. Zephyr had traveled with the likes of Jim Bridger. He knew the territory they would be traveling much better than anyone else in the party, and he eyed the Dakota scouts who had seldom been west of the James River with no small amount of suspicion.

One evening when everyone else had bedded down for the night and Zephyr sat up alone by the campfire, Aaron slipped into the warm glow of the fire. "You don't like Daniel," he said abruptly. "Why not?"

Zephyr continued whittling on the stick in his hand. Presently he squinted up at Aaron. "Not much for small talk are you, son?" When the boy met his gaze with clear gray eyes and didn't look away, the interpreter spat on the ground and said, "Guess I'm of the same mind as most of my kin." He explained, "Had me a Cheyenne woman once. Good woman. Most of the western tribes figure that after what the Dakota let the government do to 'em, they aren't worth much."

"You know better than that," Aaron said. "You know about the army and how strong it is. And you also know the same thing is going to happen to every Sioux in the West if they don't find a way to make peace. So what's the real reason you don't like Daniel?"

"It ain't that I don't like him, son. I just don't know if I can trust him."

"You don't trust any man until you know them, do you?"

Zephyr looked sharply at Aaron. "Now what makes you say that?"

"You watch everyone around you like you think they might be getting ready to jump you." Aaron pointed to Zephyr's pistol, still in the holster around his waist. "And you never take that off. Except maybe when you sleep."

"I'm not asleep yet," Zephyr said with a grim smile. Unconsciously, his hand went to his pistol. "But I probably won't take it off then either—except maybe to put it under my head as a pillow."

"Can I see it? I've never seen a Colt .44 before."

"Where'd you learn about .44s?" Zephyr asked.

"Oh, my uncle has quite a collection of pistols back home," he said. "I just paid attention when he wanted to talk about them, that's all."

Zephyr withdrew the gun and handed it to the boy. "She's loaded. Be careful."

Aaron looked down the barrel of the gun. He spun the chamber, opened it, then slapped it shut and handed it back. "Nice one. Better than the one Uncle Elliot has." He stretched and yawned, then got up.

"I thought you was going to tell me all about your friend Daniel so I'd know what a hero he is. Captain Willets already told me a few things to get my interest up."

Aaron paused and smiled. He shook his head. "Nope, You'll figure Daniel out without my saying anything. Besides," he grinned, "I'm just a kid. What do I know?"

~

The troop left Fort Randall the next day, going overland and stopping at various Yankton lodges in the vicinity. Elliot kept careful records of every visit for the benefit of Senator Lance and his committee back in Washington. He wrote that all the bands he had met thus far were "very friendly and well disposed towards the whites. They like agriculture and seem to be cheerful about planting crops with the assistance of their agent and farmer."

At each group of lodges, the troops stopped and waited. While Elliot smoked peace pipes and took notes, Daniel and Robert rode ahead scouting the area. A week after they left Fort Randall on the Missouri, they rode into Fort Thompson where more than one hundred Indian lodges were camped. With Zephyr Picotte's help, Elliot interviewed Brules, Two Kettles, and more Yanktonais. He assured them of the Great White Father's peaceful intentions towards them and impressed upon them the absolute necessity of their keeping away from the hostile bands to the north.

Several chiefs, among them Iron Nation and Two Lances, made speeches assuring Elliot of their peaceful intentions. White Bear concluded the meeting with a moving speech in which he declared that he was getting too old to fight anymore and that his many children wanted only peace. "We only wish to stir up the ground to feed our wives and children. We will trust our Great White Father to take pity on us and to help us. Send us tools for working the earth. Help us grow corn."

While espousing their intention to become farmers, the chiefs reminded Elliot that they were often visited by their more warlike brothers to the north, and that while they themselves were content, they could not promise that some of the younger warriors would not be induced to join the trouble to the north. "We cannot this year grow enough for all our families. We will still need to hunt, but we will do so in peace with all white men we may meet. We only want to find buffalo. Our women will dig roots and gather berries. We will not fight."

Robert Lawrence caught up with the party after two days into their trip up the Niobrara. That was the day Picotte's horse tossed him next to a rattlesnake hole. The trader was eye to eye with a huge rattler when Daniel blew its head off. Picotte scrambled to his feet only to hear the sound of another rattler nearby. Two more were crawling out of the hole. He clubbed one and Daniel got the other. The two men stood side by side clubbing snake after snake after snake. When the last rattler was dead, the two men stood in the center of a circle of nearly fifty dead rattlesnakes. Picotte decided Two Stars—and by association, Robert Lawrence and Big Amos—were exceptions to his rule about the Dakota Sioux, after all.

Sixteen

"To him that is afflicted pity should
be shewed from his friend . . ."
—JOB 6:14

"ENLIST? IN THE ARMY? YOU CAN'T BE SERIOUS!"
Genevieve Two Stars stared past Aaron to where his Uncle Elliot
stood looking uncharacteristically nervous. They had been traveling up the Niobrara for a week now and were about to descend
into what Zephyr Picotte called "the most God-forsaken land
you'll ever see. Makes the *Mauvaises Terres* look like Paradise." This
was where Gen had expected Aaron to head back to Fort Randall
and board a steamboat for St. Louis. He would visit family friends
before taking the railroad home to New York. But Aaron had
other ideas.

"I can't officially enlist," Aaron said. "Not until I'm twenty-one. But Captain Willets said he would treat me just like one of his soldiers and give me a taste of real army life. Civilians go along with army units all the time as volunteers. I'd be a volunteer."

One look at Daniel and Elliot told Genevieve Two Stars she was defeated and there was no reason to begin a campaign that could only be interpreted as being overprotective. She had been around military men long enough to know better than to burden Aaron with the moniker, "Mama's boy."

"You know I've wanted to be a soldier for a long time, Ma."

"You always call me *Ma* when you are set on getting your way, Aaron Dane," Gen snapped. "I don't appreciate it one bit."

"Well," Aaron said smiling coyly, "a man's gotta do what a man's gotta do. And besides that, it usually works." He tapped his foot nervously. "I don't want to displease you. But I can't see any better time or place to learn soldiering than now and here, with Daniel and Uncle Elliot to teach me. And Captain Willets is willing to put up with a raw recruit. At least I can ride. That's more than Pinky could do."

Pinky. Poor Pinky. He had met them in Fort Randall with a commission but no assignment to a specific company. The day he reported to Captain Willets for duty, he was outfitted in his version of what a half-breed guide would wear—tomahawk, sheath-knife, Colt revolvers tucked in a red sash around his waist, a Springfield rifle lying across his saddle, and enough blankets and coats piled up to nearly hide what appeared to be a very good horse. Daniel and Robert had recounted Pinky's demise so many times the troop had begun to call one another Pinky every time they made a mistake. The first time he gave chase after a buffalo, Pinky had left a trail of belongings across the prairie. When Daniel shot down a calf and it bleated with pain, its mother charged Pinky's horse. Pinky was picked up half-conscious and taken back to camp. The next day when they broke camp, Pinky was gone. Yes, Genevieve considered, Aaron Dane was a good deal more prepared to soldier in Indian country than Pinky. She wondered if Pinky had a mother that worried about him. At least, Genevieve thought, she was not sitting back East worrying about Aaron in the West.

"All right," Gen heard herself saying. "I won't fight you on this. But—"

"Thanks, Ma!" Aaron smothered her with a hug, and she was suddenly aware of just how tall he was becoming.

"You have to write Aunt Jane and tell her how you roped me into agreeing." She smiled at Elliot. "And *you,* my dear Captain Leighton, have to write Jane and tell her why this is such a wonderful idea."

Elliot removed his hat and ran his hand through his long silver hair. "I'll handle Jane," he said quickly. "She'll understand." He did handle Jane. Lucky for him, Jane was too far away for her husband to witness her blustering response when she finally read his letter. And, after considering all the options, Jane Leighton arrived at the same conclusion Genevieve had, and she understood. She didn't like the idea of Aaron soldiering. But she looked at Meg and Hope and realized that, do what she would, the children were going to grow up. And if God had called Aaron Dane to serve Him in the military, He was certainly providing excellent training for a successful career. Jane didn't need to know about Pinky to know that.

∽

June 15, 1867
Dear Amanda,

I am an expert now, for I have killed a buffalo with bow and arrow. It's true. At first Daniel and Robert would not listen to my pleas to be taught to hunt like the Sioux, but when they finally believed I was sincere, they said all right. It took them a while to find the right feathers, the right wood, the right sinew to create a true bow and arrows as their fathers taught them to make, but when it was all finished I think they enjoyed it. At least they enjoyed laughing at me and my poor attempts at target practice. But then I began to improve and finally, today, we have chased down a small herd, and would you believe it, I brought down one of the old fellows.

We are traveling through some of the strangest country. Zephyr Picotte calls it "God-forsaken" and says that it is worse than the Badlands up in Dakota. Everyone agrees that no one will ever live here but Indians and buffalo, who seem to thrive on the strange grasses that cling to the sandy earth. We call this land the Sandhills. At times it seems we are in the middle of a vast desert. Our horses' hooves sink into the sandy soil, and they labor so to get up the hills that at times we must dismount and lead them and then we all flounder along. Then at the top we may have to take a different route because on the other side of the hill there is a crater, like God reached down from heaven and scooped a huge amount of sand up. The wind creates these "blow-outs," and there is plenty of that.

Gen rides in the cook wagon, and lately we have left most of the cook's things on the pack mules so the wagon will be lighter and the wheels don't sink so. Zephyr Picotte says that when we reach the Platte we will have a road so wide to travel that we will think the Corps of Engineers has gone ahead of us to make a perfect wagon road.

We have not seen a tree for three days now. That should tell you something about how dry it is. The horses and men suffer greatly from alkali water and the dust and grit blowing in our faces.

I will post this letter when we reach Fort Laramie. When you receive it, Miss Whitrock, I ask that you think fondly of the one who sent it, who today carved your name into a rock jutting out of the sand above our camp here in the Sandhills of Nebraska.

"He did *what?!*" Stephen Bannister dabbed his barely visible dark moustache with the corner of his napkin.

"He carved my name," Amanda said, tossing her blonde curls.

"Rather impertinent, don't you think?"

"Impertinent?! Indeed not," Amanda said. "I think it's romantic." She fluttered her eyelashes and glanced sideways at Stephen, sprawled on the silk chaise in her parent's drawing room. Pretending to shiver she said, "Just think Stephen . . . some *savage* all done up in feathers and war paint could be looking at it right this minute. Wondering what it means." She gave a sigh. "I do miss Aaron. I wish he'd come home."

Stephen stood up and stretched lazily. "Oh, I expect he will sooner or later. With all sorts of stories to entertain the ladies this winter." He smiled at Amanda. "And the rest of us poor, boring New York lads will have to take a back seat. For a while."

"*Ladies*?!" Amanda sputtered. "He's *my* beau, Stephen Bannister, and you know it. Aaron's not the kind of boy to be simpering around all the *ladies*."

"Forgive me, Miss Whitrock." Stephen bowed stiffly. "I was not aware that your interest in Master Dane was quite so intense."

Amanda tossed her curls again and looked out the window. Her lower lip trembled and a tear gathered in the corner of her eye. "I do hope he's safe," she said. "It sounds dangerous, what he's doing."

"I doubt it's very dangerous," Stephen said, reaching for his hat. "Mrs. Leighton would have her husband's head if she thought her dear, sweet Aaron were in any real danger."

"Don't, Stephen," Amanda ordered. "Don't make fun. I like Mrs. Leighton. I like *both* Mrs. Leightons. In fact," she said, getting up, "I think I'll just call on them this afternoon. I'll read Meg a story. And play with Hope for a while." She smiled. "You can escort me over there on your way home."

Stephen put his hat on and went out into the hall. "Whatever you say, Miss Whitrock." He leaned against the sideboard beside the front door while Amanda pulled a short cape over her shoulders and perched a hat atop her head.

∽

"I've a letter from Aaron," Amanda said when Jane Leighton appeared at the front door of Leighton Hall. "I thought I'd share it with you. With Meg. If that's all right." Amanda shifted nervously from foot to foot beneath Jane Leighton's no-nonsense stare. "And I wondered if it would be helpful to you if I played with Hope for a few minutes. In the garden? I've been so busy this summer, but mother finally let me off some of the chores, and—"

"Miss Whitrock," Jane said firmly, "you are welcome in this house anytime you wish to pay a visit. You don't need an excuse. We're happy to have you. But please don't insult my intelligence with all that babble about chores and your mother." She stepped aside. "We both know better. Now come in."

Amanda stepped into the entryway of Leighton Hall. Her eyes swept up the wide staircase to the Palladian window above. Once again, she was surprised at the grandness of the house. The Leightons kept their elegance to themselves, that was for certain. Passersby on the street would never have guessed the interior of the plain old house was so exquisite. Amanda removed her hat and cape and handed them to Betsy, who had been with the Leightons since she was a girl. Glancing in the gilt-edged mirror opposite the stairs, Amanda could not resist the thought that anyone would be happy to be the mistress of the grand old house, although a fresh coat of paint on the walls would liven things up a bit.

"Would you like some tea?" Mrs. Leighton was saying. She didn't wait for a reply but instead guided Amanda towards the back of the house. "We're out in the gazebo today. Meg enjoys the fresh air and the scent of the flowers." Together they stepped out onto the back porch. Mrs. Leighton closed her eyes and inhaled. "I must say the gardens here at Leighton Hall are a delight." She turned to Amanda. "I know you are uncomfortable around Meg,

Miss Whitrock. May I suggest that you forget she cannot see and simply treat her like any other one of your friends. She does get lonely, and now that her strength is returning, she is learning more and more how to manage things for herself."

They were at the gazebo. Amanda took the two steps up onto the wood platform. Meg was seated opposite her in a blue plaid dress, her hair done up in an intricate braid.

"Oh, Meg!" Amanda exclaimed. "Who did your hair? It's stunning!"

Meg reached up to lay her open palm on the back of her head. "Why, I did it, Amanda. And thank you."

"How did you know it was me?"

"My *ears* work just fine, Amanda."

"I'm sorry, Meg. I always seem to say the wrong thing, don't I?"

"Don't be silly." Meg reached her hand out into space. Amanda took it and Meg squeezed. "Sit down. I haven't seen you in ages. What have you been up to? Aunt Jane, do get Aaron's letter. I'm certain Amanda would love to hear it."

"I've got a letter too," Amanda said. "That's why I came. I thought you'd like to hear it." She looked over to where Hope sat playing quietly with a tea set nearby. "And then I thought I could play with Hope. Or read to you. Or—" She fumbled with her small drawstring bag. "But first, I'll read."

"I'll have Betsy bring you girls some tea," Jane said abruptly. She got up and went into the house. After instructing Betsy to take tea and muffins out to the gazebo, she headed upstairs to check on Mother Leighton. When she found the older woman standing on the landing staring down into the garden, she paused.

"Is that Amanda Whitrock?" Mother Leighton demanded. When Jane nodded, the older woman snorted. "What's she up to do you suppose?"

"She's gotten another letter from Aaron. She wanted to read it to Meg. And she's going to play with Hope for a while."

"Amanda Whitrock came over to *play* with Hope?" Mother Leighton shook her head. "What's come over that girl?"

Jane Leighton thought for a moment. "If I didn't know better I'd say she's actually a little lonesome for Aaron."

Mother Leighton raised her eyebrows and looked at Jane, who grimaced and shrugged. The women turned and looked down on the garden. In a moment, Hope and Amanda descended the gazebo stairs together, hand in hand. Amanda deposited Hope on the tree swing and then went back to the gazebo for Meg. She guided Meg down the stairs and settled her beneath the tree. Then she went to the rose garden and plucked a blossom. Handing it to Meg, she began to push Hope on the swing.

Seventeen

"The heart of the prudent getteth knowledge;
and the ear of the wise seeketh knowledge."
—PROVERBS 18:15

THE SANDHILLS OF NEBRASKA HAD SECRETS. THE morning after he had written Amanda about how desolate the area was, Aaron topped a hill and had his breath taken away by the beauty of an inviting, lush valley surrounded by mountains of sand. At the far end of the valley a towering lone cottonwood reigned over the scene.

"Look at that, little wife." Daniel nodded towards the sparkling blue lake nestled in the valley. "Almost as blue as your eyes."

Gen smiled at him and urged her horse forward. Daniel watched her descend the hill into the valley, his heart swelling with love and pride. The journey had been hard, but she hadn't complained once. She'd been a willing assistant to Edward Pope who had become devoted to her. She and the three Dakota scouts, along with Aaron, had continued Edward's education in the Dakota language, and many evenings now they conversed in Dakota. Some of the soldiers made fun of Edward for his stammering attempts, but he pressed on, undaunted by his mistakes and the ease with which Zephyr Picotte had learned the language.

"It ain't so different from the other dialects," he said one evening when Edward bemoaned his own ignorance. "I lived out here all my life, Pope. You can't expect to just pick it up like me." Zephyr spit into the fire. "Why do you bother, anyway?"

Edward shrugged. "Never know when it might save my life. Or someone else's." He took a drink of coffee and grimaced. "Besides that, I never been too good at anything but cooking in all my life. Didn't do good in school. Can't ride all that great." He ducked his head, embarrassed. "Back at Fort Ridgely I wanted that buckskin mare Chrisman's riding back at Fort Ridgely. He said I didn't deserve a good horse if all I was goin' to do was cook. Said she'd probably throw me and hightail it off anyways." He shrugged. "He's probably right, I guess. About the horse. But I kind of like knowing something that all the other boys don't."

"Guess I understand that," Zephyr said. And after that he had begun to help Edward, even teaching him some sign language.

The men were delighted with the campsite and the access to fresh water. Gen hid inside the cook's tent when it became apparent they did not consider one Indian woman a reason to deny themselves the pleasures of shedding their clothes and romping in the water. The entire day turned into one all-consuming laundry day and water fight until someone yelled from atop a hill about a herd of antelope on the next rise and several of the men pulled on their half-dry clothes and tore out of camp to go on the chase.

Elliot spent the evening writing reports and writing home.

Aaron wrote Miss Whitrock, which Gen observed had become something of a daily event.

As evening approached, the men settled into small clutches of activity, some playing cards, some smoking, others treating their horses to a dousing with the cold water or wading in the shallows with improvised nets, hoping to snag a fish and vary their hard-tack/bacon/biscuit diet.

Daniel spent most of the evening meticulously washing down his white stallion, who had taken on the look of a pinto after being spotted with sweat and grime over the past few days.

～∞～

Gen frowned in her sleep and brushed her cheek. A moment later, she felt something close. Something leaning over her. She opened her eyes with a start. Daniel pressed his finger to her lips.

"Follow me," he whispered. When she did, he led her alongside the lake, away from the campfires and around to the opposite side of the water where a stand of reeds hid them from the camp.

"You have a dirty face," he said, brushing her chin with his thumb. He pulled her down to sit in front of him. When she did, he began to take down her hair. From his pocket he withdrew a comb. For what seemed like an hour, he combed her long hair until it hung, sleek and shining in the moonlight. He rested his hands on her shoulders for a moment. He was so close she could feel his breath on her hair. Her heart began to race when he leaned forward to nuzzle her cheek. Then he unbuttoned the top button of her waist. "My gift to you for today, little wife. I'll keep watch while you take a bath. The water is cool and fresh. There must be a spring feeding the lake."

The black sky overhead twinkled with a million stars. Gen sighed. Cool water. How wonderful that would feel. Dust and sand had been collecting in her hair for over a week. It made her scalp itch. It gathered in the creases of her hands and along her cuffs until she despaired at the ringlets of filth around her wrists. She didn't think she smelled quite as bad as some of the soldiers, but she wondered.

"Are you sure?" she whispered.

He nudged her back. "Go."

She slipped out of her waist and her skirt. "I'm a good target for any hostiles watching from up there," she said nervously, suddenly aware of how brightly her white undergarments shone in the moonlight.

"There are no hostiles watching," Daniel said. "But there is one very *un*hostile Indian watching who thinks you had better hurry into the water."

"Or what?" Gen teased. She sunk down into the water and pulled her petticoats up and over her head. Finally, she slipped beneath the surface, sighing with pleasure as the cool water swept across her skin like silk. She lay back on the surface of the water, floating and staring up at the sky. At the sound of something hitting the water near the edge, Gen startled and rolled over just as Daniel's hands slipped around her waist. He pulled her close and they slid together beneath the surface of the cool water.

❧

"It's true, Picotte. There's a new spirit in Washington." They were sitting around a small campfire that had died down to little more than coals. Elliot had been leaning against his saddle for support, but now he crossed his legs and leaned forward earnestly. "The Peace Party has more influence now. The new treaty can change things."

A low laugh rippled across the water from the opposite side of the lake. Elliot and John Willets, Aaron and Edward, looked self-consciously at the fire. At the sound of a splash, Zephyr Picotte drug a stick away from the edge of the fire and began to whittle. "Shame one of the boys couldn't of caught that fish in his net today. Sounds like a big one." He chortled, then returned to the subject at hand. "Which treaty you talkin' about, Captain Leighton? The one from '65 or the newer version?" He flipped a wood chip into the fire. "Seems to me none of the Sioux up in Powder River country care much about either one." Laying the stick in the embers, he drew his pipe out of his pocket, lit it with the glowing stick, and leaned back against the massive cottonwood tree. "I been interpreting for peace commissions and treaty-makers since before this boy was born." He waved his pipe at Aaron. "And I can tell you that at the exact moment the most recent peace treaty was being signed down on the Missouri, the hostiles up on the Powder were having a grand old time raiding travelers along the Platte Road. At this very minute there's nearly four thousand lodges of Sioux camped up there and not a one of 'em has any intention of letting whites come through their hunting grounds. Building a road through that country means war, pure and simple. And if the government don't believe it, they better brace for a repeat of that Fetterman affair that happened last winter."

"But the Peace Party—"

Zephyr interrupted, "No offense, Major. I know you mean well. But hasn't your Peace Party figured out yet that a treaty with the peaceful Sioux loafing around the forts isn't worth much unless it's signed by the hostiles causing all the trouble?"

"Swift Bear and Standing Elk signed last year."

Zephyr laughed. "Swift Bear and Standing Elk are about as hostile as those two," he nodded across the lake to where everyone knew Genevieve and Daniel were enjoying a midnight rendezvous. He leaned forward. "Listen, Major. You got to make Washington understand they can't expect to just send a list of demands up to Fort Laramie and wait for Sitting Bull and Man Afraid to come filing in like good citizens and touch the pen."

"Touch the pen?" Elliot asked.

Captain Willets spoke up. "When they don't write, they touch the pen and someone makes their mark for them."

"But both those men you mentioned have been to other peace councils," Elliot said stubbornly.

Zephyr agreed. "So would you if the word was out that whoever came in would go home with pack mules loaded down with presents and arms and ammunition. Sure they came in. But they were smart enough to get someone they trusted to read what they were signing out loud. And the minute they realized the treaty allowed for a road through their hunting grounds, they weren't going to sign—unless it was a promise to fight anything with white skin that set foot in their territory."

"I don't mean to argue, Mr. Picotte," Elliot said. "I want to learn. To understand." He paused. "But I'm confused. I read the commissioner's report. He was there when Sitting Bull and Man Afraid refused to sign. He didn't try to hide that. He reported it." He scratched his head. "But does that really matter? Sitting Bull and Man Afraid aren't all that influential anymore, are they? The commissioner explained that Sitting Bull is just an unimportant leader of that small group called the Bad Faces. And isn't Man Afraid a peace chief?"

Picotte looked at Elliot, dumbfounded. He puffed on his pipe energetically. Then he began to cough. Coughing became laughing. Picotte slapped his knee and laughed until tears were rolling down his cheeks. "Lord God in heaven, help us all!" he finally choked out. When he had finally managed to stop laughing and puffing, he set Elliot straight. "Captain Leighton. I don't know what nonsense you've been reading, but the fact is Sitting Bull is the recognized leader of several thousand warriors up on the Powder River. He's shrewd and he's also very well aware of his considerable ability to raise an impressive battle force. The last time I saw him in council he was boasting that he has more warriors than the Great White Father, and that no one was going to take his lands against his will. Now, you and I both know that isn't true, but it's going to take some talking—or some pretty impressive fighting—to convince him of that."

Elliot pondered this new information, making a mental note to check into a certain Indian commissioner's credentials when he returned to Washington. "Obviously Washington doesn't always get trustworthy information." He paused. "That was part of the problem in Minnesota. No one back East would believe the situation was serious. Ignorance was certainly part of the reason for the Fetterman debacle. Carrington went in there honestly believing he could build that road and there wouldn't be any serious trouble." Elliot swatted a mosquito. "That's part of why I'm here. We may be misinformed, but we are determined to finally forge a lasting agreement between the people of the United States and the natives. And the more accurate information I can gather, the better the chances are that will happen. There's a very good chance those three forts up in their hunting grounds will be decommissioned soon."

"That's a start," Picotte said. He tapped his pipe on the earth beside him to clean it out. "I believe you're sincere, Captain Leighton. I'll give you that. Guaranteeing those lands without white interference is probably the only way to peace. But we both know the railroad's coming, the buffalo skinners are killing, and the whites aren't going to be content with stopping at some imaginary boundary just because a bunch of savages don't want 'em to advance. From where I sit, it's hopeless for the Sioux. But they aren't going to admit it. Not yet." He went on. "I was at Sitting Bull's camp a few weeks ago. The place is crammed full of skins and dried meat. They have more horses and mules than I could count . . . and not a few have a brand that looks suspiciously like it says, 'U.S'."

"I'm not surprised," Elliot said. "Carrington reported he lost seventy head from Fort Phil Kearney alone. That doesn't count other raids."

"Exactly my point," Picotte nodded. "At the moment those lodges are filled with very rich, very happy people. And they are fighting exactly the kind of war they like. Now why should they care about making peace with the white man?"

"What do you mean, the kind of war they like?"

"The soldiers aren't any real kind of threat. They're spread too thin over too much area and the Indians know it. They promise to be good and they get ammunition—for hunting. Then they have their buffalo hunt and sun dance. Next comes a good fight at one fort or other, or a few raids where they get more horses and goods. This autumn they'll have another hunt and then retire to their winter camps, content that the soldiers won't follow them. And they'll be right. They'll have a quiet winter and next spring it will start all over again. From their point of view, just because the enemy wears blue uniforms and has white skin doesn't change a thing. It's been their way of life for as long as their tribe has a memory and a history. Why should they care to make peace?"

Elliot smiled sadly. "Have you ever heard of an Indian named Ah-jon-jon?" When Picotte shook his head, Elliot explained. "About forty years ago the Hudson's Bay Company escorted him and a group of his friends East to impress them with the power of the United States. My father told of the transformation that took place in the old chief. In a few months time he went from being a proud warrior to a strutting dandy, complete with top hat and umbrella. But the part I remember most was that when Ah-jon-jon first headed East, he kept track of every white man's home he saw by making notches on his pipe stem. When the pipe stem was covered, he used the handle of a war club. Then he covered a long stick. It wasn't long before he threw his counters into the river."

"And your point is?"

"My point is," Elliot concluded, "that just as Ah-jon-jon had no concept of the power of the nation that was swallowing up his homeland, so it is with Sitting Bull and the warring tribes to the north. They simply do not know what they are up against."

Zephyr pointed out, "Even if they know, they won't sit and do nothing while the border whites destroy them one road at a time, one buffalo at a time. It isn't in them to take defeat without a fight. They are men, after all."

There was an awkward silence, after which Big Amos spoke up. "You can't solve all the problems for this people," he said. "Do the best you can. Like you did in Washington for us. Collect the information, learn as much as possible, and then go home and talk to your Senator Lance. As my Rosalie would say, leave the rest to God."

Zephyr Picotte spat on the ground. "If God cared about the Sioux he'd have eradicated the first white people that climbed off the Mayflower."

Big Amos thought for a moment. "There's one thing the whites brought that have done the Indian some good."

"And that would be?" Picotte challenged him.

"Jesus," Big Amos said.

Picotte spat again. "Don't tell me you're one of them Bible-totin' converts to Christianity? You of all people got to know all the things that have been done to your people in the name of sweet Jesus!"

Elliot Leighton spoke up. "The existence of fool's gold does not mean there isn't real gold in the mountains, Mr. Picotte. And the existence of hypocrites who misuse religion for themselves does not mean there isn't a God in heaven who loves His children and sent His Son to die for them." He stood up and stretched. "Never confuse professing Christians with Christ, Mr. Picotte. The former will disappoint you every time. Christ never will." Elliot said good night and headed for his tent, leaving Picotte staring at the embers of the dying fire.

Gen and Daniel came back towards camp, skirting the edges of the campfire's light just enough for Big Amos and Willets, Picotte and Aaron to see Gen's gleaming, waist-length hair rippling like a dark river as she ducked into their tent.

Captain Willets got up and excused himself, as did Big Amos.

"That little girl don't look old enough to be your ma," Picotte said to Aaron. "How come you call her Ma?"

"That's a long story," Aaron said.

"I like a good story," Picotte said. "Maybe somewhere along the way you can tell me how Jesus pulled them into the fold. Never did understand what an Indian would see in a religion like that."

"What do you mean?" Aaron asked.

"Braves are brought up to take vengeance on their enemies without mercy," Picotte said. "They need a horse, they take one. And if the taking involves deception, that's even better. Christians are told to turn the other cheek and let Jesus take care of everything." Picotte did not try to hide the sarcasm from his voice.

"I can't defend Christianity very well," Aaron said. "If that's what you want you better talk to someone else."

"Don't get riled, son," Picotte said abruptly. He squinted up at the moon and looked back at Aaron. "You tell me a story about your ma. I'll tell you a story about a moonlit night when I nearly got scalped."

It seemed an even trade.

Eighteen

"Thou shalt not covet . . ."
—EXODUS 20:17

July 10, 1867
Dear Amanda,

   I am thinking you might be interested in what the days are like now that I am in the United States Army—almost. The bugle sounds reveille at dawn, which is a little after four o'clock. (Captain Willets says that once the heat of summer comes, we will be marching from 2 A.M. until early morning and laying by during the heat of the day to save both man and beast.) By the time roll call sounds (again from the bugle) we are to be dressed and have our things in order. Breakfast as well as striking tents, packing, loading, and saddling up must all be accomplished by six o'clock so that everyone is *ready to march. The scouts head out first and actually are often already gone by the time the rest of us saddle up. Our procession is always in the same order, with half the mounted men in the lead followed by cook wagon and supply wagons and ambulance, and then about twenty cavalry as a rear guard.*

After about an hour's march in the morning, we stop for about fifteen minutes to rest. Then we march on foot, leading our horses for another quarter of an hour before remounting. About ten or eleven o'clock, if there is good grass nearby (the scouts have been out to locate this), we stop half an hour or more to feed and water and then go on. The men do not eat, only chew on a bit of hardtack or biscuit while in the saddle if needed. Once again, the scouts go far ahead of us to select a good campground for the night. We make camp some time between two and five o'clock. Tents are pitched, baggage unloaded, horses unsaddled and watered, picketed to grass, fires built, supper cooked, and then once again comes roll call. If we have corn (and we do not at the moment have any), we bring the horses inside the camp lines and feed them. Once that is done, guards are set, the counter-sign exchanged, and everyone retires. Once lanterns are out things are quiet except for the call for guard relief or the occasional howling of wolves or coyotes around the camp.

Daniel, Robert, and Big Amos, along with Captain Willets, do not go to bed until everything is still. They often go out to test the guards by crossing lines in the night to see whether they are awake and will challenge promptly and properly.

Most of the time I get five hours' sleep, and it seems enough.

My bedroll is an India rubber blanket spread upon the ground, then a buffalo robe given me by our interpreter Zephyr Picotte, followed by the small quilt Gen made for me. For the first few days that we were out in the field, I woke each morning stiff and sore, but that has passed now and I sleep pretty well.

You wouldn't approve of me at all if you saw how I am dressed today. A broad-brimmed drab-colored hat, a flannel shirt over a

muslin one, a dark blue woolen blouse, sky blue regulation pan-
taloons, cavalry boots reaching to the knees, and spurs. I have huck-
skin gauntlets, a belt with a revolver, cartridge box, cap box, etc., all
attached. I look very like an army man except that I have no saber.
Daniel tells me this makes no difference. I gather that he does not
see much value in a saber.

We eat the same things every day unless someone has luck at the
hunt, and a few of the men are beginning to show signs of scurvy.
Captain Willets says this will pass quickly as soon as we reach the
Platte, where a ranch house will provide potatoes and a few meals
of vegetables. That will make things right again. Some of the men
are riding in the ambulance because of fever or other complaints,
but no one is seriously ill.

There has been one death, a private who was thrown by his horse
gone wild because of rattlesnakes, and then bitten by one of the biggest
rattlers we have seen—and we have seen plenty. Daniel and Zephyr
personally clubbed about fifty to death one day—and all out of one
hole! We gave the poor fellow who died a proper burial with a solemn
escort to the final resting place, a sermon from Big Amos, and a fine
hymn sung by all the men. Extra volleys were fired over the grave,
which was hidden from any future disturbance. Genevieve has a little
bundle of the soldier's personal effects with her, and we will send them
home when we reach the ranch on the Platte, which is where this let-
ter will be posted to you. So while you may be missing me (and I hope
you are), think of another who will receive that unwelcome package
through the same mail service, and pray for them.

Your friend, Aaron

Within two days ride of Fort Laramie, they dropped south to
the Platte River.

"Look at that," Gen said, pointing in the distance to a shimmering flood of water seeming to fill the entire valley in the distance.

"A mirage," Captain Willets said. He had taken to riding alongside the cook's wagon from time to time while Daniel and the other scouts were out ahead of the main body of soldiers. "Watch what happens as we get nearer," he said. Sure enough, the nearer they came to the Platte River, the more the floodwaters receded, and the U-shaped expanse of bluffs that had seemed to rise from the waters appeared as they were, a few miles from the river, although no less magnificent. What had appeared as only a blue mound in the distance the day before, now took on the shape of a massive medieval city. It took little imagination to see towers and fortresses, minarets and grand halls in the rock formations, now deserted and dotted with little pines and scrub bush. Across the river and near what Captain Willets said was a road ranch, strings of white moved along towards the bluffs. "A wagon train," Willets said.

They were joined by Zephyr Picotte, who offered that traffic on the road was nothing like it had been a few years back. "There was wagons as far as the eye could see then" he said, motioning into the distance. "A steady stream of 'em. Like nothin' I ever saw before or since."

After crossing the Platte, which at this time of year lived up to its name and proved to be a shallow and very "flat water," they camped near Fort Mitchell, a rectangular adobe fort, portholed for defense with a sentinel tower at one corner and a log corral next to the river. A half-mile downriver stood the road ranch built of cedar logs. Although it boasted dirt floors and a sod roof, the ranch was large, with several rooms and a store. Knowing the store would make whiskey available to his men, Captain Willets denied them leave to visit the ranch. But once he had telegraphed their arrival at Fort Mitchell and the payroll was sent up the Platte by stagecoach, Willets was forced to relax his orders. The men flocked to the store, shoring up their outfits with buffalo robes and elk skins, buying new shirts and, to Captain Willets's dismay, whiskey.

One evening as they camped in the shadow of the mighty bluff,

Zephyr Picotte recounted the tragic story behind the naming of Scott's Bluffs. "There's almost as many versions of the story as there are tellers," Picotte said as he introduced the tale. "But I got mine from Jim Bridger himself, and he knew Hiram Scott. So I suppose I'm telling you as close to the truth as will ever be known. Hiram Scott trapped and traded for the Rocky Mountain Fur Company up on the Green. But in '28 he came down with the fever. When he got so sick he couldn't sit a horse, they made a bull boat for him at Lebonte's Cabin on the Sweetwater." He stopped abruptly and jerked his chin up at Aaron. "You know what a bull boat is, son?"

Aaron shook his head.

"It's a round contraption, made by stretching skins across a reed framework. Bull boats are clever . . . but they have their limitations. The one hauling Scott and his two companions downriver broke up among the rapids in the Black Hills. They lost everything and barely managed to keep Scott from drowning. Nine days later they arrived here, half-starved, with no provisions and no way to get any since they'd lost rifles and ammunition to the river. The two healthy bas—" Picotte looked at Aaron. He swallowed. "The two healthy scoundrels convinced themselves Scott was going to die anyway, so, telling him they were going to reconnoiter for food, they left him in the shade of the bluff with a gourd of water at his side. Then they headed for civilization." Picotte waited for the meaning of his words to sink in. "Sublette found his bones the next year," here Picotte paused and looked at the circle of men listening to the tragic tale, "nearly *one hundred miles* from where his worth-less friends had confessed to leaving him."

"No!"

"Aw, Picotte . . . now that's a tall tale," Edward Pope drawled.

Picotte withdrew his pipe and shook it at the doubters. "Think what you will," he said slowly, "but never underestimate the strength of the old mountaineers. I believe it as I heard it, gentlemen."

After a two-day layover at Fort Mitchell and with no success at finding any Indians for Elliot Leighton to interview, the company headed up the pass towards Fort Laramie. It was the most rugged land they had yet encountered, a winding and torturous ascent dotted with huge boulders fallen from above. The road cut down into the sandy clay, sometimes so deep only a single wagon could pass through.

Daniel had spent the last few weeks teaching his stallion to abide two riders. When they came to the pass, he pulled Gen up behind him and they rode through together, craning their necks this way and that, taking in the amazing formations of rock on either side, marveling at the dozens of names carved into the walls of the pass. *S. Taylor, 1852 . . . Rufus Sage, 1841 . . . E. Bird, 1854 . . . H. Carpenter . . . William A. Carter . . .*

When they stopped to rest, the two climbed up one rock wall. Gen traced a name, murmuring, "Where do you suppose *R. Burton* is right this minute?"

Daniel, who had taken shelter in the shadow of a rock and was sitting watching his wife, just smiled and shrugged.

Just then Elliot waved them over to where he had found the fossilized remains of a massive creature jutting out of the bluff. "Look at that," he said, pointing to a gigantic shell. "Ancient turtles." He waved his hand in a semicircle. "And see that? The thing that looks like a giant horn? If I'm not mistaken, that's some kind of mastodon." Elliot put his hands on his hips and looked about him. "I wonder if anyone knows what a rich store of fossils are hidden in these walls . . ." Opening his notebook, he began to make notes.

Aaron and Edward Pope decided to scale the walls of the bluff, betting one another who could reach the summit first. They ended up nearly stranded on a high ridge, but when they descended again they reported having found an eagle's nest and the skeleton of a buffalo, and they swore the sight of rain clouds dumping moisture on the Platte valley miles away was well worth their narrow escape.

That evening, Aaron wrote his adventures to Amanda. He told her the story of the ill-fated Hiram Scott and described the bluff.

> *The wind has created pinnacles and turrets and pyramids and mounds of every possible size, shape, and description here in this range of bluffs. Imagine castle walls and turrets that soar into the sky, and you will have only a small idea of what we are seeing. The trail itself looks like it has been cut by a sudden rushing of water pushing through the rock, making many twists and turns and at some points cutting out the rock beneath and leaving overhanging walls. Edward Pope and I scaled one of the walls to a dizzying height from which we saw a rainstorm pass in the valley miles below. We encountered an eagle's nest, and since the occupants were away, I took the opportunity to carve a certain name high on the bluff where it is likely only God and I will ever know of its existence.*
>
> *I will post this letter when we reach Fort Laramie. When you receive it, Miss Whitrock, I ask that you think fondly of the one who sent it, who today carved your name into the steep walls of a cliff in the West.*

"How will we ever describe this to our children?" Gen asked later that day as she and Daniel stood looking towards Fort Laramie from the highest point of the trail. Before them lay the valley of the Platte, the river itself studded with islands. The descent into that valley was made on foot. Edward Pope declined to drive his team down the torturous route but instead climbed down and tried to lead them, but more often than not he had to step aside while the team tumbled down a narrow passage while Edward's mobile kitchen pitched dangerously from side to side, banging against the steep canyon walls and threatening to break apart at any moment. Edward finally caught up with his team and decided to climb aboard, riding the rest of the descent and successfully taking his team into camp near the river that evening.

Gen and Daniel had just settled into their tent that night when Captain Willet called softly, "Hate to bother you, Two Stars, but I need you."

Daniel pulled on his shirt and pants and went outside.

"Hope it's not a problem, but look." He nodded across the river to where a party of Sioux were setting up camp.

After watching them for a while, Daniel murmured, "They don't mean any harm or we'd have been attacked by now. They are probably as nervous as we are."

"Then why don't they move on?" Willets wanted to know.

"They probably are wondering why we don't move on," was the reply.

Willets was quiet for a while. "All right," he finally said. "I get your point. What do you think we ought to do?"

"Post extra guards."

"Already done."

"Bring the horses and pack mules into camp."

"Right," Willets said.

Just as they were talking, a chorus of cries and laments went up from across the river.

"It's a burial party," Daniel said. "They won't bother us."

"Right," Willets said doubtfully.

"Can we take a delegation over to talk to them in the morning?" Elliot asked as he strode up.

"Of course," Willets said. "Good idea." He turned to Daniel. "Well then, get some rest."

Daniel brought his white stallion into camp, picketing the horse just outside his tent. Then he crawled in beside his wife and went to sleep, unaware that just across the river a young brave named Hawk had been observing the camp through a contraption he had found after a battle with white soldiers a few weeks before. He held it up to his eye and brought everything near. Carefully, he inspected the enemy camp, concluding that at least for today his people were safe and the soldiers would not attack. He saw a man with white hair seated beside a tent writing. From time to time the white-haired man looked up and spoke to a yellow-haired boy. He saw soldiers playing cards, and one that was sneaking whiskey from a flask hidden beneath his jacket. His lips curled up in a sneer when he saw the Dakota scouts.

Earlier in the evening Hawk had been surprised to see a woman among them. But when she pushed her bonnet back from her face and he realized she was Indian, his interest grew. She was beautiful. After a while, Hawk surmised she belonged to one of the scouts. He wondered if the rest of the soldiers used her in the way he had seen women used at Fort Laramie.

Hawk saw many things as the sun set and he watched his enemies. But the thing that interested him most had nothing to do with how many soldiers guarded the camp, or what their business might be. The thing that kept Hawk high in a tree observing the camp was the horse picketed next to the woman's tent. He saw the scout carry water to the animal in his own hat and hand-feed him the most tender shoots of grasses. He saw him brush and comb and clean, and while the scout did all of these things, Hawk saw the horse nudge his master in the way only a sweet-natured horse would do.

Hawk watched until it was too dark to see any more. He closed up his seeing stick and thrust it into the sash at his waist. He jumped from the tree and went to his tepee. They were few in number, this small band of Bad Faces. Their leader was aging, and he did not want to fight any more whites. Hawk thought that wise, given their lack of young warriors and the number of soldiers camped across the river. All of those things were against him, Hawk knew. And yet, as he lay in his tepee listening to distant wolves howl, Hawk determined that before many more nights, he would have that white horse for his own.

Nineteen

"Use hospitality one to another without grudging."

—I Peter 4:9

NO, THE OLD CHIEF INSISTED, HE WAS NOT GOING UP TO Fort Laramie. Bad Indians were up that way and he was a good Indian. He was taking his little band down on the Republican to hunt buffalo. Let the young fools up on the Powder River fight with the white man. He had had his day to fight and now only wanted to live in peace. Yes, he told Elliot, he would come back up the Platte when the government came again to meet, but he had already touched the pen and he only wanted to live in peace. He had come across to the soldier's camp to invite them all to a feast and to emphasize his feelings of good will.

That evening the feast was held, and Elliot Leighton smoked

the first of many peace pipes In his long career as an intercessor between the United States Government and native America. Daniel and Robert and Big Amos kept guard over the horses. Aaron came back brimming full of stories. He spent the evening alternately sketching what he had seen for Miss Whitrock and thanking his Uncle Elliot for letting him volunteer.

"Why didn't you go with us, Ma?" Aaron asked Gen later that night.

Gen was wiping the last of the cooking pots. She did not turn around, only shrugged and mumbled something about Edward needing her help.

"It was amazing," Aaron said with enthusiasm. He held out a sheaf of papers. "Look," he said. "I'm not the best artist, but isn't that dancer something?"

Gen took the papers and glanced down, trying to keep her hands from trembling. She leafed through Aaron's drawings without comment, then handed them back.

"What's wrong, Ma?" Aaron asked.

Gen shook her head. "Nothing." She set the last pot in its place in the mobile kitchen and forced a smile.

Aaron looked down as she rubbed one of her forearms. He had forgotten how badly scarred she was. He reached out and lay his hand over the scars. "I'm sorry, Ma. I didn't think—I didn't mean to bring those awful things that happened back."

"It's all right. I'm as surprised as you are it's bothering me after all this time." She blinked tears away. "I didn't think it would. But when the drums started up . . . and the singing . . ." She shivered, then forced a weak smile. "I'm glad to see it doesn't haunt you. Do you remember that day you climbed up in the tree in the rain?"

Aaron nodded. "That was after Otter tried to hurt you, and Daniel arrived just in time."

"You pushed me away. Said not to treat you like a baby," Gen said. "And then you ran outside and climbed the tree to get away from everything. I wondered if you would ever again be able to smile." She sighed. "I'm glad to see you can."

"God did that," Aaron said. "I don't know why it doesn't bother me anymore. It just doesn't. And here, I guess I'm so intent on learning—"

"You don't have to apologize for not being like me," Gen said quickly. "I wish I could be more like you." She rubbed her arms again. "It's kind of taken me by surprise that I'm so—" She stopped abruptly, unable to think of the right word to describe how she felt. Presently she looked into the darkness towards where Daniel was standing watch over the herd. "I wish he'd come in."

"I'll go get him," Aaron said.

"Don't." Gen put her hand on Aaron's shoulder. "He doesn't need a foolish woman keeping him from doing his job. He'll be sorry he let me come."

A few yards away, Zephyr Picotte was telling another one of his yarns to a group of new recruits. From where he sat listening, Captain John Willets watched the interchange between Genevieve Two Stars and Aaron Dane. He frowned when he saw Gen clutch Aaron's sleeve and shake her head. When Aaron turned to go, Willets followed him.

"Is something wrong with Mrs. Two Stars?"

Aaron paused. "No. Yes." He sighed. "She wouldn't want me to say anything." He cleared his throat. "Do you think I could relieve Daniel so he could come in early?"

"Of course," Willets said quickly. "Is she ill?"

"No. Nothing like that. She just—the parlay over at the Indian camp made her nervous. Memories and all."

Willets frowned and looked down at the ground. He pulled on his hat brim and looked out towards where the herd had been taken to graze. "I posted extra guards. I hope she knows I'm not a fool. Spotted Antelope may be peaceful, but no self-respecting Sioux could resist the temptation to run off a few well-fed government ponies. Do you think it would help if I told her that?"

Aaron considered. "With all due respect, sir, it's not the horses she's worried about."

"I know that," Willets interrupted. "I just thought I might be able to allay her fears."

"Well, sir, about the only thing that's going to do that is Daniel. But she doesn't want to admit it, and she'd be really angry with me if she knew I even told you. She doesn't want people thinking she's a fool woman."

"Go relieve Two Stars," Willets said. "Tell him I need him fresh in the morning for a special scouting assignment."

"Yes, sir," Aaron saluted and turned to go.

"And, Dane—"

"Yes, sir?"

"Just for the record, I think Mrs. Two Stars is about the least foolish woman I've ever had the pleasure to meet. Don't tell her I said that. But don't be afraid to let me know if there are any concerns affecting her that I could help."

"Yes, sir."

As he watched Aaron mount up and ride towards the herd, Willets poured himself a cup of terrible coffee and headed for his tent. He thought back to his temporary acquaintance with Miss Parker back in Minnesota, trying to imagine her on such an expedition as this. The image made him smile and shake his head. No, Willets realized, Miss Parker was not the sort of woman one would expect to head West. She would never have climbed Scott's Bluffs to see fossils and would have had no curiosity about the whereabouts of the people who had carved their names along Mitchell Pass. Minnesota was about all the frontier Miss Parker and women like her would willingly endure.

The image of Genevieve Two Stars's shining dark hair falling down her back that night when she and Daniel came back from their late-night swim flashed in his mind.

A man would be crazy not to admit Daniel Two Stars was one lucky man. And what could be wrong with acknowledging a woman's admirable qualities, Willets argued when his conscience hinted that he had been watching Mrs. Two Stars and admiring her a little too much lately.

"Just hold me," Genevieve whispered.

Daniel wrapped his arms around her as they lay together in their tent. "What is it, little wife?" She was trembling. He felt her forehead with a sense of dread. "Are you sick?"

"No," she muttered. "I'm not sick. It's—oh, I don't know," she sighed. "I don't know. The music tonight. The drums and the dancing . . ." she buried her face in his chest and sobbed.

Not knowing what to do, Daniel did the right thing. He let her cry.

"I should have stayed with Nancy," she finally said. She pushed herself away and wiped her tears with the back of her hand. "Then you wouldn't have to put up with me." She began to cry again. "I'm sorry. I don't mean to be so much trouble."

"You are no trouble, Blue Eyes," Daniel said gently. "You are my love." He said a silent prayer for understanding, and waited again.

"I didn't think I'd be afraid," she finally murmured. "But when I saw the tepees and the fire—"

"There have been other campfires and other villages since we left Fort Randall," Daniel said.

"I know," she sat up and he followed suit. "I know. But this . . . this is different." She looked at him. "You know it's different. We've only met peaceful Sioux up until now. There hasn't been any threat."

"I don't think Spotted Antelope's band is a threat either, Blue Eyes."

"Then why did Captain Willets post extra guards around the herd?" she said abruptly. "Why are the men staying in tight clusters around the campfires? Why aren't they joking as usual?"

Daniel smiled and shook his head. "Why aren't you a little less watchful, Blue Eyes? You would worry less." He sighed. "Aaron noticed one of the young braves perched in a tree early this morning looking our camp over with a spyglass. It's probably nothing. But Captain Willets wants us to be more alert. And that is wise." He grinned. "In the old days, Blue Eyes, I don't think *I* would have been able to resist a few good army horses." He reached out to touch her hair. "But they are a peaceful band and we are watching the horses. I doubt there will be any trouble." He began to hum the Dakota courting song, tracing her hairline with his finger as he did so. "Don't be sorry you came, little wife."

"I don't want to be a burden to you," Gen said.

"You are not a burden," Daniel whispered, enfolding her in his arms again. "You are my life." He kissed her.

❦

"A woman? You brought a woman on your expedition?" Doctor Beaumont's sterling gray eyes flickered angrily. "What were you thinking, man! You know this season has been one long skirmish after another with the Sioux or the Cheyenne or both. Why, I've threatened to send Libby downriver a dozen times, and if it weren't for her being a stubborn old battle-ax, she'd have been safe and sound in Omaha weeks ago."

Willets smiled. "Now, Henry. I'm glad to hear you and Mrs. Beaumont are still so fond of one another."

"Harrumph," muttered Beaumont, tugging on his moustache. He frowned. "She's a tough old bird, John. I never knew just how tough until I tried to get her to leave this spring. Says she won't be sent away and that's that. Says if she's to be scalped then so be it but she isn't leaving me to the wiles of the desperate women in this God-forsaken place. As if there's any danger of that!" Henry Beaumont twirled the tip of his graying moustache in an unsuccessful attempt to hide his sense of pride in and love for his wife.

"Well, as I said, I'm glad to see things haven't changed between you two. That's exactly why I know you'll want to help me out by having Mrs. Two Stars as your guest for a few weeks while we go upriver. It's only a few weeks and her husband will be back to take her home—wherever that ends up being."

"What do you mean, wherever that ends up being?" Beaumont asked quickly.

"If you'll offer me a cup of coffee, I'll tell you the whole story," Willets said.

Beaumont waved Willets into a chair. He strode to the door, cracked it open and hollered, "Libby! Libby Beaumont!"

Presently a stately, gray-haired woman swept into the room. Ignoring their visitor, Mrs. Beaumont leaned down to give her husband a peck on the cheek and cooed, "What is it, dear?"

"We've company. And we need some coffee." With a secretive smile, Beaumont waved his hand towards John, who rose to bow just as Mrs. Beaumont turned around.

"John Willets!" Libby clapped her hands together. "*Captain* John Willets!" She grasped him by the arms and inspected his uniform. "My, my. When did that happen?" Without waiting for a reply, Libby headed for the door. She waggled her finger at her husband. "The next time you want coffee, Doctor Beaumont, see to it you say *please*." She winked at John. "He's still an insufferable old poop, John. Hasn't changed a bit." She closed the door behind her. They could hear her laughing out in the hall.

After serving coffee to her husband and John Willets, Libby Beaumont settled into a chair opposite them. She stayed to hear Willets tell about Genevieve Two Stars and the Minnesota Sioux Uprising, about Daniel Two Stars and prison, about Simon Dane and his children, and lastly, about Abner Marsh and his dogs.

"Mrs. Lawrence and the new baby went to the reservation on the Niobrara. Robert settled her with friends there. But Genevieve—Mrs. Two Stars—insisted on coming with her husband."

"I like her already," Libby said, winking at the doctor.

"I have to admit that I sort of planned we'd impose on you once we came to Fort Laramie. Of course we hoped things would be more peaceful, but—"

"Well, they aren't," Beaumont interrupted. "I've treated more arrow wounds than scurvy in the past two weeks."

John frowned and gulped coffee. "We're supposed to be here for the September 1st parlay. As long as the weather holds in Nebraska, we'll head back along the Platte after that. Unless, of course, my orders change."

"You're just itching to get some real action, aren't you?" Beaumont said. "Hoping you'll be ordered to stay out here."

Willets shrugged. "Nothing worse than an army man stationed where there's no need for army. Fort Ridgely isn't going to be attacked again. Settlers are pouring in. There's not much to be done back there."

"And not much hope of another promotion unless you see action, is there, Captain?" Libby interjected.

John smiled. "Well said, Mrs. Beaumont." He stretched his legs. "One thing you should know about the Two Stars. They aren't your typical Indians. At least not what you're used to out here. They're Christians."

Libby and her husband exchanged glances.

"No," Willets said. "I mean it. They are real Christians. Like you two."

"What do you mean, like us two?" Libby asked. "You sound like you're describing a common disease."

John laughed softly. "I mean they read their Bibles every day and they try to do what it says." He thought hard, then cleared his throat. "When they first came to Fort Ridgely and I heard what that homesteader did to Genevieve, I was all set to take a few men to his place and, as I put it, 'put the fear of God' into him. Daniel wouldn't have it. He said everything in him wanted to do just that, but he couldn't. He said he'd leave it with God. That he wasn't going to live a life of vengeance anymore."

"I'm honored, John, to think you connect that kind of faith with me," Dr. Beaumont said. "Honored and touched."

"If I didn't know better," Willets said suddenly, "I'd think God was ambushing *me* with true Christians." He laughed at his joke, but neither Doctor nor Mrs. Beaumont did. He swiped his hand over his goatee. "Big Amos and Robert Lawrence are Christians, too. I reckon they'll be in church on Sunday if you have a minister preaching."

"We do," the doctor said. "And they'll be welcome. So would you, John."

Willets set his empty coffee cup on the serving tray and stood up. "I'll be bringing Daniel and Genevieve by to meet you, then."

"Why not come to dinner after church tomorrow?" Mrs. Beaumont asked.

"That your way of making it harder for me to skip church?"

"No," Mrs. Beaumont shot back as she bent over to pick up the serving tray. "But if I'd thought of it, I would have used it."

Willets opened the door for her.

"We'll see you in church then, John," Doctor Beaumont

said, smiling. "Ten o'clock. Bring all your friends. Bring the whole company if you can."

Willets nodded and stepped outside. The sun was dipping behind Laramie Peak in the distance, casting long shadows in the valley. Unhitching his buckskin gelding, he stood for a moment, reins in hand, looking across the parade ground towards the stone church. The cross at the top of the steeple was still illuminated in bright sunlight. He smiled. His mother would be so pleased.

Twenty

"What time I am afraid, I will trust in thee."

—PSALM 56:3

"OH, AARON," GEN SWALLOWED THE LUMP IN HER throat. She put her hand on the boy's arm. She hadn't noticed before, but as she looked down now, she realized Aaron had his father's hands. How had that happened? She looked back up at him. The goatee he had been nursing along for the past few weeks was actually beginning to show. His hair was longer, too, but pleasingly so. Blond ringlets spilled over his forehead. He hated the curls. The women at Fort Laramie did not. Gen had seen them turn their heads as he walked by. She patted his arm and squeezed it. "I know how much it cost you to say that. And I love you for it. But I wouldn't dream of keeping you from your duty."

She blinked away the tears gathering in her eyes and looked up at him. "You're a man now, Aaron. You aren't that little boy who climbed the tree to get away from all the horrible things happening around him anymore. You want to be in the middle of the action." She inhaled deeply. "And I want you to go." *Do all mothers lie at times like this?*

"You're sure?" He could hardly keep the excitement from his voice. "You're sure, Ma?"

"No," Gen said, making herself laugh. "I'm not at all sure. Now get out of here before I change my mind. Go tell Captain Willets you'll be with the company heading up to Phil Kearney."

Aaron kissed her on the cheek, grabbed up his hat, and headed for the door. He paused just outside. "I love you, Ma."

Gen nodded. Then she buried her face in her hands and wept.

❧

"Aaron told me what you said." Daniel put his arm around her. "You still surprise me at times, little wife."

"Somehow, sometime this summer he became a man. I didn't even see it happen." She paused. "He has Simon's hands. But I think Ellen is in there, too. There's a gentleness about him." She sighed. "I hope he never loses that."

"We'll take good care of him."

She said nothing, only wrapped her arms around him and rested her head against his chest. "I am trying very hard, best beloved."

"I know you are." He brushed his lips across her forehead before hugging her fiercely. "Let's walk."

They exited the tiny adobe cabin Gen would call home for the next few weeks and headed for the foothills in the distance, walking past a collection of tepees inhabited by friendly Indians called "loafers," natives who never left their camping places around the fort. Loafers, Gen had learned that day, were looked down upon by the whites as lazy and by their own people as too accepting of white handouts. Making their way towards the river, Daniel and Gen sat down beneath a fringe of low brush in full view of the water.

"I read from Philippians this morning," Gen said abruptly. She recited, "For I have learned, in whatsoever state I am, therewith to be content. I know both how to be abased, and I know how to abound: every where and in all things I am instructed both to be full and to be hungry, both to abound and to suffer need. I can do all things through Christ which strengtheneth me." She paused. "You wouldn't think abundance would require learning anything about contentment. But when I was in New York at Leighton Hall, I had to work on it. I wasn't truly happy, but I felt God wanted me there." She wrapped her arms around her knees and gazed towards the other side of the river. "Then I got what I wanted and came home to you. It wasn't the way we expected it to be at the Grants. But I was learning to be content."

"Even if we didn't own the land?" Daniel asked.

Gen shrugged. "That never mattered to me. We had what we needed." She swallowed. "And now, I know He is still with us. But—" she sighed and shook her head. "I'm not content." She hid her face against her knees and talked into her skirt. "I don't want to be in this place without you." She raised her head and looked up at her husband.

He put his hand on the back of her neck and pulled her over to rest against him. "I'm sorry, little wife. This isn't the life I wanted to give you."

Gen put her hand over his. "Don't apologize. You're doing what God gave you to do. If it means we have to be apart for a while, I should be content and concentrate on the blessings. But I can't seem to get to that place." She laughed sadly. "I'm such a hypocrite."

"What makes you say that?"

"This morning while you were out with the horses, Mrs. Beaumont came to camp. She said she thought it was wonderful the way I was trusting the Lord."

"She seems nice," Daniel offered.

"She is." Gen sighed. "How amazing that God provided a Christian sister for me all the way out here." After a pause, Gen said, "But, Daniel, she said she *admires* how well I'm taking your leaving."

"What's wrong with that?"

Gen shook her head. "The only reason she admires the way I'm handling this is because I'm a very good hypocrite. I manage to hide the crumbling walls inside."

"I don't think being content means you don't feel anything. Doesn't that verse say Paul *learned* it? That means he wasn't always content, either."

They were quiet for a while. Finally, Gen spoke up again. "I won't believe God is letting this happen without a purpose. I'm thinking there's something I can only learn by staying behind. But I don't want to learn it. Not this way."

"There is a plan, Blue Eyes. We just can't see it."

"All right. So then the question is, how can this be made good for you and me? If God causes all things to work together for good, then how is this expedition and your going up to Fort Phil Kearney going to work for good?"

"If we knew that, little wife, we probably wouldn't have to go through it. We'd be onto the next lesson."

"You mean we'd still be back in Minnesota enjoying our little cabin and our friends?"

Daniel smiled sadly. "Maybe."

"Ooh," Gen balled her hands up into fists and pounded her head. "Why do I have to be so *dense?!* Why does God have to make the lessons so *hard?!*"

"I love you, little wife." Daniel pulled her close.

"I'm a terrible student and a rebellious child. I'm mad at God. And when I tell you all that . . . *that* makes you say you love me?"

He kissed her cheek. "Of course. If you are a terrible student and a rebellious child . . . and just a little bit angry at God, then it brings us closer together, because I am all of those things and worse." He grew serious. "I'm not looking forward to going up that river into hostile territory, Blue Eyes."

She pushed away from him. "Daniel Two Stars . . . are you admitting you're *afraid*?!"

He looked down into her eyes. "I am." When she nestled against him again, he said, "You have been concentrating on a verse about learning to be content. The one I have been thinking about talks about 'momentary light affliction.' It talks about how these things are nothing compared to the 'eternal weight of glory' we will enjoy someday. Those two phrases keep pounding in my head. But no matter how often I tell myself this is momentary and light . . ."

"It doesn't feel momentary or light at all."

"No, it doesn't."

Again, there was silence, until Daniel began to pray. "My Father. We have come out here to help our friend Elliot on his mission for the government. Thank You for giving me this work. But, Father, we are afraid. I don't want to leave Blue Eyes alone at this fort. I want to be with her forever and always. But I have to go. And when I come back, Father, where will we go then? We don't know. We can't return to Minnesota. Must we go to the reservation in Nebraska? When I think about all these things, and about Aaron being a soldier and all the other troubles in our lives, Lord, I am afraid. Blue Eyes says she is not content. And we do not feel that all of this trouble is momentary or light. I don't know anything to say, Lord, except that we are Your children and we want to do what is right. Show us the way. And when You have shown us, give us the courage to walk it."

~⌒~

"You take this." Daniel pulled the small leather money bag he wore around his neck and put it over her head. "Buy that red calico at the sutler's store and make a new dress to wear when I come home." He touched her chin and kissed her lightly before whispering, "Not too many buttons, though."

She followed him outside, barely managing to help Edward pack up the camp kitchen while she tried to see everything Daniel did. She watched him as much as possible, trying to memorize him. Once, she caught Captain Willets watching her. He smiled and nodded. It made her blush and feel self-conscious to think he had been watching her watch Daniel.

Aaron and Elliot joined them for the last breakfast, served just as the sky was blushing pink at dawn. They talked about nothing and everything, filling the air with words just to keep the silence from accenting everyone's nervousness. When at last the bugle sounded "boots and saddles," there was a certain amount of relief in the call to duty. Big Amos and Robert gave Gen letters to send down the trail to Santee with the next mail stage. Aaron and Elliot had already posted letters home. They said their good-byes and went to mount up, leaving Daniel and Gen a moment to themselves.

Daniel's white stallion bobbed his head up and down and danced sideways.

"He's ready to go," Gen said nervously. She looked up. "I guess you are, too. You don't have to kiss me . . . the men are watching."

"Are they?" Daniel said, staring down at her. "Good." He pulled her close and enjoyed a long, slow kiss, ignoring the stallion's impatient whicker until the animal head-butted them apart.

"Well," Gen said breathlessly.

"Yes," Daniel said, cupping her face in his hands. "You," he

STEPHANIE GRACE WHITSON

said, "are the best thing that ever happened to me." Gen stepped
away. When he jumped astride the horse without using the stir-
rups, she teased him about showing off.

"If you think that's showing off, just wait until I get back." He
leaned down to brush his finger along her jawline. "Don't forget.
A red dress."

"And not too many buttons," she answered back.

"I love you, best beloved," he said.

"And I, you." She smiled up at him, intent on being brave.
Almost, she succeeded. Until she caught a glimpse of the tears
welling up in his dark eyes. Swallowing hard, she backed away.
He urged the white horse forward and joined the men. She bent
over and picked up the bundle he'd left behind and stood watching the men file out of the now-deserted camp. As the last horse
disappeared in the distance, a white horse came thundering back
along the column. Just barely, she saw him stand up in the stir-
rups and lift his hand. She waved back. In a moment, he wheeled
the stallion around and was gone.

Mrs. Beaumont found her, sitting on the bundle that repre-
sented everything she owned in the world and nothing that mattered, sobbing as if her heart would break.

❦

"Oh my dear, my dear girl," a voice was saying.

Gen swiped at her cheeks and stood up. Bending over, she
grabbed a strap and hoisted the bundle off the ground. "I'm all
right," she said.

"Of course you are," Mrs. Beaumont said. "And I'm the
Queen of England. Pleased to make your acquaintance. Will you
come to tea?"

Gen looked up at the woman uncertainly.

"If it makes any difference," she said gently, "I felt the same

193

way the first time Dr. Beaumont left me alone at a fort." She tucked a wisp of gray hair behind her ear.

"And it gets easier?" Gen said hopefully.

"No. It never gets easier. Not if you love them." Mrs. Doc sighed. "But, you learn to bear it."

"Without making a public spectacle of yourself?" Gen looked around her, hoping the cluster of women standing by sutler's had just arrived.

"Oh, I can't promise that. But there's something about a man and wife who love each other that makes an impression on the world, my dear. Too many marriages are built on convenience. Too many are loveless. I like to think God can use those of us who know His love to woo onlookers into the kingdom." She patted Gen's arm.

The women started off together, but when Gen headed towards the parade ground, Mrs. Beaumont stopped. "Are you going somewhere, my dear?"

"Just to my room. Captain Willets arranged for a room over on laundress row."

Mrs. Doctor smiled. "Is that what they told you?"

Gen frowned. "You mean I don't have a room?"

"Why, of course you have a room. Your husband made the arrangements last week. And I am delighted. You shouldn't be so secretive about yourself, my dear."

"I'm afraid I don't know what you are talking about," Gen said.

"We have a little school for the native children," Mrs. Beaumont explained.

"Yes," Gen replied. "I knew about that."

"Your husband told us about your background. At Miss Bartlett's in New York?"

Gen nodded. "But I don't see what that has to do with—"

"We need a teacher, Mrs. Two Stars. I can't keep up. We can't pay you, but Dr. Beaumont and I would be honored if you'd accept our hospitality for as long as you are here."

"Daniel . . . did this? For me?"

"Now, now, you're going to start crying again," Mrs. Beaumont said. "Let's get you home," and she took Gen by the arm and guided her towards the lovely, two-story white frame doctor's residence. As they walked, she maintained a one-sided conversation on the trials of army life, the goodness of God, and the weather.

By the end of the week, Gen had settled into a routine.

By the second week, she had learned Mrs. Beaumont's life story.

And by Monday of the third week, Mrs. Beaumont had become Libby, Gen's good friend and personal prayer warrior.

Twenty-One

"For by wise counsel thou shalt make thy war:
 and in multitude of counselors there is safety."
—PROVERBS 24:6

"JUST REMEMBER: WHERE YOU DON'T SEE ANY INDIANS,
that's where they're thickest."

Zephyr Picotte packed his pipe with tobacco and lit it before
settling back against a tree. Aaron considered his advice, looking
from Daniel to the other scouts. When he saw them nod and smile,
he, too, nodded. Captain Willets joined their campfire. It was three
days since they left Fort Laramie, and other than a long-since-aban-
doned camp and occasional smoke signals, they had seen no signs
of Indians, either hostile or friendly. Each night they pitched three
tents; first, a large square one with a flap that created a shaded
"porch" for Captain Willets; then two Sibley tents, accommodating

seventeen men each; and lastly a small tent for Edward Pope and the scouts. They ate in the open air around their campfires and could set up or take down camp in a matter of minutes.

By their fourth day in the field, Elliot was beginning to think he was wasting his own time and the U.S. government's money. Picotte was inclined to disagree, and said so. "Remember what I said the other day. We don't see 'em, but you can be sure they see us." Picotte's advice proved true the next morning when it was discovered that several horses had been run off, right from beneath the picket guards' noses.

They traveled over hills covered with blooming flowers of all colors. Once, after they had crossed a particularly beautiful spot, Daniel dropped back behind the main party just long enough to pull his Bible from his saddlebags and tuck a few blossoms between the pages. *She will know I was thinking of her.* He paused long enough to appreciate the beauty and to envision a little cabin just up on the hillside. But then he saw smoke signals rising from a bluff in the distance. Slipping the Bible back into his saddlebag, he mounted up and galloped back to the column.

Each night they camped by crystal-clear streams filled with fish. The men gorged on freshly caught fish and when they tired of fish they hunted, dining on elk, deer, antelope, or jack rabbit. Aaron declared fresh antelope the finest meat on earth and made it his daily goal to acquire a bearskin "for Miss Whitrock's Christmas gift." Although they saw bears every day—one so large Aaron mistook it for a buffalo—he did not succeed in taking one down until Big Amos and Robert Lawrence determined to help. The three brought in a fine specimen and Aaron had his bearskin.

Despairing of any chance to talk to Indians, Elliot decided to make scientific observations and began sketching, trusting Zephyr Picotte to supply the names of plants and wildlife. "I can tell you what the Cheyenne call that," he said once, when Elliot pointed to a blue wildflower. "But I got no idea beyond that."

Six days out of Fort Laramie, the expedition crossed Clear Creek, skirted Lake De Smet, and struck the Bozeman Trail. Soon, they were approaching the plateau where Fort Phil Kearney stood above a broad stretch of fertile, grassy meadows and clear mountain creeks. It was impossible to imagine a more ideal location for a military fort.

Intended to house one thousand men, the six-hundred by eight-hundred-foot rectangular fort was enclosed by a pine stockade standing eight feet high. Blockhouses with portholes for cannon at diagonal corners were complemented by flaring loopholes at every fourth log along the entire length of the stockade. All the gates were massive and constructed of double planks with substantial bars and locks. Inside this main stockade were an impressive parade ground and the usual complement of log or lumber buildings including hospital and chapel, bakery and laundry, cavalry yard and stables, officers quarters and battery. The commanding officer's quarters was a two-story building topped by a watchtower. East of the fort proper, a rough palisade of cottonwoods enclosed the mechanics shops and the teamsters' mess, more stables, the hay yard, and the wood yard. From this stockade, the "water gates" opened, providing access to the nearby Little Piney Creek.

For natural beauty, Fort Phil Kearney had few equals. To the West rose the Panther Mountains, to the south the Big Horn range, and far to the east, the Black Hills. Only a few hundred yards from the fort rose Pilot Hill, whose conical summit provided a natural watchtower from which the picket guard could signal danger by waving a flag—and, the men heard later, the flag had been waved much too frequently since the Fetterman disaster last December.

Once the company had been welcomed inside, Captain Willets met with the post commander who explained, "The plan seems to be to harass us constantly. They run off the stock. They try to entice my men away from the stockade in hopes of cutting them off. It's all minor, and there haven't been any serious battles recently, but hardly a day goes by without some engagement or, at the very least, a threat in the form of smoke signals or war whoops from the hills." He scratched his beard and shook his head. "We're spread too thin, Captain." He looked at Elliot. "You write that to Washington, sir. If they expect us to hold the Bozeman trail, they've got to send more men. We're supposed to house a thousand. I've fewer than four hundred."

The first night, Aaron could not sleep for the chorus of howling wolves outside the stockade. "They come up after the leavins' in the slaughter yard by Little Piney," Picotte explained the next morning. "Last year the Injuns caught on to that and came in after sundown under wolfskins." He pointed up to the wall where a guard was walking towards one of the blockhouses. "Shot a sentry right off that wall before anyone guessed they weren't all wolves out there." Picotte paused. "You hear any wolves, Aaron Dane, you listen for the echo. I learned it from Jim Bridger himself. The howl of a real wolf don't echo in these hills. You hear an echo, you get ready to shoot, 'cause those wolves got braids and bows under their fur."

The commander dashed any hopes Elliot had of traveling still further north to Fort C. F. Smith. "There's not a Sioux chief in this country interested in talking peace, Captain Leighton." He looked at Willets. "I'm sorry, Captain, but even if there were some men here foolish enough to head off with you under a white flag, I couldn't spare them. My main concern right now has to be protecting the woodcutters down on Piney Island. We've got to get more wood in if we're to survive the winter."

"May I offer my men to support you?" Willets said.

"What you ought to do is pack up and take yourselves back down the trail to Fort Laramie."

"You said you didn't have enough men to hold the fort. We aren't many, but my men are hard fighters."

Powell studied Willets' face for a moment. "If you don't mind my asking, Captain, do you have any experience fighting Indians?"

"In Minnesota."

He jerked his head towards where the Dakota scouts stood listening. "What about them?"

"Do they have experience?"

"If they're Sioux, they know how to fight. The question is, who will they fight *with* when the shooting starts?"

Daniel stepped forward. "I swore allegiance to that flag, sir," he said, nodding towards the American flag hanging on the wall. "And I keep my word."

Big Amos and Robert Lawrence nodded their agreement.

Powell studied the men, who met his gaze. "Well then," Powell said. "As long as we understand each other." He nodded. "The woodcutters just got started last week. Already they're threatening to quit. Can't say as I blame 'em. One of 'em was found scalped yesterday."

"We'll go," Daniel and the scouts said at once.

Powell nodded. "See you at dawn."

❧

When they arrived at Piney Island, they learned that the woodcutters had been divided into two parties. One group was camping on a bare plain, the other in the thick of the pine woods about a mile away. Powell sent twelve of his men to guard the camp in the woods and thirteen to escort the wood trains to and from the fort, before establishing his headquarters on the open plain. It was here on the open plain he requested Willets and his volunteers build a strange kind of fort.

"The woodcutters only use the running gears to transport logs. Their wagon boxes are over there." He waved in the distance. "I want those boxes positioned like this." Holding a long stick in his hand, Powell outlined an oval in the dirt. "Put a complete wagon here," he scratched an X at one end of the oval, "and here," a second X went to the opposite end of the oval. "It all needs to be up there," he indicated the highest point on the plain.

"Do we set 'em on their sides?" Willets asked.

"No." Powell shook his head. "I want the men to be able to lay inside them. We'll drill holes about a foot above the ground."

"Portholes," Willets said, nodding.

"You got it. If we end up defending ourselves inside those wagons, I don't want a man to have to raise his head out of the wagon to shoot."

Captain Willets and his men got to work, arranging the wagon boxes, piling sacks of grain and logs—anything that might stop a bullet—between the wagons, dragging all the camp supplies inside the corral and distributing rifles and ammunition.

"They don't know what they're getting into if they attack," Powell said, demonstrating the Springfield's tremendous range and power by firing at a distant target. But what was even more amazing about the Springfield was how fast it could fire. No more long pauses to reload. "Who's your best shot?" Powell asked Willets.

"Picotte. The man can hit a dollar at fifty yards. I've never seen him miss."

"All right, then. If it comes to a fight, give him the most guns." Powell nodded at Aaron. "You get beside Picotte and reload as fast as he can shoot. Can you do that, son?"

Aaron nodded. He looked at Daniel and gulped.

High on a hillside overlooking the island, Hawk watched the soldiers get ready for battle. He was painted for war, but he was more concerned about watching the movements below than fighting. He'd joined the warriors recently, having broken away from Spotted Antelope's band. He'd followed the soldiers to Fort Laramie and then beyond. He was certain they had no idea he was following them, but even so there had been no chance to accomplish his goal until now. One of the first things the warriors would do in an attack would be to run off the mules and some horses. Hawk was perfectly positioned now to do that. He settled back against a tree and waited, confident that by day's end he would own a white warhorse.

❧

Aaron Dane kicked at a clod of dirt. He knew he was acting like a spoiled child, but Captain Powell had trusted him enough to assign him to load Zephyr Picotte's guns in the fight, and he resented Daniel's interference.

"Go help guard the mules," Daniel had said that morning within Captain Willets's hearing.

When Aaron protested, Captain Willets's had made Daniel's suggestion an order. Aaron couldn't disobey. And so he went.

"I know what you're doing," he told Daniel before he left. "The hostiles will be more intent on running off the herd than shooting, and I'll have a better chance of getting away. You're putting me where it's safer."

Daniel had looked at him steadily and, without expression said back, "Head for the fort as soon as there is any shooting."

"I'm not going to run away like a coward," Aaron said quickly. "I'm not a boy."

"Then do a man's job and go for reinforcements," Daniel shot back. "Be a hero."

Aaron had climbed aboard his pony, only partially mollified. Now, as he sat with the morning sun on his back watching the mules graze, he grew more and more resentful of being sent away from where the real fighting would take place.

Suddenly a mounted party of braves swept down to stampede the herd of mules. At the same time, Aaron heard shots from the direction of the wood train a mile away. Hostiles were attacking two fronts at once.

Daniel heard the shots in the distance. He saw smoke rise from the direction of the woodcutters camp. Yelling at Robert and Big Amos, he ran for his horse. Without bothering to saddle up, he mounted the white stallion and headed off towards the herd, nearly burying his face in the stallion's mane to keep himself low.

Up on the hillside above the action, Hawk watched the stallion streak across the earth, nodding with satisfaction. When the horse entered the fray, Hawk waited for the rider to fall, but no one managed to kill him. Instead, Hawk saw the horse brought alongside a soldier on a gray pony. He saw the two racing away together towards the fort.

But then, to Hawk's delight, the white horse wheeled around. While the soldier on the gray pony headed for the fort, the white stallion tore back across the plain towards the fighting. He mounted his pony and, raising his coup stick in the air, headed down the mountainside in the direction of the white stallion.

❧

While war whoops filled the air a short distance away, the thirty-two men inside the wagon-box corral prepared for battle. Supplies stored in the only two complete wagons were broken into, and when all the arms were passed out, each man had at least two rifles at his disposal.

"If you aren't a good shot," the word was passed, "then just reload for a man who is. Make every shot count."

Powell had taken some men and gone out to deflect the

charge from the woodcutters' camp. While he was gone, while the men were passing out ammunition and getting ready, Aaron Dane came charging up on his gray pony. He pulled the animal to a sliding stop, dismounted, and found Picotte, who grabbed him and dove into a wagon.

"Where's Daniel?" Aaron asked, raising up to look around.

"Get your head down, boy, if you mean to keep it." He ignored the question about Daniel, concentrating instead on getting ready for battle. "Cover up," Picotte ordered, throwing a blanket at him. Aaron obeyed without question. "A good blanket can stop an arrow. I got away from a war party once wrapped in a blanket. When I finally got free and pulled it off, there was a dozen arrows in it. Blanket saved my hide."

Aaron nodded. His hands were shaking so badly he wondered if he would be able to help Picotte at all. He peered through the porthole before him. What he saw made his blood run cold. In all his dreams of battle, this was never what he envisioned.

"Have you seen Daniel?" he whispered.

"I saw him streak out towards the herd. Haven't seen him since. I assume he came after you. Looks like he got ya." Picotte studied Aaron for a moment. "Look at me, son." When Aaron obliged, the older man said, "Just fight. Worry later."

Aaron swallowed hard and peered through the hole drilled in the wagon. "How many are there?" he whispered.

"Enough," Picotte said. "You know how to eat an elephant, son?"

Aaron looked at him, puzzled.

"One bite at a time." He grinned. "It's the same way here. One at a time. We make every shot count."

"No one fires until I give the order," Powell said, just loud enough for his men to hear.

Big Amos and Robert exchanged glances. "I'm glad Captain Leighton didn't ride out with us," Big Amos said. "He was a good soldier, but only one hand is not enough for a day like today."

Robert nodded. "Did you see Daniel come back?"

Big Amos shook his head.

The two men stared towards the enemy coming slowly across the plain, mounted on beautiful war ponies, painted for war, bedecked with feathers, intent on annihilation.

"Hold," the commander ordered. "No one fires until I give the order."

The Sioux quickened their pace, raised their lances, and gave the war cry designed to unnerve the enemy.

"Hold," Powell shouted, never taking his eyes off the advancing warriors.

One hundred yards, then ninety, then eight, and still Powell told his men to hold. Not until his men could see the designs painted on the breasts of the horses did he finally allow them to fire, but when they did, a continual stream of bullets poured out of the little corral.

The advance divided and swept around the corral, ringing the men with fire. Later it was reported that the battle raged so close that sometimes two enemies were killed with one bullet. Finally the Indians retreated, leaving in their wake scores of the dead and dying on the ground around the wagons.

Inside the corral, one private and one officer lay dead.

Picotte nodded at Aaron who had pressed himself against the corner of the wagon box and was trying his best not to vomit. "You did good, boy," Picotte said. "Now get yourself collected. They'll be back."

"H-h-ow many are there?"

Picotte shrugged. "Lots more'n there is of us." He looked at Aaron. Presently he picked up a Colt revolver, inserted a bullet, and spun the chamber. He held the revolver out to Aaron. "You listen to me, boy. You pay attention to what's happenin'. If we lose this here fight and you're not dead yet, you put this to your head and pull the trigger. You hear me?"

Aaron's eyes widened in horror.

"I mean it," Picotte snapped. "You do not, I repeat, you do not want to know what they will do to you if they take you alive." His voice softened. "It probably won't come to that, son. I'll take care of it for you—if I live long enough. But you promise me if I mess up and don't get the job done in time, you'll do what I say. You hear?" Picotte grabbed Aaron's shirt and shook him. "Listen to me. That Injun mama of yours is going to need the comfort of knowing you didn't suffer. So you do it for her, even if you can't do it for yourself." He shook Aaron again.

Aaron nodded. "All right," he croaked. "I will." He moistened his lips. "I will." Then, he leaned over the edge of the wagon box and vomited.

In the next wave, unadorned warriors crept forward along the ground, using every depression in the earth as protection. Once near the corral, they let loose a volley of bullets and arrows. The defenders ignored them. Zephyr's insistence that Aaron stay covered with a woolen blanket paid off, as an arrow struck, but failed to penetrate the blanket just above his left shoulder blade. Bullets crashed against the wagon boxes until it sounded like they were inside a tin-roofed building in a hailstorm. Still, the soldiers resisted useless firing.

When only silence emerged from the corral, the main body of Indians mounted another attack. Once again a great semicircle of warriors advanced slowly, filling the air with war songs. Artists would one day try to capture the terrible beauty of streaming warbonnets, buffalo-hide shields, painted faces, and war ponies, all advancing beneath the majestic mountain backdrop. But Aaron Dane was not an artist and he saw no beauty in the scene. He felt the Colt revolver against his side, he wondered about Daniel, and a horrific sensation of fear crept inside him.

In the end, the Springfield rifles made the difference. The attacking warriors circled the corral waiting for the pause when the enemy would have to reload. That pause would be the end of the battle, for they would easily overwhelm the soldiers then. But the pause never came. Instead, the enemy kept firing almost constantly. With modified Springfields, the soldiers could eject empty cartridges and slap new ones on, almost without even needing to take their eyes off their targets. Constant gunfire was causing too many Sioux to fall on the battlefield.

After a brief retreat and war council, a final attack on foot was launched. Screaming warriors streamed out of a ravine just north of the corral. Some fired guns, others sent flaming arrows into the hay piles in the middle of the oval.

"Get the canteen!" Picotte screamed at Aaron over the din. "Keep the barrels cool!" He snatched up another rifle while Aaron obeyed, one hand on the canteen, one on the Colt revolver in his belt.

In an instant, in a lifetime, the warriors broke and retreated, carrying what dead and wounded they could off the battlefield with them. Unnatural silence descended. Momentarily bugles sounded in the distance. Help was coming.

Across the open plain, the Sioux chiefs ordered their men to break off. They had had a good fight, captured a great many horses and mules, and killed a few whites. It was a good day to die.

"Always loved a good bugle serenade," Zephyr Picotte said, smiling at Aaron, who peered through his porthole and closed his eyes to keep tears of relief from running down his cheeks. It was the most beautiful thing he had seen in a long time, Aaron thought; a long column of men dressed in blue, flags flying, rifles blasting, pounding across the earth to the rescue. They divided in half and swept around the corral. The men inside the corral raised up as one and cheered as the regiment swept by in pursuit of the fleeing enemy.

Within the hour, the gates of Fort Phil Kearney opened to admit the twenty-eight survivors of what was to be called the

Wagon Box fight. Among the wounded were two scouts named Robert Lawrence and Big Amos. Their wounds were slight and would keep them from their usual duties for only a short while. Their wounds concerned no one, least of all Aaron Dane and Elliot Leighton. Not because Aaron and Elliot didn't care about their friends, but because when the fight was over, when the casualties were collected, Daniel Two Stars and his white stallion were missing.

Twenty~Two

"Doth the hawk fly by thy wisdom,
and stretch her wings towards the south?
Doth the eagle mount up at thy command,
and make her nest on high?"

—Job 39:26–27

Running. They were always running these days, it seemed. But running didn't always keep bad things from happening. Nowhere was there a safe place. Even the hunting grounds near the mountains were being invaded by whites. And all the while they spoke of treaties and what the *Lakota* should do to keep the peace. Two Moons giggled madly to herself. What the people could do, she thought, was die. They were doing that well, she thought. Certainly her husband High Hand and their child had done it well. High Hand had raised a white flag and an American flag over their tepee and told her not to worry. He was standing under those flags when a soldier thrust a long sword through his heart. Two Moons had covered her arms with cuts trying to cause enough pain that she would forget the look in High Hands's eyes when he fell to his knees. But although she slashed her arms repeatedly, she did not forget.

Their baby died, too. Two Moons had run into the tepee and grabbed up the cradle board before lifting the side of the tepee away from where the soldiers were and slipping away. She was at the edge of the camp when the sound of galloping made her turn—just in time to have the cradle board ripped from her arms. What happened next made her scream. At least she thought she probably screamed. She wasn't sure. She must have screamed . . . but then she fainted, and the blood from the baby splattered across her face so that they must have thought her dead because they left her alone.

She woke in the night and crept away, certain a soldier would catch her—and not really caring if one did. But by some act of the spirits that ruled time, she was not noticed and she got away on a pony so ancient the soldiers had not bothered to round it up with the herd. She had been wandering for weeks, she thought, although she wasn't sure. Whenever the pain became too much, she would stop and pick up a sharp rock and slash her arms again. Now, as she staggered up the narrow canyon towards winter camp, she wondered if that had changed, too. Maybe her people would not be able to spend the cold moons in their usual valley.

Two Moons paused and looked about her. Up above, the birds were circling. She knew what that meant, and she decided to lie down and wait for death to come. Two Moons swooned in the heat. She dropped her pony's lead, and the creature ambled away slurping noisily from the river.

When no birds came to her, Two Moons opened her eyes. She did not rise from the earth. Still, lying as she was, she could see the birds were beginning to drop from the sky . . . after something that must lay on the canyon floor just out of sight. No matter, she thought. If she stayed here, she would be a meal for them soon enough. She slept.

At some time in the night, a mountain lion screamed high above her, and Two Moons awoke. She shivered with fear and sat up, clutching her arms to her sides. When things were quiet, she bent down to take a drink from the river. Her pony was there, swaying as it stood half asleep by the water's edge. Presently, Two Moons plunged her hands into the water and brought some of it to her face. The coolness of it was pleasant, and before long she had slipped out of her dress and moccasins and into the river, sighing with pleasure as the water flowed gently over her. Once she closed her eyes and sank beneath the current, but she could not will herself to remain and popped up, sputtering and coughing, looking around foolishly as if she expected someone to scold her.

She emerged from the water clean and feeling ashamed. She remembered that her own mother had lost a young lover to the Crow and lived long enough to send several children into the spirit land. She was being weak, Two Moons scolded herself. Pulling her dress back over her head, she put her worn moccasins back on and sat, watching the shadows on the canyon wall. Her stomach growled. Again, she drank. Again, she slept.

When the canyon walls were gray with morning light, Two Moons woke and sat up. She picked up a rock and pressed it against her arm as had been her custom every morning for the past few weeks. But this morning she did not cut herself. She was distracted by the birds again, and as the canyon began to glow with morning light, she caught the old pony and ventured to the place just out of sight that seemed to be attracting them.

Expecting to find the carcass of some animal, Two Moons caught her breath when she saw a dead horse and the body of a soldier. At the sight of him, all the evil came back. She crouched down and grasped a huge rock, hesitating long enough to relish what was coming. She would do to him what had been done to her child, and it would help. Revenge always helped. She lifted the rock overhead and ran towards the dead soldier, raising her voice as she did so in an unearthly wail that echoed from the canyon walls and came back to her even as she came down with—

Barely, just barely, she missed him. The rock landed with a thud beside the man's head and she knelt down, trembling with the realization of what she had nearly done to a brother. Even if he was dead, he was Indian. A scout, she realized, and her mouth curled up in derision. One of those who helped the white army locate and kill. She despised him. Still, her mother had taught her healing ways and made her promise never to willfully harm what the great Wakan had created. Two Moons sighed—so she would not dash out his brains. But she would not bury him. Let the birds have him and the white pony that lay nearby, its neck twisted at an odd angle.

She stepped over the dead Indian and hurried to the horse. Working quickly, she removed the blanket and the bags tied behind the saddle. She could not get the one that was beneath the animal out from under him. But she opened the one that was available to her and grunted when she found nothing of value, only some kind of book, its pages stained with bits of pale blue dried flowers tucked inside. Two Moons put the book back inside the bag, more of an object of curiosity than of value. She finally managed to drag the other bag from beneath the horse. She removed the bridle and every other piece of equipment that might be of use. There was a water holder and a gun and bullets, although she wasn't certain how to load the gun. Still, she lay these things in the blanket and made a bundle to tie on her pony's back.

She was just getting ready to continue her journey towards winter camp when she thought she heard something. Her heart racing, she backed against the canyon wall, expecting at any moment to see a column of soldiers coming towards her. But the sound had been too slight to warn of coming soldiers. When she heard it again, she frowned and stepped towards the horse.

Things were quiet. She decided to inspect the soldier for any-

S T E P H A N I E G R A C E W H I T S O N

thing she could use and began by putting his hat on her own head. Regretting the size of his boots, she decided to take them anyway. When she began to pull and tug on the boot, he groaned. The sound sent her scurrying away in terror. But when he did not move, she told herself she was a fool to be hearing a dead man protest the taking of his boots and she returned to the task. But this time, when she moved the foot, the man yelped with pain. She went to his head, leaned down to his face. His breath was shallow and fast, but he was indeed breathing.

"Who are you?" she said.

He opened his eyes, but there was nothing there but pain.

"I am Two Moons," she said. "I thought you were dead." When it appeared he didn't understand her, she looked him over. There was no blood except for a few clotted scratches. Reaching for the knife in his belt, she cut away the cloth above the boot she had tried to remove, revealing a sight that sickened her—a ghastly wound that would likely kill him. The tip of a bone was sticking up out of a hole in the man's leg. She would need to get it back inside where it belonged . . . preferably close enough to the other bone that the two could meet and grow together again. But she knew from watching her mother that someone would have to hold him down when she tried that. It would leave an even bigger hole and cause more bleeding, though—he would likely die from the black sickness she had seen spread over a man's leg in the past.

He coughed and barked out in pain, lifting one hand to his chest. Those bones must be broken, too. Two Moons looked above her. He must have come over the edge up there. She shuddered to think of what else might be wrong inside his broken body. It was no wonder his eyes stared blankly when she asked questions. He might never be able to answer questions. She remembered a brave who had taken a fall on a buffalo hunt and never been the same. Sometimes, he clutched his head and roared with pain. At others,

213

he would wobble through the village laughing at nothing. No one knew how to help him. One night, he disappeared without a trace.

A noise brought Two Moons back to the present. The man raised a trembling hand to his forehead. The effort made tiny beads of sweat break out on his skin. He grimaced and whispered something. He licked his cracked lips. She went to the river, filled his water bottle, brought it back, and then dribbled the tiniest bit of water into his mouth. He swallowed, opening his mouth like a bird, begging for more. Against her instincts, she gave it but he became sick. Agonizing pain caused by the vomiting made him pass out.

Two Moons was glad. His being unconscious made it easier to clean him up. She opened the collar of his shirt and, using the part of his pant leg she had cut off, bathed him, carrying water back and forth from the river until she had done what she could.

I should let him die, Two Moons argued with herself. He had been a scout helping the army. A symbol woven into the beaded necklace she'd found when she unbuttoned his shirt indicated he was Dakota. Everyone knew the Dakota were cowards or they would never have let the army drive them out of their lands in the east. Now they were all on some reservation being treated like animals. Word had traveled among the camps years ago of what had happened to those Dakota who helped whites against their own brothers.

This Dakota was beautiful, though, and not old. The thin gold ring on his small finger signified that he was married. Two Moons wondered if he had children. It was the thought of children that finally decided her course of action. Enough children had lost their fathers. She fingered the scars along her arms while she thought. Maybe what she had heard about the Dakota wasn't true of them all. Certainly people thought things about her people that were wrong. And her mother had made her promise to use the healing ways whenever she could. Two Moons looked up at the canyon walls around her. Surely the Great Wakan must think well of this man to have brought her here.

Overhead, the cry of a bird caught her attention. An eagle landed on a precipice and looked down upon them. Presently the great bird soared lower and lower until it came to rest along the river opposite them. It looked at her boldly for a moment before rising again to the blue skies and disappearing.

Yes, Two Moons thought. *That must be it. The Great Wakan has brought me here and sent the bird as a sign.* Her mother had taught her to use the healing ways to help any who came her way. Even an enemy.

The man opened his eyes.

"I should let you die," she signed. "You work for the soldiers."

Whether it was because he was beautiful, or because of the eagle, or because when she said she might let him die there was no sign of fear in his eyes, Two Moons worked the rest of the day fashioning a rickety travois from the crooked trunks of a few straggly trees growing along the river. She used the horse's bridle and the cinch from the saddle and some other pieces of leather to lash them together. She doubted her ancient mare could pull the injured man very far on the contraption, but she would do what she could. Every mile she managed was a mile closer to winter camp.

She had relished the idea of sending a rock through his skull when she thought him already dead. *Whatever I am*, Two Moons thought, *I will not kill a wounded man. Perhaps this was a test from the Great Wakan*, she thought, *to see if I would still live by the rule of kindness to the helpless that has reigned among the People since the day they were born from Mother Earth.*

Yes, Two Moons thought. *That must be it.* And even if she was wrong and the Great Wakan was not testing her, at the least it appeared that he had provided her with another man. Perhaps this one was actually fleeing the army when the horse fell over the cliff. *If he was fleeing the army, and if he does not die . . . well*, Two Moons thought as she pulled the travois bearing the wounded soldier along the canyon floor, *then we will see.*

Twenty-Three

"But love ye your enemies, and do good,
and lend, hoping for nothing again . . ."
—LUKE 6:35

"NOW LISTEN HERE, SON—"

"Don't call me that! I'm not your son and I don't have to listen to you!" Aaron yelled at the top of his lungs, shoving Zephyr Picotte's hand off his shoulder. He appealed to Elliot. "Make him listen, Uncle Elliot. Make him understand."

"I do understand, Aaron," Zephyr said. His voice was almost gentle.

"You don't," Aaron spat back. "You can't. If you understood, you wouldn't be standing here telling me we can't go look for Two Stars. He's not *like* other Indians. Why won't you believe me?"

"It's got nothing to do with Two Stars," Picotte said. "I wouldn't volunteer a hunting party to go look for the baby Jesus today, not with what just happened. It's likely the warriors haven't even gotten all their dead off the battlefield yet. And you're running on nervous energy right now. By evening you're probably going to collapse. And it's not just you. A battle like we fought today takes it out of a man." Picotte grunted and sat down. He kicked a chair in frustration and looked across the room at Elliot. "Maybe he'll listen to you."

There was quiet in the room while Elliot swept his hand through his long white hair, thinking. He had just come from the commander's office where reports were being prepared on today's fight. He had listened carefully, using all his military experience to try and gain a clear picture of what had happened. He had looked over the men's shoulders when they drew diagrams and listened to at least a dozen different accounts of events. The only explanation for why any of the men inside that corral had survived seemed to be a miracle in the form of a Springfield rifle. That was the only thing he could figure, but nothing gave him any clear idea of what could have happened to Daniel. Someone thought they had seen the white horse headed off towards the woodcutters' camp. Someone else had seen him take part in the small charge against the force firing the camp, but that force had retreated to inside the corral, and it was at that point in the morning all trace of Daniel Two Stars seemed to disappear.

"Tell me what happened again," he said to Aaron. Then he waved toward an empty chair. "But first, sit down."

"I've already told you everything I know," Aaron said wearily, as he slid into a chair. After a moment, he repeated it all again. "I was mad because Daniel didn't let me stay with the men at the corral. He sent me off to help guard the herd. I knew what he was doing. He knew they would probably try to run off some mules and ponies first, and he figured that would give me time to get away. He told me at the first sign of trouble I was to head for the

fort. He made it sound like I'd be helping by going for reinforcements. But what he was really doing was trying to keep me out of
the fight." Aaron rubbed his forehead with his fingertips. He continued with a trembling voice. "They did stampede the herd first.
Just like Daniel said. Only he didn't stay put in the corral to fight.
When he saw how many Indians there were—"

"How many?" Elliot asked. The reports he had heard ranged
anywhere from two hundred to a thousand, depending on the
individual soldier and his stomach for battle.

"I don't know," Aaron said. "I think most of the men think it
was maybe two hundred." He cleared his throat. "It seemed like
more, but two hundred is probably about right. Anyway, when
Daniel saw what was happening, he came and got me. Didn't
even take time to saddle his horse. Just climbed aboard bareback
and streaked into the fight. I'd only fired my rifle a couple times
when he road up alongside and hollered for me to come to the
fort." Aaron scraped his boots across the wood floor nervously
and leaned back in his chair. He looked at his uncle dully. "But I
didn't. I pretended I was going, but I doubled back. When the
Indians stopped to burn the woodcutters' camp, that gave me a
chance to get inside the corral. Then the fighting . . . I asked
about Daniel, but there were too many things—"

"Nothin' we could'a done anyway," Picotte interjected. He
scratched his beard, thinking. "Doesn't make sense, him just dis-
appearin' that way."

"What if he's wounded, Uncle Elliot?" Aaron's voice was
edged with desperation. "We can't just leave him out there." He
added, "Robert and Big Amos would go after him."

"They would," Elliot agreed. "But neither of them can. Big
Amos has a bullet hole in his shoulder and Robert got creased
here," Elliot brushed his head above his ear. "Doctor's worried
about infection. Said he had a patient once where everything
seemed fine, then a few days later the poor soul went into a coma

and died. Autopsy showed a brain abscess. He wants to keep a close watch on Robert in the hospital."

"So we don't have our scouts and Zephyr won't go," Aaron put his head in his hands.

"I didn't say I wouldn't go," Picotte said. "I just said I'm not heading out tonight. We'd be nothing more than fresh meat for those warriors tonight. Or wolves."

"I'm not afraid of wolves," Aaron blustered.

"Well you should be," Picotte said. "A pack of a hundred wolves would bring that pony of yours down without giving you notice, boy." He waved his hand at Aaron. "I know, I know, you're not a boy. Quit actin' like one and think like a man. Men don't behave like emotional women when bad things happen." He stood up. "We'll ride out tomorrow when the men go to reconnoiter the battlefield. See what we can see." He shrugged. "Who knows, maybe Daniel will come in himself before morning. He could just be layin' low, waitin' to make sure he can make it back to the fort before he comes out of hiding." He made for the door, pausing on his way out of the room. "Don't think on it anymore, Aaron. You'll go around and around with it in your head and nothing good will come of it."

"I should have come to the fort like he told me," Aaron muttered. "We needed reinforcements. We really did."

"Maybe that's so. But the fact is, what you did or didn't do probably didn't make all that much difference with what happened. Maybe Two Stars would have stayed inside the corral if you weren't so stubborn. Maybe he'd been the one shot in the head the minute the battle started. Maybe not. This isn't battle practice, son. It's the real thing. And when the real thing happened, Two Stars did what he had to do, and you fought like a man. You can hold your head up and no man has a right to tell you otherwise. So don't you tell yourself some foolishness that'll only weigh you down with guilt." Picotte closed the door behind him.

"People make decisions in the heat of battle, Aaron," Elliot said quietly. "Some of them are good, some are bad. In the end, a soldier does the best he can and learns to live with the results. We all have to do that, or we'd all end up crazy. Now get to bed. You won't do Daniel one bit of good if you aren't rested tomorrow." Elliot got up and scooted his chair back beneath the table.

Aaron followed suit, pausing at the door. "What are we going to tell Ma, Uncle Elliot? What if we don't find him?"

"She's a strong woman," Elliot said quickly, "with a strong faith. She's been through hard things before. She'll bear up."

Aaron nodded. He headed off towards his bed in the bunkhouse shared with several other enlisted men. Elliot watched him go, thinking to himself that, while his hair had not gone white nearly overnight, Aaron Dane looked at least a decade older. He put his good hand out and leaned against the log wall for a minute, wishing he felt as confident as he had sounded when he predicted how well Genevieve might do in the face of Daniel's death. *She'll bear up.* Elliot thought about it.

The wolves were at it again, fighting over the scrapple in the slaughter yard. Elliot listened to their snarls for a few minutes, then, as he crossed the parade ground, he paused and looked up at the inky black sky, praying with all his might for a miracle so that he would not be forced to take news of Daniel's death to Genevieve Two Stars.

❧

So he was alive. Barely, he realized, but the searing pain meant at least alive. High above him the sky was blue. He was in some kind of deep ravine. He could feel the frame of a travois beneath him, hear the scraping of the frame as it moved along what must be the canyon floor. It wasn't a smooth ride, and with every bump it took all his energy not to yelp like a wounded animal against the pain that coursed through his body.

He wondered why they hadn't killed him. But consciousness didn't last long enough for him to work that out, and he slipped away.

The next time he was conscious long enough to think, Daniel realized he was inside a tepee. The sun was shining and blue sky shone above through the smoke-hole at the top. He could hear dogs barking, children laughing. He could feel the softness of some kind of animal pelt beneath him. Not a buffalo robe, but something else. There was someone in the tepee with him, but when he tried to turn his head the pain was too great. Breathing hurt, too. He kept his eyes closed, trying to concentrate on each part of his body. Every time he was tempted to fall asleep, he fought it. He managed to stay awake long enough to take inventory. Breathing was all right as long as he didn't try to take in too much air, but every breath still hurt. His arms seemed all right, too. And his left foot, since he could move it. But the right one didn't respond at all. He couldn't feel his toes. If he tried to move his foot the pain shot up his leg and into his back and nearly knocked him out. He took inventory twice, coming to the same conclusion each time. When he sensed he was thirsty, someone read his thoughts, and moisture dribbled into his mouth. He swallowed it greedily, but he didn't have the energy to open his eyes or even grunt to let whoever was tending him know he was awake.

❧

"He will die," the old man said. He had been inside Two Moons's tepee and assessed the damage. "Everything will mend but the leg. The black sickness will come into the skin and he will die."

Twenty~Four

"He woundeth, and his hands make whole.
He shall deliver thee in six troubles: yea in
seven there shall no evil touch thee."
—JOB 5:18–19

LITTLE BY LITTLE, HE WAS REMEMBERING. A WAR CRY
had lured him up into the pines above the battlefield. He had a
flashing memory of what he'd heard about Fetterman and wondered if the war party they had seen was only a decoy. He had
wondered if maybe a few thousand more warriors were waiting
just over the hill to swarm down and annihilate the men inside
the corral, and he had been determined to find out.

All he'd seen was a flash of war paint in the trees up ahead,
and he'd charged after it. Once he'd realized there were no other
warriors and it was just the two of them, he'd pulled up, meaning to go back and join the fight. He had been near the rim of

a canyon, and as he wheeled the stallion around to head back, he shuddered involuntarily as he neared the edge of a particularly tall cliff. Nudging the stallion's sides, he was heading away from the rim of the canyon when a war cry sounded from the hill above and a single warrior on a dun pony came charging at him out of the pines.

The surprise attack had caught him off guard and thrown him off balance. He fell off his horse and landed with a thud that both stunned him momentarily and gave the enemy the chance he needed to grab Daniel's horse.

But the white stallion was not a horse to be ridden by just anyone. His master was lying in the dirt and when the strange rider tried to climb aboard, the stallion sidestepped. That was all the time Daniel had needed to leap back to his feet and attack the horse thief. He had been enraged—he should be in the battle, not grappling with some fool over a horse.

What happened next was still fuzzy, but he remembered a howl from a mountain lion and the white stallion rearing up and going over backwards. Somehow Daniel lost his balance and stepped backwards into nothing but blue sky, gray canyon walls . . . and falling. After that, he didn't remember anything until he woke on the travois.

He was better, he realized. The pain had confused him at first. So had the dream of colors and that feeling of flying. He understood both now.

Brown eyes had been the next thing that confused him. If he was sick or hurt, Blue Eyes should be here. A woman was here, but not Blue Eyes. He understood that now, too, of course. He was in some Indian camp being tended by a stranger. He could see the worry in her eyes.

When he finally managed to push himself up onto his elbows and look himself over, he worried, too. He still couldn't feel his leg, and he could see enough of it to know it was swollen and red.

He lay back on the skins, which he now realized were antelope, and inhaled deeply. Moving still hurt, but he could bear it.

The next time the woman was in the tent, he opened his eyes to let her know he was awake. "Where am I?" he said in Dakota.

Her gaze was not unkind, but it was clear she didn't understand him.

It took so much effort to sign his question he could hardly keep his eyes open to watch her answer, which was no help at all, because she simply signed, "With me."

She signed, "You are Dakota."

He nodded.

"I am your enemy," she signed, and then giggled and smiled. When he frowned, she added, "I am your friend." She left and when she came back, she had filled a skin with water. She hung it near his head and handed him a tin cup before she left the tent.

He drank and went back to sleep.

❦

The smell was bad inside the tent. *It couldn't be me*, he thought, *the woman washed me.* She had even combed his hair with her small, gentle hands. He raised up on his elbows again. This time, he managed to sit up and what he saw made his midsection tighten with fear. His leg was worse. Sweat poured down his face from the effort to sit up. *Maybe the sickness from my leg is spreading inside me and causing me to smell of death,* he thought.

The little woman came in and saw him sitting up looking at his leg. She saw the sweat on his forehead and made him lie flat. She washed his face and offered him soup.

"I am going to die," he signed.

She didn't answer and looked away.

The next time he was awake and the little woman was beside him, he tried to make her understand that he wanted something from his saddlebags. Eventually she understood and brought him the little book with the pressed flowers tucked inside.

At the sight of it, the wounded man blinked tears away from his eyes. He opened the book, turning the pages. He seemed to be searching for something. Two Moons realized he must be able to read the white man's words. Presently he took the gold ring off his hand, tucked it between two pages, and handed the book back to her.

"For my wife," he signed.

Two Moons took the book from his trembling hands, and nodded. His wife was called Blue Eyes and men at the fort would know her. She put the book and the ring back in his bags and left the tent. She walked away from the camp towards the snowcapped peak in the distance, thinking, *He hasn't begged for anything. He hasn't complained or even seemed afraid.* In the days she had tended the wounded man, he had only seemed intent on getting better. He had accepted her care, but he was always somewhere else in his mind. *Waiting,* she thought. *Waiting to go somewhere.* And when he realized he might be going to the spirit world instead, all he did was mention his wife and lie down to wait like a warrior who went into battle singing, "It is a good day to die."

The medicine man said the doctors at the fort would cut off the bad leg. He said he had seen soldiers hobbling around on one leg, an awful life—but it was life. If she could give this one man life, then maybe it would somehow make up for all the death in her past.

Two Moons looked up toward the white mountain peaks. The snows were coming. Nights were cold now. She might have already waited too long. The fort was many days away. The black sickness hadn't started in the man's leg yet, but it was coming. She knew because the skin on his leg was tight and shiny, and the liquid running from the wound had begun to stink. That must be how he knew he was going to die.

Well, he wasn't going to die, not if she could help it. Even if he did, then at least he would be at the fort where someone might know how to get the words and the ring to his wife, wherever she was. Maybe she was one of the loafers around the fort. That could be it.

She, Two Moons, had nothing from her husband or her child, except the scars on her arms to remember them by. She remembered the beads High Hand wore around his neck. Her hand went to her chest and she wished she had those beads now.

Two Moons hurried back to the tent. In less than an hour she had struck it down around the wounded man. She signed that she was taking him to the fort, but she didn't know if he understood. The fever was on him and he was suffering more. It was late in the day. She would travel all night. She had to.

The old women in the village gathered around, offering advice she didn't want or need. Did they think she didn't know she was being foolish? Did they think she didn't know they would both likely die going out alone?

The children had grown to like her stories, so they helped her tie her bundles in place on the travois behind her ragged pony. But when it came to getting the wounded man on the travois, she didn't know what to do. She didn't want to hurt him any more. It hadn't mattered before. But now she knew he was brave and he had a wife somewhere—a wife who cared to know that he was alive or dead.

Just when she was despairing of how she would load him, the medicine man arrived. He examined the wounded man's leg and looked at her with the death message in his eyes.

"I am taking him to the fort. You said the doctor there would be able to help him. You said you had seen men who had lived, even when the black sickness was on them."

The medicine man grunted. "You are crazy, Two Moons."

She looked at him with sad, dark eyes, and said gently, "Is not all of life a kind of craziness?"

He squinted at her for a moment. "If you are a spirit woman come to test me, you will see that I have passed your test," he said, and he helped her load the wounded man on the travois.

The men made their way along the old, well-worn trail, heads down, hearts discouraged. Visiting Lakota camps had not proven dangerous, after all. But it had been useless. No one knew anything about a white horse or a Dakota scout. The five of them had been wandering the hills for two weeks now. Unless they wanted to spend the winter with the Lakota, they'd better head back. It wouldn't be long before a storm could blow down from the Big Horn Mountains and make travel almost impossible.

Elliot had gathered more information about the "hostiles" than he'd dreamed possible. Of course he hadn't written any of it down. He didn't want the mission to appear "official" in any way, for that might risk too much. But this foray up the Tongue River had taught him things he'd use for the rest of his life. He wondered if that was why this had all happened. If Daniel were dead, at least it would bear lasting fruit in Washington.

Aaron had paid attention and learned, too. He'd picked up a fair number of Lakota phrases by listening to Picotte. Growing up around the Dakota had taught him a lot about Indians in general, but he didn't remember them before they had been "civilized" and taken onto the reservation. These Lakota had made it their duty to stay as far away from whites as possible. They were nothing like the Dakota Aaron had grown up with. If nothing else, he realized he had much yet to learn about Indians. And he'd been reminded of that sense of "a calling" Aunt Jane had told him about. The Indian Question was far from being answered, and Aaron had begun to think he could easily give his life to help find answers that could somehow preserve this proud, beautiful people. He wondered if that was why this had all happened. If Daniel were dead, at least it would bear lasting fruit in Aaron's life and, through Aaron, on behalf of the Indians.

Edward Pope had learned he was neither the coward he thought he was, nor was he stupid. He could do a lot more besides cook, although he watched the Lakota campfires with inborn curiosity and decided feasting on dog wouldn't kill a man. He surprised himself with what Picotte called "amazing powers of observation," and discovered a knack for setting people at ease, more than once saying something in a meeting that lightened the mood when things were getting tense. The Lakota weren't fooled. They knew Aaron and Willets and Leighton were army. But Edward Pope eased their suspicions and made them almost believe their story about being deserters and looking for one of their friends named Two Stars who was going to join them for the winter up on the Little Bighorn.

Captain John Willets soaked up Zephyr Picotte's wisdom and experience. From Aaron and Elliot he learned what true friend-ship and love among men of God looked like. It didn't take him long to realize both Aaron Dane and Elliot Leighton were the "Two Stars kind of Christian." Picotte had made it clear he didn't want any part of their religion, and to Willets's surprise they both respected that and didn't shove their beliefs at him. Still, there were times when he looked at Elliot or Aaron and would have sworn the men were praying silently. He watched them closely, wondering what would happen to their faith when they realized they weren't going to find Daniel Two Stars.

He thought too much about Genevieve Two Stars, and he didn't like it but he couldn't seem to do much about it. She was there, behind every thought he had of Daniel, a shadow beside her husband, and more often than not the reason he kept look-ing. If he was going to have to tell her Daniel was gone, he wanted to be certain he'd done everything humanly possible to prevent it. She was going to need someone to watch out for her if Daniel was gone. He wondered if she would go back to New York. He knew she hadn't really liked it there. But he couldn't let himself think of her beyond making certain Genevieve Two Stars would be well cared for. It was, after all, his duty to his men to do what he could for their families.

Twenty-Five

"It is good for me that I have been afflicted;
that I might learn thy statutes."
—PSALM 119:71

THE MAN ON THE TRAVOIS NOW HAD A RAGING FEVER. He hadn't really been behind his eyes for hours, and the leg was worse. Two Moons lifted the blankets and what she saw sickened her. All she could do now was hurry. Faster and faster she went, running until she could no longer stand the burning in her lungs, yet slowing only long enough to catch her breath before running again. She had kept moving all night. She thought they were only another day's journey from the fort, but she didn't know if it would matter. The wounded man had been delirious for a while. Now he was silent, his face a gray mask, his breathing shallow.

Two Moons stopped only long enough to let the pony walk.

She was worried about her old mare. She had been surprised when the horse managed to get the wounded man to camp the first time. Asking her to pull him back again might be too much. Some time in the night the pony began to wheeze and gasp for breath. Two Moons made her keep moving, and although she didn't want to, she prodded the little mare every now and then with a stick when she threatened to stop.

Only when she could no longer force herself to put one foot in front of another did Two Moons rest. She pulled a blanket off the travois and, wrapping herself in it, slept. She would not lie down lest she sleep too soundly. She had had no reason to live for a long time, but now that she had one, she was obsessed. She drove herself and willed the man to live. She prayed to her own spirits and whatever spirits the man believed in to come to her aid.

On the second day she was tugging the mare down a steep incline when the old creature stumbled and went down onto her knees. Two Moons yelled and screamed at the pony, pulling with all her might until the old girl wobbled upright and walked on. But sometime that afternoon, the pony went down first on her knees, then on her side, threatening to spill the travois as she sank down, wheezing and gasping.

Two Moons pounded the pony with her fists and wailed at the wind. When she realized the little mare was dead, she untied the travois poles from atop the pony's withers. Unloading everything except the man and his book, she braced herself against the poles. Straining everything in her, she managed to pull the travois along, inch by impossible inch, down an incline. She made progress for a while, until they reached another hill. Evening was coming on, and at last Two Moons gave out, completely spent. She sank beside the wounded man, looked down at her scarred arms, and closed her eyes. Then, as the sun set behind the mountain peaks, she lifted her voice in a death wail.

"Shhh." Picotte held his hand out and cocked his head, listening. He looked at Captain Willets. "You hear that?"

Willets lifted his chin slightly, closed his eyes, and listened. "The wind. Not human."

Picotte took his pipe out of his mouth and squinted, working at listening harder. "The wind's bringing it, but it's human. A death song, if I'm not mistaken."

"Where? From what direction?" Willets opened his eyes, suddenly wide awake in spite of their long day.

"North." Picotte listened again. He sniffed the wind like an animal. "Wolves, too. But it was human at first."

Willets scrambled up. He went to where Leighton and Aaron had bedded down atop a cushion of pine boughs. "Elliot." He shook Elliot's shoulder. "Need to check on something."

Aaron lifted his head. "What? What is it?"

"Don't know. Picotte thinks he heard a Sioux death wail. We both heard some wolves in the distance."

The men scrambled out of their bedrolls.

"You'ns go and check on it." Edward Pope was up, too, stirring up the fire. "I'll keep the extra horses here. And I'll have coffee when you get back."

In less than half an hour the four were on the trail, grateful for the bright moon, hoping the sound was more than their imagination, trying to follow it through the night.

When the wolves first appeared, Two Moons was ready. She had built a fire to keep herself and the man from freezing in the night. It was a strong flame, and although the creatures surrounded her, she thought she could stave them off. There were only a few. But as the night went on and the flames grew small, Two Moons realized more wolves had come. They were restless, and they watched her with glowing yellow eyes, waiting for the flames to die. She untied the travois and worked to get one of the poles free. She would use it as a club and fight as long as she could. She and the man were entering the spirit land tonight, but they would not go until she had fought the wolves. She shivered with fear, hoping they would kill her quickly.

When the first creature lunged at her, snarling and snapping its jaws, it was only playing at the attack and she fended it off easily. A second one came and she landed a good blow across its head. It yelped and trotted away, shaking its head like a child after its mother boxed its ears.

Two Moons sang, hoping it would frighten the creatures and for a time it did. She punctuated her song with shouts, and the wolves backed away. But as the night wore on and the fire began to smolder, the wolves grew bolder. One of them charged at the wounded man. Two Moons landed another crushing blow across the animal's back and it tumbled over and then scrambled away. She positioned herself across the man, one foot on either side of his body. The wolves came closer. More than one, this time. Two Moons raised the stick over her head and screamed just as three of them lunged.

There was the blistering roar of a rifle, and one of the wolves fell dead across the wounded man. A second was thrown back and slunk away, yelping from pain. The others disappeared. The third wolf slashed Two Moons's leg as it streaked across the wounded man's body. Two Moons lunged at it with her stick, but she tripped on the man she was trying to protect and fell. She covered her head with her arms and, curling into a ball, waited to die.

But she didn't die. She heard men's voices and another gunshot. Someone grabbed her arm and said words she didn't understand. She looked up and thought he must be a forest spirit, for his face glowed red in the darkness. She shrunk away, hiding her face in her hands.

Then she realized his face glowed red from her dying fire. He was white. And that made her more afraid than if he had been a forest spirit. She scooted away from him, stammering that she had not hurt the man on the travois, she was only taking him to the fort to get help. She had found him and she didn't mean any harm. She was nearly hysterical, and she grabbed the man's book up and shook it in the face of the yellow-bearded man who was holding her arm.

Suddenly someone said in Lakota, "Hush, woman. We won't hurt you. We have been looking for this man."

As suddenly as she had begun to talk she was quiet. The one who knew her language was the old one with the gray hair. Her eyes stayed on him, ignoring the others who were babbling in their own tongue.

"Why is he sick?" the old one asked.

"He fell. I found him broken at the bottom of a high wall."

"Broken? What is broken?"

"Ribs. His leg."

Picotte lifted the blanket covering Daniel's lower body. What he saw made him close his eyes and swear to himself.

"Ask her when she found him," Aaron wanted to know.

"There's no time for that," Picotte said. "We've got to get him to the fort." He looked at Aaron. "He's probably not going to make it, son. But we're going to do our best. That leg's infected. Gangrene maybe already have started. It works fast. Help me get this travois rigged—" he looked at Captain Willets. "Which horse is least likely to raise a fuss?"

"Mine," Elliot said.

"Then let's get it rigged and get moving." He turned to the little woman. "What is your name?" When she answered, he smiled. "All right, Two Moons. Can you help me with the travois? These white men don't know how to do it."

Relieved to have something to do, Two Moons stepped over a dead wolf. She motioned for Picotte and another to help her and in moments they had the travois lashed to Elliot's gray mare. True to Elliot's prediction, the mare snorted and stared, but she tolerated the contraption without kicking. Two Moons scrambled up behind Picotte and soon they were moving quickly towards camp.

At the camp, Edward Pope had coffee waiting, but no one wanted to drink it. Instead, Elliot and Aaron kept on towards the fort while Picotte and Willets helped Pope break camp by the light of the moon.

"You take the girl," Picotte said. "You've got a younger horse and we'll go faster that way." He said a few words to Two Moons, who nodded and walked obediently over to Willets. He started to lift her up, and for the first time noticed the deep gash the wolf had made across the top of her foot.

"Wait a minute, Picotte," he called out. "She's hurt."

Picotte started to get down, but Two Moons shook her head. She called to him, pushing Willets hand away and motioning towards the fort.

"She says to leave it."

Willets wouldn't listen. "It's deep. Needs tending now."

"Fair enough," Picotte said, and he translated for Two Moons, who stared down at Willets with an odd expression on her face, but submitted to his attention. Edward Pope produced a bandage and a canteen of water.

"You got everything in that kitchen of yours, Pope?" Willets joked.

"Just about," Edward said. "A man's got to be prepared." He finished packing his kitchen while Willets tended the little woman's bleeding foot. While he worked, he pondered his first sight of her, one foot planted on either side of Daniel's body, her eyes blazing in the firelight, poised to take on a pack of wolves with a stick. He'd never seen anything like her for bravery in a woman, that was certain. Unless maybe it was Genevieve Two Stars.

Two Moons flinched when Willets washed the slash across the top of her foot. He apologized and tried to be gentler, thinking about the dainty feet of women back in Minnesota who whined if their dance slippers got muddy. One of them in this situation would have been wolf bait in less than a minute. One of them, he realized, would never have had the guts to try to bodily drag a man to a fort after her pony gave out. He wrapped Two Moons's foot and prepared to mount behind her, but she slid back behind the saddle.

"Don't want a white man's arms around you, eh?" Willets mumbled. "Fine. But I hope you can manage to stay on." He kicked his horse's flanks and headed out at a smart trot.

❧

Dawn presented a gray sky and cold winds. The men spread more blankets atop Daniel and picked up the pace.

Once, Daniel opened his eyes and Aaron leaned down trying to get his attention. "You hold on, Daniel. We're taking you to the fort. The doctor will help. Just hold on."

They rode in grim silence, churning out the miles. Willets rode up alongside the travois. He talked to his friend, trying to encourage him, hoping that if he couldn't hear the words, at least he would hear the respect and caring and respond. "Don't give up, Daniel. We're almost there."

A few minutes after Willets talked to Daniel, he was aware of Two Moons's hands holding lightly to his coat. He caught up with Aaron. "Good time to pray, young man," he said gruffly.

"What do you think I've been doing all morning?" Aaron said testily. "Maybe you ought to try it, too."

"Maybe I will," Willets shot back.

Aaron looked at him sternly. "Why should God listen to you? You probably haven't spoken to Him in years. You don't even know Him. You said that yourself."

"I didn't know God played favorites when it came to prayers," Willets said, half joking.

"He doesn't. But He's pretty plain about who He does and doesn't listen to. So unless you're serious about knowing Him, I'd suggest you just whisper a prayer to the wind, or whatever else it is you believe in." Aaron nudged his horse forward and caught up with Elliot.

Willets pulled his horse behind the travois, frowning and thinking. *Who was Aaron Dane to tell him God wouldn't listen to John Willets's prayers, anyway? Who did he think he was? It was Daniel's life they were talking about.* And John Willets valued it as much as anyone else. Surely they all knew that.

A cool wind began to blow. Willets sensed rather than felt the little woman behind him shiver, although she seemed to be leaning a little closer to him now. Up ahead, Aaron pulled his horse up and dismounted just long enough to untie his bedroll. When Willets and the woman rode by, he held a blue-and-white quilt up for the woman and said something in Lakota. Two Moons answered him gently and draped the quilt across her shoulders.

"Captain," Aaron said, catching up with them quickly. "I— I'm sorry about what I said back there."

"No problem," Willets said abruptly.

"No, that's not true, sir. I'm worried about Daniel, but so are you in your own way and I shouldn't have taken it out on you. Of course I've been praying. And you can, too. Only—"

"Only what? Only I'm not holy enough for it to do any good?"

Aaron was quiet for a minute. He swallowed hard. "It's not that, sir. No one's holy enough that God wants to hear what they have to say about anything. That's not it."

"What *is* it, then, Dane? I'm all ears." Willets did not try to keep the sarcasm out of his voice.

"Well, sir, the way I understand it is this: sin puts a gap between the sinner and God. And since we're all sinners, we're all separated by that gap. The Cross is what closes the gap. Jesus did away with sin by taking it on Himself at the cross. Once we make it personal, it's as if our own sins were with Him when He died. So our sins are all forgiven and the gap is closed. There's a bridge we can ride across. And when we get to the other side, there's no gap anymore between us and God, because Jesus took the sin that was keeping us separated."

"And then God hears our prayers and does what we want?" Willets said.

"No, sir, not exactly," Aaron said. "I mean, yes, once we accept the Cross for our sins, the sin gap goes away. He hears our prayers then. But He still might not do what we want."

"You telling me God might not answer your prayers for Daniel?" Willets snorted. "If you think that, why do you bother to pray?"

"Oh, I know He'll answer," Aaron said. "I just don't know how He's going to answer. He does what He wants."

"Well, good for God," Willets said. "If He just goes around doing what He wants, then I don't think I'll bother to get in good with Him."

"Well, sir," Aaron cleared his throat, "I can see how you'd feel that way. Lots of people say they believe in Jesus just because they want to get in good with God and have Him do things for them. They kind of think of Him like He's magic or something."

"But you don't think of God that way, do you Dane? Neither do Two Stars or his wife."

"No, sir. It's different for us."

"I know it's different," Willets snapped. "But you can't seem to explain it so a man can understand it."

"I'm sorry, sir."

Willets shook his head. He sighed. When he finally spoke, his voice was kinder. "It's all right, boy. It probably can't be explained. Religion gets confusing, even for theologians. Don't be too hard on yourself."

"Can—can I just tell you what it means to me, knowing Christ and all?" Aaron asked shyly.

"Fire away," Willets said.

"Well, it's like this. I was raised by missionaries, so I learned a lot about the Bible and God. And I knew about Jesus dying on the Cross and it was for the sins of mankind and all that. I knew it in my head anyway. But then the outbreak happened and I saw all those terrible things. It really threw me. I just couldn't see how God could be in all that." Aaron paused, thinking hard. "I think I hated God for a while because I knew He could stop it, but He didn't. I couldn't understand it."

"And now you do?"

"Oh, no, sir. I still don't understand it all. But I think I got enough little pieces to get me through." Aaron brushed his hand down his jaw, rubbing the stubble growing there. "All these bad things that happen, they aren't God. They're sin in the heart of man. And God doesn't want it any more than we do. But unless a man knows Him, he sins and sins and sins again. But when a man goes to God and gets his sin forgiven, God puts a new man inside him. Someone who has the power to look evil in the face and choose good. That's why Daniel can make all the choices he makes, like not taking vengeance against Abner Marsh when everything inside him wants to do it. And being worried about me in a battle. That's why he can love like he does. There's a new man inside him."

"You telling me Jesus is the reason he and Genevieve love each other so much?"

"Sure. God's love pours out of the new man if Christians let it. And when you know God, you learn He does things different from humans. I mean, if He acted like us He wouldn't be God, would He? He's working things out for our good and His glory—there's a promise like that in the Bible. But sometimes that means things happen we don't like. And we just have to trust He knows what He's doing."

"Seems to me you just take your faith blindly, Aaron," Willets said. "You look at the world and you interpret it through your faith, but when things don't match up, you just say 'that's God'." Willets meant it as a criticism and a challenge. He was surprised when Aaron nodded and agreed with him.

"Exactly, sir. We walk by faith. Not by sight."

"Faith in a God who doesn't make sense," Willets said.

"Faith in a God who tells us everything we need to know in His Word—and expects us to live by it."

"Oh, so now I have to believe in God *and* the Bible," Willets said.

"Who wants to believe in a God they don't know? And how are you going to know who God is unless you read His Book, sir?" Aaron said. He was amazed that Willets even asked the question.

Willets shook his head. "Don't think I'm ready for that, son. The Bible doesn't make a whole lot of sense to a whole lot of people, me included."

"How much of it have you read?" Aaron asked quickly.

"Enough to know I don't understand it."

"You ever ask God to explain it to you?"

"You just told me God isn't listening when reprobates like me talk to him," Willets said.

"Maybe I'm wrong about that. Maybe you should ask Him and find out." Aaron nudged his horse ahead and leaned down to say something to Daniel.

Willets closed his eyes momentarily. He was tired. His mind

was scrambled with doubts and questions and fears and uncertainty. And he didn't like the feeling one bit. Presently he urged his horse into a canter and caught up with Picotte.

"I'm thinking I should ride on ahead to the fort and get the doctor on notice we're coming in," he said.

Picotte frowned. "I don't know about that. Not so sure there isn't a party of warriors trailing this little gal." He nodded at Two Moons.

"If there is, they'd have attacked by now," Willets said. "We're pretty obviously defenseless."

Picotte considered. Finally he shrugged, "fine. If you're willing to take the risk, go ahead."

"Can you tell her what I'm doing?" Willets said. "Let her stay here if she wants."

Picotte and Two Moons exchanged a few phrases. Then Picotte nodded. "Go ahead. She'll stick with you. She says just don't let the soldiers hurt her."

"Tell her she's safe with me," Willets said.

"I reckon she knows that," Picotte answered, but he translated anyway.

Willets felt the little woman's arms encircle his waist. He took that as permission to leave, and in a moment the two were galloping away from the group of travelers, headed for Fort Phil Kearney.

◦◦◦

Late in the afternoon Willets came thundering back, leading two dozen soldiers and a military ambulance. The ambulance pulled up and the rear doors were opened. Elliot led his mare so that the travois was positioned just beside those opened doors and all Daniel's friends gathered around while the fort surgeon examined Daniel. After one look at the leg he said, "That has to come off." He looked up at the circle of friends. "Now."

"Now?" Elliot asked. "Out here?"

"The sooner the better," the doctor said. He looked at Elliot's hook.

Elliot raised his hand. "Antietam," he said. "Bloody Monday. Cannonball."

"Think you can assist in a surgery?" the doctor said. He stood upright and reached for a box in the back of the ambulance.

"If I have to," Elliot said.

"Well someone has to. There's signs of gangrene around this ankle." He pointed to a black circle the size of a coin. "Every minute counts." He looked up at the sky. "And there's a storm moving in."

"Let's get started," Elliot said.

A field examining table was pulled out of the ambulance and set up in the open air. When Two Moons appeared at Daniel's head, the surgeon frowned. "Get her out of here."

Two Moons spoke quickly to Picotte, who translated. "She's been taking care of him. Says he has two broken ribs and a fractured collarbone. The leg bones were showing out the hole when she found him. She pulled them back inside and has been treating him. She says he didn't have a fever until a couple of days ago. He'd been pretty clearheaded the whole time until then."

Dr. Grainger looked down at the splint. "Did she do this?"

"She did," Picotte said without asking Two Moons.

Grainger stared at Two Moons for a moment. She met his gaze.

"Ask her if she's ever seen a man's leg cut off before. I don't want her fainting and causing a distraction."

Picotte translated again, but when Two Moons answered, he hesitated before giving her answer.

Grainger, who was opening a box of tools that looked very much like carpenter's saws and drills, didn't look up. "Well?"

"She's never seen a man's leg cut off before. But soldiers cut out her husband's heart and beheaded her baby. She thinks she can handle this surgery."

Suddenly, it was very quiet. Grainger looked at the woman and she looked back.

"Tell her I am sorry for what was done to her family," the doctor said slowly. "Tell her if she would stand at the man's head and soothe him if he stirs, it would be very helpful."

Two Moons stood at Daniel's head. She began to stroke his temples and his forehead. When the doctor soaked a piece of cotton with ether and put it to Daniel's nose, Two Moons stood back, but the minute the doctor turned his attention to the leg, she leaned down and, putting her head next to his, began to sing quietly.

Twenty-Six

"I trust in the mercy of God for ever and ever."
—PSALM 52:8

"FIRST TIME I EVER OPERATED TO THE SOUND OF MUSIC," Grainger muttered.

"I'll make her stop if it bothers you," Picotte offered. He was standing leaning against the ambulance, his back to the operating table, but near enough he could translate between the doctor and Two Moons as needed.

"No need," Grainger said. He was making his first cut into the skin as he said, "Some people believe if a healthy person holds the hands of the sick, it gives the sick new strength . . . as if health can pass from the healthy body to the weak. Maybe she can pass on some healing while she sings."

While he talked, he pulled the skin away from the muscle tissue, explaining as he worked, "It's been my experience that a straight cut through the calf muscles gives a pain-free stump." Blood rolled down the table and dripped onto the earth at the foot of the table. Grainger lay his knife down atop Two Stars's shirt.

"Saw," he said, and Elliot handed him the saw. "It's a terrible sound, I know," he said. Sweat formed on his brow as he worked. "Just remember that sound is the only thing standing between this man and the pearly gates." Elliot closed his eyes so he wouldn't see the lower half of Daniel's leg leave the table.

"File," Grainger said, and worked to smooth the end of the bone. "You need to open your eyes now, Captain Leighton. I'm going to need an extra hand. And whatever you do, don't faint on me."

Elliot looked down and grimaced. Bile rose in his throat.

"You going to be all right?"

Elliot swallowed and nodded. "Get on with it."

The doctor nodded. "Good." He pulled the skin flap up and stitched it shut. "Neater than stitches at a quilting bee, eh Major? Now brace your hand under the thigh—yes. Just so." He packed the end of the stump with cotton padding and put more over the knee. "Bandaging is important. Two turns around the stump end—always from behind. Keeps the tension so the skin flap is pulled forward. Prevents ulcerations over the end of the bone." Grainger worked while he talked. He'd inserted a piece of tubing in the wound before closing. "Drain comes out in two days if it goes all right. We'll have him moving tomorrow. Assuming he wakes up, of course." Grainger felt Daniel's forehead. "Fever's pretty high." He spoke to Picotte. "Ask her if she'll ride with him and keep his face cooled off with water."

"'Course she will," Picotte said.

Daniel was loaded into the back of the ambulance. Two Moons scrambled up behind him, canteen in one hand, cloth in the other. As she bathed his face with cool water, she talked to him.

The surgical table was rinsed off, folded up and put away. The doctor ordered two of the detail from the fort to bury "the specimen." He washed his hands in the creek and, seemingly oblivious to the bloodstains on his uniform, returned to the ambulance and climbed up alongside the driver for the trip back to the fort.

The military detail lead the way, followed by the ambulance, Picotte, Willets, Leighton, Pope, and Dane. They traveled along in unnatural silence until Willets said something to Elliot and galloped off towards the fort.

"Where's he going?" Aaron asked.

"To get Genevieve," Leighton said.

❦

Genevieve Two Stars leaned against the doorframe of the Beaumont's residence looking out on the Fort Laramie parade ground. The men were drilling in exact precision, the flag was flying, it was a beautiful fall day, and Genevieve was trying her best not to let the tears out. *Be thankful,* she reminded herself. *The children you've been working with are good. Libby and the doctor have been kind. You have food and clothing . . . and with these you should be content.*

Movement off to the left attracted her attention, and she smiled to see a young antelope peering around the corner of the house at her. It watched her for a moment, its ears flicking first one way, then the other.

"Come here, Beggar," Gen reached into her pocket for a few grains of corn and held out her hand. One of the soldiers had brought a fawn in this past spring after he found it nestled next to its dead mother. Libby bottle-fed and hand-fed until the little guy learned to walk. Now they couldn't make him leave. He went from house to barracks to the sutler's and back again, begging and charming. When Gen sat down at the edge of the rough board porch, Beggar stepped up and accepted her grain offering, then rubbed his head against her shoulder, nearly knocking her over. "Hey, you," Gen protested. "That's all there is. Go charm someone else."

Rolling thunder made her look up towards the mountains. Sure enough, storm clouds were moving in. One of these days the clouds would hold snow. Gen's eyes wandered to the gates. Her new red dress had been finished for weeks. She had made a blue one, too. And three shirts for Daniel. She'd bought him a new pair of pants and boots . . . and still there was money left in the leather pouch around her neck.

She was beginning to wonder if they were going to spend the winter at Fort Laramie. She was, she told herself for the hundredth time, not worried. Didn't God say not to be anxious for tomorrow? Didn't He say He would never give her more than she could bear? She clung to those truths every day—sometimes every moment when she was particularly lonely. She was changing, she knew. She dared not hope that her secret might be true, but she longed for Daniel in a new way, longed to whisper the secret only to him and to have him share new wonder at God's goodness.

Sighing, Gen got up and headed for the little stone church. Three children were waiting on the stairs, pointing up at the clouds. When she approached, they once again begged for the story of Daniel in the lions' den. "Inside," she said, rubbing her arms briskly and following them up the stairs. "Rain's coming." The three young boys ran to the front of the little church and clustered on the front pew. Gen sat before them on the stage, wondering if any more would come. Half a dozen children usually joined her each morning.

Rain began to fall, gently pelting against the church windows. Gen began the lesson, teaching her three pupils a few new words in English. She had forgotten how quickly children could learn.

Since she didn't speak Lakota, their beginnings had been slow. But Libby had already taught them some English as had the soldiers, although Gen found herself trying to *un*teach some of those words. It was difficult for them to understand the concept of swearing. Lakota had no such words.

When the moments passed and no more children came, Gen asked about those absent. They were gone, she learned. Gone to be with relatives up north in winter camp before the snows came. Gen nodded, once again reminded of the mixing of two ways of life, wondering how it would end for those Lakota who spent their time divided between the white man's world at Fort Laramie and the old ways in winter camp.

When the rain began to click against the window, the children ran to watch small ice crystals sliding down the glass. Gen watched too for a moment before calling them back to the front pew.

"So," she said, smiling, "now I teach *one, two, three.*"

"*Four! Five! Six!*" the little ones shouted back at her.

She held up her fingers as they counted and had just arrived at ten the second time when she heard someone run up the church steps, with spurs. Her heart pounded as she watched the door. The children turned round, peeking over the top of the pew. The door opened. John Willets stepped in, dressed like a trader. He was alone. He took his hat off and held it in his hand, and then he just stood there staring at her.

The children turned back around, looking at their teacher with wide eyes. Her voice trembling, Gen said they should go.

"Later?" one asked.

Gen glanced down at him, a young boy with gentle brown eyes and a winning smile. She shook her head.

"Tomorrow?" he persisted.

"Ask Mrs. Doc," Gen said. She was looking back at Willets as she spoke.

The children filed down the church aisle. They stared up at

Willets as they walked past him and out the door. Gen sat, clasping her small hands in her lap, watching Willets walk towards her. "Is he dead?" She knew it was her voice, but it was as if she were listening from some place far away.

Willets shook his head. "No. But he took a bad spill. Broken bones. He's up at Phil Kearney."

Gen stood up. "How far is that?"

"Six days' ride."

"You'll take me." She didn't ask. Somehow she knew he would.

❧

She had packed quickly, and by the time she was finished Willets had bought supplies at the sutler's and was waiting outside the doctor's house with a fresh horse for himself and a dapple gray mare with a charcoal mane and tail for her. It was still raining, but the temperature had warmed enough that it was just rain now. When Libby protested their leaving in such weather, Gen insisted they would cover themselves with India rubber blankets and they would be fine.

"You be careful," Libby said, patting Gen's arm. "This isn't a good idea, you know."

"It is what it is," Gen said, forcing a smile. "I'm healthy. It will be all right."

"You shouldn't be traveling alone with a single man," Libby said.

Gen smiled at her. "I'm only a Sioux squaw, Libby. No one cares." She nodded at Willets. "They'll think he's a squaw man, but I suspect he can handle that."

Libby blinked a few times.

"It can't be helped, Libby. Don't you see?" Gen's voice pleaded for her to understand.

"Of course, dear." Libby patted her arm. She hesitated, then leaned close and whispered, "You should tell him." She nodded at Willets. "So he knows not to make it too stressful. This rain is going to make things slippery. Easy to fall. Tell him."

Gen shook her head. "No. Daniel hears it first."

Libby patted Gen's arm again and looked at Willets. "You take care with her," she said firmly.

"Yes, ma'am," Willets said. He handed Gen a wide-brimmed hat. "To keep the rain from running down your neck. You'll thank me if the storm gets worse."

"I'll thank you now," Gen said, forcing a smile and pulling the hat down over her ears. She said good-bye and mounted the gray mare. Libby helped her arrange the India rubber blanket so that it covered saddlebags stuffed with the red calico dress and Daniel's new clothes. At the last minute, Libby tucked a suspicious-looking bottle in with the red dress.

"Wild plum wine, dear. To keep the chill off."

Gen raised her eyebrows in surprise.

"It has medicinal value," Libby insisted.

"Thank you," Gen said. "I'll remember that."

"And remember you are welcome to stay the winter with us. Both of you." Libby raised an eyebrow and winked. *"All* of you."

Beneath the India rubber blanket, Gen's hand went to her waist. She swallowed hard, croaked her thanks, and headed after Willets, who was already waiting at the gate.

When they had ridden outside the fort and were headed north, Willets asked, "You all right? Mrs. Beaumont seemed worried."

"I'm fine. She worries about everything. The horse slipping and dumping me in brambles. Snow. Daniel. She's just that kind of person." It began to rain harder. Gen pulled the rubber blanket down over her skirt as far as it would go and bowed her head beneath the hat.

"You get tired, you say something," Willets half shouted. "Just keep your eyes on me and don't worry about anything." He took his horse up the trail. Gen fell in line behind him, not even bothering to look behind her before Fort Laramie was out of sight.

Toward evening the rain let up. They stopped long enough to roll up the rubber blankets and tie them in place behind their saddles. Gen took her hat off and let it hang from the saddle horn. After a brief rest, they mounted up again, riding a few more miles before lengthening shadows in the valleys signaled the need to make camp for the night.

They had eaten their cold supper and were sitting by a dismally small fire when Gen cleared her throat and asked, "Is he—is he going to die? Is that why you came for me?"

"Of course not," Willets lied. He stood up abruptly and pretended to check the stakes supporting Gen's tent. "But broken bones take a while to mend, and you might as well not be sitting down at Fort Laramie worried. Everyone agreed."

"Tell me what happened," she demanded.

"It was the day of the Wagon Box fight—"

"Wagon Box fight? You were in a battle?" Her voice wavered. "You didn't tell me you were in a battle. What of Aaron? Elliot? Were they hurt?"

"Elliot wasn't even in the fight. Aaron did himself proud. Didn't get a scratch."

"Robert? Big Amos?"

Willets described the two scouts' injuries, hurrying to say, "But when I left they were on the mend. In fact, Robert was really angry I wouldn't let him come for you." He made an attempt at a joke. "Guess he didn't think a white man could travel fast enough."

"The Wagon Box fight. Tell me," Gen said. She was concentrating on the clouds in the distance while she waited for him to answer.

"Right. Well—" Willets spent the next half hour or more detailing everything he knew about the fight. "Aaron's going to be a first-rate soldier. He's a good shot and he didn't lose his nerve.

Even Picotte thought he did well, and Picotte doesn't hand out praise lightly."

Gen nodded. "Now tell me how my husband was hurt."

"Near as we can tell, he went off a cliff with the stallion. Two Moons found him at the bottom of a canyon, said the stallion was alongside him. Dead, of course."

"Two Moons?" Gen frowned and looked at John.

"She's Lakota. She found Daniel and took him into some camp. Probably saved his life."

"And this Two Moons is where?"

"Still at the fort, I guess. At least she was there when I left. Wanted to watch over Daniel herself."

Gen looked up at the gray sky, then back down at her hands. She held them out toward the fire. "How long was Daniel missing?"

"Less than two weeks."

Gen rubbed her hands together and looked up at Willets. "Are you telling me the truth, or is Daniel already dead and you are afraid to tell me?"

When he wouldn't look her in the eye but instead searched the hillside behind her while he swiped his hand over his blond goatee, Gen covered her face with her hands.

"No—no, Genevieve. Don't. Don't cry. It isn't—" Impulsively, he reached over and pulled her hands away from her face. He lifted her chin and shook his head. "It isn't that. But there is something I haven't told you." When her blue eyes filled with tears he swiped them away with his thumb. "Doctor Grainger came out to meet us when we brought Daniel back. He," Willets gulped, "he said Daniel would die if he didn't operate."

"Operate?" Gen said the word as if she had never heard it before. "What kind of operating?"

"His leg, Genevieve. Doctor Grainger had to take it."

For a moment it was as if the words didn't make sense to her. She looked down at John's hands holding hers. Then she snatched her hands away. "*They cut off his leg?!*"

"Only below the knee. Had to. Gangrene was starting. Do you know what that is?"

Gen nodded. "Blackness. When I was in New York, some of the men they sent back from the battlefield—" She closed her eyes and shuddered. When she opened them again, there were no tears. She began to ask questions rapid-fire.

"Where was the gangrene?"

"His ankle."

"And the wound?"

"One just below the knee. Another down at the ankle."

"Where did the doctor cut?"

"Just below the knee."

"Show me." She reached over to his leg. "Here?" she touched a spot. "Or here?"

"Just there," Willets said, sliding his hand across his leg about three inches below the knee.

"What did Daniel say?"

"He doesn't know. At least he didn't. He wasn't awake when we found him."

"Unconscious, you mean."

"Yes."

"For how long?"

"Only a few hours."

She nodded. "Does he know I am coming?"

"No."

"And does he know they took his leg?"

"No. At least he didn't when it happened."

"Hurry," she said, "we must hurry."

Twenty~Seven

"Be thou my strong habitation, whereunto
I may continually resort: thou hast given
commandment to save me; for thou art my
rock and my fortress."

—Psalm 71:3

Six days they had been on the trail. She had had six days to pray and prepare, but when she stood at the foot of Daniel's bed, she wasn't prepared at all. He looked small and weak. His breathing was shallow and rapid, and he hadn't responded at all to the sound of footsteps approaching. Beneath the blankets she could see the outline of what was left of his leg. They had it elevated on a pillow. She could also see where it ended, and that, combined with the smell of alcohol and medicines in the room, made her stomach lurch.

His bed was near a window against the far wall, but it was

dark and the only thing visible in the window was the reflection of the oil lamp burning low on his bedside table.

And Two Moons was there, for Gen knew it must be her, the small dark-eyed woman sitting on a chair beside her Daniel's bed.

The woman named Two Moons looked at Gen without expression, as if to say, "So. You are here." But she didn't offer to get up and give Gen her chair.

"Two Moons," John Willets whispered. "This is Daniel's wife. Genevieve."

Genevieve reached out. "You saved him. Thank you."

Two Moons nodded and shrugged, as if to say, "It was nothing."

Gen looked at her wondering what it was that had inspired her to care for a stranger from another tribe—a tribe her people considered cowards. She had wondered about Two Moons before, and the only answer she was able to invent was that Two Moons was God's answer to all her prayers for Daniel. Now, as she stood looking at the woman, she felt a little unsure of herself. Sorry that Two Moons was so young. John hadn't mentioned that. Hadn't mentioned she was pretty, either.

"Blue Eyes?" His voice was barely audible, but she heard her name and all the thoughts about Two Moons dissolved in the joy at hearing what she thought at that moment was the most beautiful sound on earth. She leaned down to kiss his cheek. "I am here, best beloved," she whispered. Just barely, his lips turned up at the corners. Beneath the blanket, his hand moved. When she pulled away the blankets and slipped her hand beneath his, he took a deep breath and fell back to sleep. Someone slid a chair up behind her. She sat down and rested her cheek against his hand on the bed.

When next Gen opened her eyes, gray light was filtering through the windows in the hospital. She stayed still for a moment, listening to Daniel's even breathing with her eyes closed. Her back ached and she grunted softly with the effort to move. When she pushed herself upright, she rubbed her sore neck and stretched, then watched Daniel for a few moments. On the opposite side of the bed there was a table with assorted bottles and bandages neatly arranged beside a water bucket. She took a drink, then used a second cupful to dab at her face. She was horrified at what came off her face onto the towel. She must look awful. She looked over her shoulder at her sleeping husband.

"Two Moons?" he croaked.

"No. It's me." She kissed his cheek, then his forehead, brushing his dark hair away from his face.

He frowned slightly, as if trying to comprehend. "I thought I was dreaming." He opened his eyes and when they focused on her face, he smiled. "A good dream." He asked for water. When she slipped her arm beneath his head to help him drink, he tried to help himself sit up, but after two gulps of water he had to lie back down, exhausted. She thought he was asleep until he moved his good leg and winced.

"What is it?" she asked.

He grimaced. "Leg hurts."

"I'll get the doctor."

"No. Don't—don't go. He'll come." He took a couple of deep breaths and fell back to sleep.

Later that morning Dr. Grainger took Gen aside and explained everything that had been done, everything to expect. "It's infected, but wounds always get infected. It's getting better. The drain is out. I left a few stitches in, but we can take those out soon."

"He complained of pain," Gen said. "He never complains about pain."

"Phantom pain," the doctor said. "His brain doesn't realize the leg is gone. Everyone experiences it. And it can be fairly intense."

Gen nodded. "What can I do for him?"

"Just what you are doing. But you certainly don't need to spend every minute in here. I told Two Moons the same thing. He's out of danger."

"Where else would I want to be?"

"Well," Grainger said, "some wives in this situation would want to be anywhere but the hospital."

"Then I guess I am not 'some wives.' Can you show me how to change the bandage?"

"Of course. Is there anything you need?"

Gen shook her head. "Only for my husband to be all right."

"Because of the other injuries, this is going to take a little longer, but usually we can fit him with a wooden leg by the end of the third week."

Gen gulped and nodded.

"It won't be long before we can get him up. Picotte is quite a hand at whittling. I've got him working on something." He smiled and nodded encouragement. "I know this seems a terrible tragedy, Mrs. Two Stars. And it will take a while for him to adjust. But I've seen men do so well you would never guess they've had the surgery." The doctor looked over Gen's shoulder. "It looks like he's resting comfortably. There's half a company of men outside waiting to see you."

Gen followed the doctor outside. Robert Lawrence had a permanent part just above his left ear and Big Amos would have a weak arm for a few weeks yet, but they were healthy and anxious to return to their wives in Nebraska before snowfall.

"We'll get him up and moving," Robert promised. "We're not leaving without you."

"I've several letters for you," Elliot said. "Jane is hoping you and Daniel will come back to New York with Aaron and me. He can recuperate under our doctor at home." He held up his hook. "Obviously the man knows what he's doing with this sort of thing."

Even Edward Pope had come to say hello, his head bobbing up and down nervously as he promised an unending supply of soup as soon as Daniel's appetite returned.

But Aaron. Seeing Aaron opened the floodgates.

"Ma!" he swept her up into his strong arms and whirled her around and set her back down after a fierce hug.

Gen reached up to pat his cheek, now covered with a week's growth of beard—he had decided just a goatee like Captain Willets's was not quite enough, he explained nervously. She put her hands on his arms to "get a good look" at him and felt the rock hard muscles beneath his uniform, and she burst into tears because he was all grown up now and he was a man who didn't need a mother anymore and he had been in a battle and could have been killed but here he was, growing a beard and laughing and happy, and suddenly she realized again that she could have lost not only her best beloved but Aaron too, but God had been good and brought them both through and oh, Lord, if only Daniel would weather this trial, everything would be all right.

The joy and relief and the fear washed over her all at once. She laughed and said it was all right, but she could not make herself stop crying. John Willets, who had been in the background of it all, handed her a clean white handkerchief. She hid her face in it while the men looked on nervously. Finally, she waved them all away with a promise to let them see Daniel in the afternoon after Dr. Grainger's visit.

Everyone left except Aaron. "Come on, Ma. Let's walk over to the barracks. The fresh air will do you good, and you can see a little of Fort Phil Kearney."

"I've seen all of Fort Phil Kearney I care about," she said, "but a walk will do me good." She put her arm through Aaron's and allowed herself to be led away. Behind her, she saw Two Moons slip into the infirmary.

"Tell me what you know about Two Moons," she said to Aaron as they walked.

"Captain Willets seems to think she's some kind of healer or something. She hasn't had much to say about herself. She told the captain she had a husband and a child. Apparently the army killed them, although we can't figure where. Doesn't seem possible she was at Sand Creek, but from what she said happened, it must have been there. But that was Cheyennes, not Lakota. And she only talks Lakota. She seems a little—odd."

"What do you mean, *odd?*"

"Like something just isn't quite right—up here," he tapped his temple.

"If her family really died that way," Gen said quietly, "it's no wonder. Remember the women in the outbreak—the ones the worst happened to?"

Aaron was quiet for a moment. "Yes. Of course." They walked on silently while Gen looked around her. Finally Aaron offered, "She's amazingly gentle with anything hurt. Animals and people alike. Doesn't matter which. There was a dog last week that got chewed up pretty good in a fight. Two Moons has it in a box over at the sutler's and tends it. The thing won't let anybody but her near it. But it's tame as Amanda's lap dog with her."

Amanda. So he still thinks about her. Gen shoved the topic of Amanda Whitrock to the back of her mind. "Is that where she's been—Two Moons, I mean—since I came?"

Aaron shrugged. "Probably."

"Tell me about yourself. John said you were in something they are calling the Wagon Box fight. He said you're becoming a good soldier."

It was all Aaron needed. For the next few minutes he talked nonstop and in that time Genevieve realized, with a sense of dread, that Aaron Dane had indeed found his calling. He was a born soldier. Part of her was filled with regret for the sake of his father, who would no doubt have preferred him to be a missionary. And it almost seemed that he had the heart of a pastor in ways. His faith was strong. He punctuated his speech about the fight with thankfulness to God for protecting him. He even mentioned concern for a few of the men he had gotten to know since being at the fort. It was obvious he had a sense of God's hand in the details of his life. But Aaron Dane was never going to make a missionary—at least not in the traditional sense of the word.

They circled around the parade ground and then headed back to the infirmary. As they mounted the steps Two Moons appeared at the door and sidled down the stairs to leave.

"Wait," Gen called. "Don't go." Frustrated by the language barrier, she asked Aaron to get Picotte to translate for her.

"What do you want to tell her, Ma?" Aaron said, smiling a boyish smile. "I've been learning Lakota."

"I just need to thank her. To tell her she must come and visit any time she likes. And I want her to know that my saying the words is not enough." Gen's voice wavered. "Somehow I want her to know that when she saved Daniel she gave me back my life. I will never be able to repay her."

Aaron began to talk. But he had only spoken a few words when Two Moons held her hand up, interrupting him. She said a few words and touched Gen's arm. Smiling shyly, she headed for the sutler's.

Gen watched her go, then turned to Aaron for an explanation.

"She watched your face when you were talking," Aaron said. "And she saw Daniel's face when he realized you were here. There is nothing else to say."

∽

"Blue Eyes."

It was early afternoon. Gen had closed her eyes and was nearly asleep sitting upright in the chair beside Daniel's bed. She started awake, and when she opened her eyes he was looking at her with a real smile.

"Did you make the red dress?"

Gen nodded and leaned forward to rest her elbows on the edge of the mattress. "Of course. And a blue one. And some shirts for you. And we have money left."

But Daniel wasn't asking for an accounting of the family finances. He was feeling better and his mind had wandered to other things. "Did you remember—about the buttons?" There was a hint of the old Daniel in the brown eyes.

Gen nodded and blushed.

He grinned. "Can you help me sit up?"

When she leaned across him to grab an extra pillow, he wrapped his arms around her and kissed her neck. "I love you, little wife," he whispered.

"And I love you," she said breathlessly, "but Dr. Grainger is due in here any minute and—"

"Oh, all right," he muttered, letting go. Wincing and grunting with the effort, he raised up on one elbow so she could tuck an extra pillow behind him. When he was comfortably propped up, he opened his arms to her. "Now come back here," he ordered, "just for a minute. I promise not to embarrass you in front of the good doctor."

Gen closed her eyes while he held her, wondering if it might be the right moment to tell—she felt his arms stiffen. "What? What's wrong?" she asked. He was looking towards the end of the bed. He pushed her away just enough to see her face. He was frowning as he looked from her, to the bed, and back again. She followed his gaze and sat up.

"It's all right, best beloved," she said, touching his cheek. "You're going to be fine."

"Take the blanket off," he said between clenched teeth. "Let me see."

She slid off the edge of the bed and onto her chair, patting his hand. "This afternoon, Daniel. When the doctor comes."

"Now." He didn't look at her at all, but began pulling at the blankets. "I want to see it now."

With trembling hands, Gen helped him lift the blankets away. She closed her eyes briefly, then turned her back to the wounds and watched her husband's face. He frowned as he slowly rubbed the back of his hand against his chin. He grunted and must have tried to lift the stump, because he winced and let out a big breath and lay back against the pillows. He said, "All this time it's been hurting and it isn't even there."

Gen explained, "Dr. Grainger said it's called phantom pain. It's normal."

"Normal." His voice was bitter. "Normal doesn't quite seem the word to describe it." He grimaced and looked away. "Cover it up."

Gen did what he asked, talking while she arranged the blankets, fluffed his pillow, walked around the end of the bed to pour a glass of water. "Dr. Grainger said he has known men who get along so well you can't even tell they've had it done. Picotte is carving a wooden leg. And if everything looks all right when we change the bandage today, Dr. Grainger said you can get up and—"

"I want to be alone for a while, Blue Eyes."

She set the cup of water down on the table and turned to face him.

"Please."

"All right, best beloved," she whispered. She kissed his cheek. He grabbed her hand and kissed the palm.

"You know it doesn't matter. Not to me," Gen said.

He looked up at her. "But it matters to me."

She cleared her throat. "We'll face it together. Like—"

"Don't." His voice was sharp. "Just—don't, Blue Eyes. Leave me alone now."

Gen left.

Early that afternoon, Elliot visited. He explained phantom pain and proposed that Daniel's recuperation could be effected much more quickly at Leighton Hall.

Aaron came and prayed with him.

Edward Pope brought soup.

Robert and Big Amos said he and Genevieve should stay with their families on the Niobrara for the winter.

And Doctor Grainger came, changing the bandage, answering Daniel's questions, assuring him there was no reason he could not have a good life.

While everyone was visiting Daniel, Captain John Willets was looking for Genevieve. He found her in the corner of an empty stall in the stables. She was sitting on the hay with her legs drawn up and her arms around her knees. Her head was bowed and she was crying as if her heart would break.

As for Daniel, after all his visitors left, he longed for Blue Eyes to come back. He wondered if he would ever be the man she needed again. And he, too, cried.

Twenty-Eight

"Hear my cry, O God; attned unto my prayer.
From the end of the earth will I cry unto thee,
when my heart is overwhelmed:
lead me to the rock that is higher than I.
For thou hast been a shelter for me,
and a tower strong from the enemy."

—PSALM 61:1-3

"GET OUT! GET OUT AND LEAVE ME ALONE. JUST *LEAVE me alone!*"

Intending to pay Daniel another visit, Elliot had just reached for the infirmary door handle when he heard his friend yelling at the top of his lungs. But it wasn't the anger in the voice that kept Elliot from going through the door. It was a memory; the memory of his own seething anger when he woke in a military hospital without his left hand. It was the memory of the fear and desperation that visited every amputee in turn like a dark fog creeping in the hospital ward windows at night and swirling from bed to bed. Some wounded men gave the fog added substance and shrouded themselves in it. These men might leave the hospital healed in body, but they would be forever enveloped in darkness. Others convinced themselves they would be better off dead. Elliot was amazed at how often, in spite of healing wounds, these men died. And then there were the men who fought battles with the darkness and came out victorious. They were the heroes, Elliot thought—the men who accepted the reality of missing limbs as a challenge, conquered their limitations as best they could, and used their experiences to help others. Elliot did not count himself that kind of hero. He had, after all, only lost a hand when others must learn to live without both legs . . . or, what was worse in his mind, both arms. But in the world of wounded veterans, he was at least what a pastor had once called a wounded healer—someone willing to relive his own horrible history if it would help another.

When he heard Daniel's outburst, Elliot waited outside, praying for words to help his friend. The silence on the other side of the door was deafening. Daniel might not be yelling anymore, but Elliot knew that anger wasn't really the problem anyway. The real problem was the other emotions—the fear and desperation. He'd heard them both in his own voice for months after his hand disappeared with a cannonball at Antietam.

How long, O Lord? He's been through so much already. Elliot prayed for Daniel. *You know all things . . . I know that You know what You are doing . . . but forgive my unbelief, Father, when I ask, are You* sure *You know what You are doing . . . he is young, and he has already endured so much . . .*

From inside the hospital, Gen's voice sounded to interrupt Elliot's prayer. "Please, Daniel. Just let me—"

Anger once again obscured his fear and desperation as Daniel shouted back, albeit not quite so loudly as before, "I said *no!* Now go away and leave me alone!" Bitterness crept into his voice. "Go find Captain Willets. He's what you want, anyway."

"What on earth are you—" Now it was Genevieve's voice that was tinged with fear.

Accusation was flung into the room. "Don't think I don't see you two walking together," Daniel said.

Elliot grimaced and formed a prayer for Gen. *Help her to stay calm, Lord. You and I both know meeting anger with anger won't help.* He was relieved when he heard the gentle reply.

"I go out to walk around the parade grounds because you won't let me stay when Dr. Grainger changes your bandage. I don't see what difference it makes if John Willets—"

"Since when do you call him *John?*"

"He asked me to." She tried to explain. "Daniel, he saved your life. We owe him—"

"I may owe him my *life,*" the voice spat out. "But I don't owe him my *wife.*"

Gen's voice was still reasonable, but Elliot could hear the frayed emotions just below the surface when she said, "You're upset. You don't mean what you're saying. Please, dear, just let me—"

"I said *no!* Now get out and let me be."

Elliot heard footsteps hurrying towards the door. In a moment it was flung open and Gen rushed out of the infirmary, tears streaming down her face. She looked at him with such desperation he could feel sympathetic tears gathering in his own eyes. He opened his arms and Gen collapsed on his shoulder, sobbing.

"I—don't—know—what—I—did—"

"Shhh, Genevieve, shhh," Elliot patted her shoulder. "You did nothing. It's *him.*"

"But he thinks—"

"No, he doesn't. Not really. He's angry, confused, frightened, and a little desperate. All normal reactions."

Gen finished crying. She pushed herself away. Taking a deep breath, she leaned back on the porch railing, then turned away to look off toward the snowcapped mountains. "Well, he isn't the only one feeling confused and frightened." She swiped at her cheeks with her palms.

"Maybe I can help," Elliot said. "I'll try." He put his hand out to pat Gen on the shoulder.

Gen put her hand over his. She looked up at him, but her lips trembled and tears threatened again, so she just shook her head and turned away.

"Take all the time you need," Elliot said gently. "I'll stay with him until you come back." He smiled. "I'm bigger than he is. He won't be throwing *me* out. In fact, why don't you go on over to visit with Mrs. Grainger. She can show you that room she thought you and Daniel could use. I suspect you'll be needing it in the next couple of days."

"I—" Gen swallowed hard. "I thought I might go over to the chapel and just—pray."

"Good. And when you feel better, stop at the doctor's." Elliot shoved her gently towards the stairs. "It's going to be all right, Genevieve. Really."

She nodded, inhaled deeply, and headed for the chapel. When she heard the infirmary door open and close behind her, she turned, half-expecting Elliot to come out again—or to hear something else crash against the door. Daniel had already flung a tin cup across the room in frustration. She wouldn't be surprised if he did it again. But there was nothing. With another glance up at the mountains and a fleeting concern about snow and being forced to spend the winter here at Fort Phil Kearney, Gen headed for the chapel.

❧

The sawmills just beyond the stockade walls were working hard today, and as Gen sat on the chapel steps, the high-pitched whine of blades slicing through logs filled the air. She knew she should be inside praying but she was exhausted. At the moment she didn't know what to say to God or to anyone else. And so she sat, looking around her, wondering why life had become one eternal list of unanswered questions. Just over her shoulder, a guard marched back and forth along the walkway constructed along the stockade wall. Between the officers' quarters strung along the parade ground she could see the battery composed of several mountain howitzers. Soldiers were drilling on the parade ground. She could hear their drill sergeant shouting orders from time to time. She shivered involuntarily, but just when she stood up to go inside, John Willets hurried up.

"What's the matter?" he demanded, frowning. "Two Moons said she heard a crash and shouting over at the infirmary. She saw you come out and Elliot go in. I've been looking for you. What's wrong?"

"He was trying to use Picotte's leg and fell. It made him angry." She forced a smile, disconcerted that she had noticed Willets had cut his hair and trimmed his beard. John Willets was looking especially handsome today. "If Two Moons heard a crash, that was it." She grinned feebly. "Unless she heard the tin cup he threw across the room."

The blue eyes were flecked with anger as Willets blurted out, "He threw something—at *you*?" Without waiting for a reply, he added, "Someone needs to inform him he can't treat you like that."

"Of course he didn't throw anything at *me*," Gen said quickly. The entire confrontation was making her uncomfortable. There was a possessive tone in Willets's voice she didn't like. It was new, she thought—or was it? Perhaps she'd missed something.

"I appreciate your concern, but it isn't necessary. Honestly. Elliot arrived at just the right minute. He's gone in to talk to Daniel, and I've come over here to pray. We'll work it out. We always do." She forced a smile and opened the chapel door.

STEPHANIE GRACE WHITSON

"Isn't there something I can do for you?" Willets asked.

Gen shook her head and looked down for a moment at Willets's polished boots. When she met his gaze again she noticed how very blue his eyes looked now that he was once again wearing his uniform. And now she was feeling not only uncomfortable, but also a little guilty. "You must be about your business now, Captain Willets. And my husband and I must be about ours." She clasped her hands at her waist lest she reach out to put her hand on his shoulder and be misunderstood.

"And exactly what is your business?" Willets asked. "What are you going to do?"

"Well," Gen said. "Dr. and Mrs. Grainger have invited us to stay with them for a few days. Then I suspect we'll be leaving for Fort Laramie."

"And then?" Willets asked. He swiped his hand across his goatee in a gesture that had become familiar. "I—I care what happens to you, Genevieve. I want to know you'll be all right."

"You've been a good friend, Captain Willets," Gen said carefully, "to both Daniel and me. We owe you a debt we will never be able to repay. And we'll never forget you."

The blue eyes searched hers. "But where will you go, Genevieve? Daniel's a good man, but a man with one leg—life could be hard. What's going to happen?"

Gen shrugged. "I'm afraid I don't know." She smiled. "But it doesn't really matter all that much, as long as I have my Daniel."

"Aren't you—aren't you at least a little afraid?" Willets asked. "Or does your faith take care of that, too?"

"I'm a Christian, John. Not inhuman. Of course I'm afraid. So is Daniel. That's what's at the root of those crashes Two Moons told you about." She smiled at him. "But—*What time I am afraid I will trust in thee.*"

"That's it, huh?" His voice was gently mocking when he said, "Just trust in God and He'll fix everything."

"Not exactly," Gen replied. "He doesn't fix everything. He's not going to give my husband a new leg. At least not a flesh and blood one."

"So where's the good in your faith?"

Gen thought for a moment. "I think perhaps the good is in the fact that while He doesn't fix every*thing*, He can and does fix every*one*."

"I don't know what you mean."

Gen glanced past him towards the infirmary while she groped for an answer. "My faith in God isn't some ticket out of trouble. It helps me *through* and *in* the trouble. God doesn't fix everything for His children so they don't have difficulty. Actually, now that I think about it, what God does is something better than that. He promises to go *through* it with us. He says, *I will never leave you nor forsake you.* Think of that, John. If you know the God of the universe is right beside you, then you can pretty much take anything the world can throw at you."

Willets nodded his head in the direction of the infirmary. "Seems to me Daniel forgot that."

Gen nodded her head. "You could be right. What's wonderful, though, is that whether or not Daniel remembers God is there, God hasn't forgotten him. He's still there in that infirmary with him." Gen smiled. "Eventually Daniel will remember that."

"So God was next to Daniel when old Doc Grainger was sawing away, huh?" Willets said. When Gen winced, he stepped forward and touched her sleeve. "I'm sorry, Genevieve—I shouldn't have—"

"No," Gen held her hand out to him. "No, that's all right. But let me answer you. The answer is yes, John. Yes, God was there. And since I think I know your next question, I'll say yes, God could have blinked His eye and restored Daniel's leg. But here's how I think about that: since He didn't, that must mean He has something Daniel must learn that he could only learn with one leg." Gen broke off. Tears gathered in her eyes. "Oh, John," she said, "I only wish you could understand what I'm talking about. To you it probably sounds like a lot of nonsense. But I'm so glad you let me say it, because it was exactly what *I* needed to hear."

"Can I—can we talk again sometime—about what you just said?"

Gen shook her head. She blushed as she said, "Daniel is concerned about—about our—friendship. There isn't anything for him to be concerned about, but he is my husband and—"

Willets searched her eyes for a moment before nodding reluctantly. "Of course. I understand."

Gen tucked a stray lock of hair behind her ear and flung a plea for wisdom to heaven. Finally, she put her hand on his shoulder. "If God is calling you, John Willets—and I think He is—you aren't going to be able to get away from Him. There are others who can answer your questions and give you answers. At least to the questions that *have* answers."

"And what about the ones that don't have answers?"

"Why, that's what *faith* is for, John," Gen said quietly. She patted his shoulder and then took her hand away. Now she could smile at him with true warmth. The something that had made her uncomfortable had been removed. She was free to care about John Willets's soul—and only his soul.

"Who do I ask for that?"

"*Let him who lacks wisdom, ask of God,*" Gen recited.

"Aaron says God doesn't listen to infidels."

"Then stop being an infidel and come to Him with what little faith you already have. That's where it all begins."

He took his hat off and smoothed the brim. He cleared his throat. "I'll never forget you, Genevieve Two Stars," he said quietly. "And I'll be thinking on what you've said. And, listen, if I've done anything—well, maybe I've thought—"

"Stop," Gen said. "Don't say anything more. You're a good man, John. If there is any fault in our friendship, we both own it."

He looked up at her, surprise shining in his blue eyes.

"But it stops here. I won't be taking any more walks around the parade ground with you, Captain Willets. That was foolish of me, and I should have known better."

Whatever John Willets might have been thinking in his moments of contemplating Genevieve Two Stars, he now realized that, like Genevieve, he had been foolish. But in his case, there might even be an element of sin in what he'd done. He smiled wryly at the thought of such a religious concept rising in the thoughts of an avowed unbeliever. Pulling himself to attention, he saluted her. "My respects to you and your husband, Mrs. Two Stars," he said.

Gen smiled and nodded. She thanked him again and went inside the chapel, aware that, whatever her interchange might have done in John Willets, it had accomplished a far better work in her own heart. She made her way to the front of the chapel and knelt at the altar. *Father in heaven. Thank You for bringing John Willets over here so that I could share my faith with him . . . and be reminded of it myself.*

Genevieve prayed for a long time. She asked for guidance, and she prayed for wisdom in how to help Daniel. But most of all, Gen poured her heart out in thanksgiving to the God who never left her side and who worked His will in all things for the good of His own . . . *I don't know how You are going to work things, yet, Lord. But I believe that You've brought this into our lives because there are things we must learn that can be learned only if we endure this trial. Help me know what to do. Show me the next thing and I'll do it.*

At that moment, Gen felt something new. A flutter of movement so fleeting she thought she must be imagining things. She stopped praying and waited, concentrating, almost breathless with anticipation. *Yes.* She scooted back on the front pew, smiling.

John Willets allowed himself one last, wistful glance at the chapel door before heading across the parade ground towards the sutler's. He felt strange, almost like he did right before a battle. There was the sense that something profound was about to happen, and the anticipation of it was exhilarating. He glanced up at the mountains in the distance, noticing their beauty in a new way. *How can a man look at that and not believe in God.* Aaron Dane had said that one morning when they were arguing about religion over their early morning coffee. Now, as Willets looked at those same mountains, he was inclined to agree. *All right,* he thought. *There is a God.*

He looked at the mountains again. *You are there. I am here. It might be interesting to know if You are hearing this. And if You are . . . if You will send someone to talk to me about crossing the gap between us.* At the moment he had the thought, John remembered another conversation with Aaron Dane where they discussed the gap between man and God and how Jesus Christ had provided a way to cross it. He couldn't recall everything Dane had said that day. Perhaps they would have to discuss it again.

Twenty-Nine

The steps of a good man are ordered
by the Lord: and he delighteth in his way.
Though he fall, he shall not be utterly cast down:
for the Lord upholdeth him with his hand.

—PSALM 37:23–24

JUST INSIDE THE INFIRMARY DOOR, ELLIOT BENT DOWN and picked up a tin cup before walking down the open center aisle towards Daniel's empty bed. The patient was huddled on the floor leaning against the wall, his arms folded, his good leg bent, his forehead resting on his knee.

"Go away," he said without looking up.

"You may be able to chase your wife away but I am not so easily ruled," Elliot said, as he placed the tin cup on the bedside table. He perched on the edge of the hospital bed. "Now suppose you tell me what's going on?"

Two Stars leaned his head against the wall and didn't answer.

Elliot sat down on the floor beside him. Seeing the blood seeping through the bandaged stump, he said, "Should I be calling Dr. Grainger?"

"No," Daniel said miserably. "He took the rest of the stitches out today. He even said we could leave the infirmary. It doesn't hurt that much. I'm sure it's fine."

"Better take a look anyway," Elliot said. "You want some help?"

"I'll check it later," Daniel said. "When I'm alone. Please, Elliot, just leave me be."

"Forgot the leg wasn't there, I suppose. " Elliot looked around him. The bed had been shoved away from the wall. The chair Gen usually sat on was lying on its side and the bedcovers hung over the side of the bed touching the floor, testament to Daniel's trying to catching himself and failing. "That must have been some fall." Touching the curve of his metal hook, he said, "I used to reach for things all the time. Can't tell you how many glasses of water I knocked over with this hook before I remembered I didn't have a hand anymore." He was quiet for a moment. "And I didn't want anyone to see the stump, either."

Daniel turned his head and looked at Elliot, then down at his stump. He pounded his thigh with his fist. "God has done a lot of things for me I should be thankful for. And I am. But this. I just don't understand why He had to take my leg."

"I used to wonder the same thing about my hand," Elliot said. "At the time it seemed like the worst thing that could possibly happen. I thought my life was over." He paused. "It wasn't. I thought I'd never be happy again. I was wrong." He grunted as he remembered something else and considered whether or not he should mention it. Suspecting he had just discovered the crux of Daniel's fears, he decided to say it. "And, being the shallow kind of man I was, the thing I worried about most was women. I didn't think a woman would ever have me. I could always think my way through dinner and small talk without the hand, but when it came to—well, to closing the bedroom door at night and—well, you know what I mean. I just didn't think a woman would be able to stand the idea." He took a deep breath. "But, as it turned out, I was wrong about that, too." He cleared his throat before adding, "Hardest thing I ever did was let Jane see the stump. Repulsive, I thought."

"It *is* repulsive," Daniel said.

Elliot nodded. "But you know what Jane did, Two Stars? She didn't shudder or pull away. Just cupped it in her palm and said nothing. When I looked up at her, she was crying."

"I don't want pity."

"That wasn't pity, you fool. It was love. The purest kind. The kind that looked at my hurt and felt it and mourned it." He paused. "I don't think I ever loved Jane Williams more than at that moment. When she looked at what I thought was the ugliest part of myself and didn't retreat—" Elliot gulped and paused. Then he said quietly, "Most people live their whole lives without ever knowing that kind of love."

"Jane never knew you when you had two hands." Daniel said. "It's different for Blue Eyes and me."

"You do Genevieve a great injustice if you really believe that," Elliot said. "Listen to me, Two Stars: that little wife of yours thinks you *hung* the stars. And I'm fairly certain she still believes you could hang a few more . . . even with just one leg."

"I can't even get myself out of bed and take a step," Daniel said miserably.

"Why not?"

"I can't maneuver that leg Picotte made. It's like hauling a log around. That's what made me fall." He pounded his thigh again.

"Then think of a better way," Elliot said. He leaned over and nudged Daniel on the shoulder. "You lost a leg. That's terrible. But you know something? It's happened thousands of time before you, and if men continue to be idiots and fight wars, it will likely happen thousands more. Whether it proves to be a minor inconvenience or the end of your happiness is up to you. But I'm telling you from experience that making it a minor inconvenience is the much better choice."

When Daniel didn't move to get up off the floor, Elliot stood up. "Look, my friend, I spent months in a hospital having subsequent sections of myself hacked off while the doctors tried to stop the gangrene creeping up my arm. Thankfully the third operation did the trick. You know what I finally learned from all that? In the end, the awful thing that happens isn't what life is about. Life is about what we *do* with the awful thing that happens. Of course we feel terrible. We wonder about the future. We're afraid. We grieve. But there's a season for all those and then there's a season to get a grip and get on with life. Think about what the two of you have already been through together, Daniel. Are you going to let this destroy it?"

"Ask Blue Eyes," Daniel said, "and John Willets."

Elliot snorted. "You know what you are thinking just isn't true. Not because of him, but because of *her*."

"I don't want her to see me this way."

"It's too late, best beloved." Gen's voice sounded from where she stood at the end of the bed.

Daniel looked up. He braced himself against the wall, pushed his hands flat against the floor and closed his eyes.

"Elliot," Gen said, "if you'll excuse us, I need to speak with my husband." She waited for Elliot to leave before stepping across Daniel and sliding down the wall to sit beside him on the floor.

"I have to ask your forgiveness," she began. "I knew you were worried about John Willets. But I let you worry. I thought it might make you want to get better. That was wrong." Daniel started to speak, but she interrupted him. "No. Just let me talk. I've never seen you this way before. I don't mean the leg being gone. I mean the anger and the hurt. And whatever other feelings you have that you won't share with me. I don't understand why you won't share them, but I just want you to know I won't be walking with John Willets anymore."

She moved to where she could look up into his face. "I love you, Daniel Two Stars. It doesn't matter how angry you get, you can't send me away and you can't push me out of your life. You don't have to love me. You don't even have to talk to me if you don't want to. But I'm not going away. Ever again."

She stood up. "Now get yourself back onto the bed. There's some blood on the bandage and we didn't bring you this far to get a new infection and to start all over again. Elliot and Aaron and Robert and Big Amos say they won't start for home until you are ready to come with them. So you owe it to them to take care of yourself. I'm going to go get some fresh water. When I get back, you need to be back up in bed."

When Gen returned with the fresh pail of water, Daniel was waiting in bed. When she began to unwrap the bandage, he braced himself. He watched her while she worked, waiting for the quick breath, the moment when she would look away and break his heart.

When the last strip of cloth fell away from the wound, she did indeed take a deep breath. And she did look away from the stump . . . to look directly at him. Her eyes were shining with tears, but still she smiled. "I don't think you really even need a bandage anymore. The blood is from a little tear where there was a stitch. It's nothing."

He didn't realize how tense he'd been until he relaxed and slumped back against the pillows. His hands were shaking as he brushed his hair back off his shoulders and clasped his hands behind his head. "Elliot—Elliot thinks we might be able to think of a better way for me to walk."

"I know you can," she said.

He took a deep breath. "I've been thinking I can probably ride a horse whether I can walk or not. I mean," he said, looking down at his legs. "Most of the gripping is done with the knees. I'm weak, but I think I might be able to do it on a gentle horse."

"You've always liked a horse that had spirit," Gen said.

"What if I fall off and land on my bad leg?" he said.

"Then you get up and try again. And again. And again. Until you find a way." She busied herself with the bandages, with smoothing the blankets at the foot of his bed, with lighting the lamp beside the window. She positioned her chair beside the lamp and lay her Bible on the table.

"I'm going to walk over to the mess hall and see if it's too late to get you some supper," she said.

When she walked by the bed, he grabbed her hand. She caught her breath and waited, her heart pounding.

"I'm not hungry," he said.

"All right," she said. "Then I'll—I'll read to you?"

"That would be nice," he said gently. "In a minute."

She looked down at him. With his free hand he motioned with his index finger. "Come here, Blue Eyes. If you don't mind a kiss from a one-legged coward."

As it turned out, she didn't mind. And it wasn't just one kiss.

❦

The next morning when Elliot stopped in to visit, Daniel ordered Gen to go away. "Don't go away angry, best beloved," he grinned. "Just go away. I need to talk to Elliot."

"Mrs. Grainger is making a new dress for the Thanksgiving ball," Gen said. "I'll see if I can help her with any handwork."

When Gen was gone, Daniel swung his leg over the edge of the bed and sat up. "I'm weak as a newborn foal, Elliot. But I'm wondering . . ." and he laid out a plan.

Elliot smiled. "We can do that," he said. "But let me get Robert and Big Amos and Aaron over here. They might have ideas, too."

The men spent most of the morning together. Then they summoned Picotte and gave him a new carving assignment. As soon as he left, Daniel began to practice walking with a crutch. He was dizzy and he almost fell more than once, but Big Amos kept up a hilarious running commentary, and by the time Gen returned, Daniel met her at the door smiling. He put his arm around her and pulled her to his good side. "How's that?" he asked, grinning at Aaron.

"Seems like old times," Aaron said.

Gen blushed.

Over the next week Daniel began to eat more. He headed outside with his crutch and finally was strong enough to walk all the way to the stables and back on his own. Every day he grew stronger and better able to balance on one leg. When the infirmary beds began to fill with soldiers with various complaints, he and Gen moved into the room offered by Dr. and Mrs. Grainger.

"I think you've walked a few miles today," Gen said one evening. She ran her hands over his shoulders and arms and commented on the muscles. "That's the man I fell in love with," she whispered, leaning close to kiss him. He returned the kiss. She closed her eyes and wished for more. It was not given.

He stayed away longer during the day. The grayness disappeared from his face, and by the end of the second week, when they joined the Graingers at their supper table, she looked across at him and realized every trace of what had happened was gone . . . except for the crutch.

There was talk of returning to Fort Laramie. Robert and Big Amos wrote letters saying they would be home for Christmas. Aaron and Elliot wrote the same news to New York. But Daniel said nothing about what might happen with the two of them after Fort Laramie. Gen tried not to question. She thanked God for his healing and the strength returning to his body. And she longed to tell him her secret . . . but held back. She didn't know what she was waiting for, but it was a gift for a special moment. She would know when the time was right. And it was not right. Not yet.

Thirty

To everything there is a season and a
time to every purpose under the heavens . . .
a time to weep, and a time to laugh;
a time to mourn, and a time to dance.

—ECCLESIASTES 3:1, 4

THEY WERE LEAVING. GOING TO FORT LARAMIE, AND
then through Mitchell Pass again eastward to Fort Randall. From
Fort Randall, Robert and Big Amos would head home to
Nebraska. Aaron and Elliot would board one of the last
steamships to navigate the river headed for St. Louis—if the river
wasn't frozen over by then. If it was, they would head out on
horseback to Sioux City and the railroad. Either way, they would
be home for Christmas and Miss Amanda Whitrock would have
her bearskin rug.

But Daniel didn't say what they were doing. When she asked, he
shrugged. "Be patient, Blue Eyes. All things come to those who wait."

"But what comes after Fort Laramie?" she finally asked. "We're leaving tomorrow, and I don't know where we are going."

"We are going to Fort Randall," Daniel said.

"I mean after that."

He smiled. "Well, after Fort Randall you are spending the rest of your life with me."

She stamped her foot in mock anger: "Tell me."

"I can't. Not today." He pulled her down onto his lap and kissed her. "Just wait until later. I'll tell you everything then."

"All right. I'll wait," she said. "But I just want you to know you are not the only one in this family with a secret." She jumped up. "And I'll bet mine is better than yours."

Elliot appeared at the door. Daniel grabbed his crutch and went out. And Gen packed. It didn't take long to collect her clothing and Daniel's and tuck them into a bag. She left the red dress for last, fingering the lace at the neck and remembering how he had teased her about it. She'd never worn it. She had begun to fear she never would.

There was to be a dance that evening. This was nothing new, for the post band often provided music for entertainment on Friday nights. The men lamented the lack of women. Sometimes drawing straws relieved the shortage. Those who drew short straws began the evening as surrogate women, tying yellow ribbons on their sleeves and agreeing to follow rather than lead for half the evening. When the band took a break, the armbands were traded and the "men" spent the rest of the evening dancing as women. It was cause for good-natured joking and not a few fights. But then a fight or two provided entertainment, too, and no one appreciated good entertainment like men about to spend a winter alone in "the howling wilderness."

Gen and Daniel had never participated much in the normal fort activities—Gen because she was taking care of her husband

and Daniel because he couldn't. So when Robert Lawrence came by after lunch and told her Daniel wanted her to get ready for the dance, Gen was surprised.

She donned her blue calico for the dance and waited. And waited. She could hear the band tuning up and see people headed for the empty barracks where the dances were always held. Still, there was no sign of Daniel—or the others, for that matter.

Mrs. Grainger and her husband left for the dance, but they didn't ask her to join them. Instead, they suggested she enjoy the sunset from the rocker on the front porch. And they smiled mysteriously.

She had gone inside to get a book to read when there was a knock at the door and Aaron called out, "Ma, you there?"

Gen headed for the door, worried when it was only Aaron with Big Amos and Elliott. Daniel was nowhere to be seen.

"Where's Daniel?" she asked. "Is something . . . ?" She stopped in mid-sentence, for Daniel was there after all, riding towards them astride a spirited chestnut gelding. *Riding.* So that was the secret he had kept from her. He had overcome his fear of falling and learned to ride again. A horse with spirit. Just the kind he liked.

He was wearing a bright blue shirt with a scarf knotted at the neck and thigh-high leather boots. He looked wonderful, and when he smiled at her, there was such joy in his eyes she wanted to cry. She started down the steps, but, as it happened, there was more to Daniel's surprise for his wife.

He held up his hand. "No. Stay there. I'll come to you," he said and, pulling the horse up, he dismounted—carefully, but without help. When his wooden foot hit the ground, he wobbled a little. Gen held her breath when he grabbed the stirrup to steady himself and the chestnut sidled away. But he regained his balance in time, handing the reins to Aaron before taking a deep breath and heading for the porch.

Gen watched him approach, her hands clasped beneath her chin. Her Daniel was walking. *Walking without the crutch. Without even a cane.* When he stepped up on the porch and put his arms around her, she began to cry.

"I can't dance yet," he whispered, "but I still want to take you over to hear the music."

"You never *could* dance, best beloved. At least not the way white people do."

He chuckled. "Come to think of it, you're right about that. All right, then. No dancing. Just walking. Together."

Robert and Big Amos, Elliot and Aaron went on ahead. Daniel took Gen's hand and together they walked towards the barracks on the opposite side of the post. Daniel explained how Picotte had carved three legs before they found wood light enough for him to manage. "The real inspiration, though, was when Aaron had the idea of these high boots. They seem to help me balance."

"What about riding?" Gen asked.

"That came back immediately," Daniel said. "The only thing that bothered me was maneuvering a foot I can't feel into a stirrup. I have to put it in with my hand, which is a nuisance. But I can bear with that."

When they arrived at the barracks, he put his arm around her waist as they went through the door. Doctor and Mrs. Grainger greeted them. Someone else offered punch, and before long they were standing in a corner talking with Robert and Big Amos about the journey home.

"Which one of you is to be the woman tonight?" Daniel teased, holding out a yellow ribbon.

Big Amos took the ribbon, but then he gave Robert an odd

look before making some strange excuse and disappearing. Robert followed suit.

"Good to see you up and around," a familiar voice said. Daniel turned around just as John Willets walked up and held out his hand.

Daniel shook it and thanked him, aware of the slight pressure on his back as Gen moved her hand up and down between his shoulder blades. *Don't make a scene. Please.*

"Mrs. Two Stars," Willets said. "I hear you are leaving in the morning."

Gen nodded.

Awkward silence followed, until Daniel cleared his throat and said, "I suppose you came to ask my wife to dance."

Willets blue eyes widened with a mixture of surprise and concern.

"No—I only—"

"I'm glad you did," Daniel said. "Dancing isn't quite on my menu yet." He looked down at Gen. "How about it, Mrs. Two Stars? There's a shortage of women. Why don't you help out? It's been a long time since you used what you learned at Miss Bartlett's back in New York."

Amazed, Gen looked up at him. She frowned slightly. "Are you—are you sure?"

"I'm sure," Daniel said. He held out his hand to Willets. "You've been a good friend, John. Thank you—for everything. Now go dance with my wife."

He bent down and kissed Gen on the cheek. "Just one dance, Blue Eyes."

❧

"But it's only just started," Aaron protested when Daniel and Gen got ready to leave. He was wearing a yellow ribbon around his sleeve and had been a good-natured partner to several half-drunk soldiers that evening.

Daniel knew Aaron was right. The band was just taking its first break of the evening, and the music would likely last until long past midnight. And in the morning more than one soldier would mount watch with a splitting headache from too much punch and too little sleep. "I'm getting stronger, but my leg—"

"I'm sorry," Aaron said quickly. "I forgot about the leg." He looked down at Gen. "Good night, Ma." He hugged her and went back inside.

Moonlight flooded the parade ground with light so bright they could have seen the flag at the top of the flagpole, had it still been flying. As it was, the flagpole cast a long shadow in the general direction of the battery and the mountain howitzers.

Daniel was limping slightly by the time they reached the Graingers. A wagon waited outside already loaded with provisions for the trip south. "We'll be at Fort Laramie before snow falls," Daniel said as they made their way alongside the wagon towards the Graingers' front porch. He grunted with the effort to climb up on the porch and sat down with a sigh of relief in one of the two rocking chairs the doctor's wife had brought with her to her husband's new assignment a few months ago.

"I hope you didn't overdo tonight," Gen said gently.

"I did," Daniel said. "But it was worth it. I'll likely be sore for a few days . . . but I'll be in the saddle for most of the next few days anyway. That will help." He laughed softly. "Although I suppose my backside will be sore from that. And who would have ever thought Daniel Two Stars would get saddle sore like a fresh recruit."

Gen was standing behind him, rubbing his shoulders. "That feels good," he said, reaching around for her hands. He pulled her around and down onto his lap. Tracing the line of her jaw down her throat he lifted her chin and kissed her. "Don't you think it's time you told me?" he asked, nuzzling her ear.

"Told you—what?" she gasped softly, closing her eyes, praying he wouldn't stop.

He lifted her free hand and kissed the Palm. "Blue Eyes," he said softly, "earlier today you said I wasn't the only one with a secret." He kissed her lips gently. "You even hinted your secret was better than mine. Well, now you know mine. I can ride a horse again. I can walk." He put his hand on her waist. "There's nothing I can't do, Blue Eyes." He looked into her eyes and whispered softly. *"Nothing."*

She caught her breath and returned his gaze. When she saw the answer to her unspoken question in his eyes, her heart leaped with joy. She could feel her face grow warm as she blushed, and she laughed nervously.

"I think I know your secret," he said.

"You do?" Her voice wavered.

"You brought the red dress. . . the one I teased you about the day I left Fort Laramie." His hand traced the line from her chin to her waist. "The one without too many buttons."

She shook her head. "That's not what I was talking about."

"What then?"

She sat up straight, stroking the back of his hand while she spoke. "That night when we camped in the Sandhills by the spring-fed lake. You remember?"

He laughed softly. "Of course I remember."

"Well . . . you . . . we . . started something."

"We—what?"

She pressed his open palm against her waist. "We started a family."

Daniel took in a sharp breath. "Are you—sure?"

"Of course I'm sure." When he didn't say anything more she began to worry. "I know it isn't the best time. I—I'm sorry if —"

"Sorry? Don't say you are sorry, little wife." He pushed her off his lap and hobbled to the edge of the porch, leaning against the railing while he stared up at the sky. "Come here," he said quietly, pulling her into his arms. "I think," he whispered, "that I must be the happiest man beneath the moon this night of nights." He kissed her. After a few moments he asked, "Do you still have that red dress?"

Her heart thumped. "Of course."

"Good," he said, leading her across the porch and inside the darkened house. "It will come in handy." He stopped at the door to lean down and kiss her once more before muttering, "Another time."

❦

November 3, 1867
Dear Amanda,

This will be my last letter from the frontier. We are in Fort Randall, and if all goes as planned we'll be on board the steamship Belle and headed home tomorrow morning.

Captain Willets stayed at Fort Phil Kearney, as did Picotte. It's been snowing, and we made the last day of our journey across Nebraska with a cold wind at our backs. I think we must have left Fort Phil Kearney just at the right moment to keep from getting snowed in. Behind us in the distance, a wall of dark gray clouds promises winter is coming. Picotte told some truly hair-raising stories about winter storms . . . but there will be time for those once I am back in New York.

I don't think Gen will mind if I tell you some wonderful news, and that is they are going to have a baby. Gen says in the spring. They have gone to Santee with Robert and Big Amos, and so will be with friends when the baby is born. But I know they won't be staying—Daniel could never be happy farming.

When we were crossing Nebraska earlier this year we camped at a veritable oasis in the sand hills. Daniel thinks there is a future in those hills for anyone who cares to raise cattle. It's an interesting idea. Everyone seems to think Nebraska is a wasteland. Some of the maps label the very place where we found an oasis as the Great American Desert. I wonder what future generations will think.

Will you meet the train, please? Uncle Elliot and I will telegraph our arrival date. I would like it very much if Stephen Bannister stayed home this time.

Your Aaron

"He hath made everything beautiful in his time."
—Ecclesiastes 3:11

Epilogue 1877

THE OLD WARRIOR TRUDGED UP A HILL. ONCE HE HAD fought with thousands. Thousands had become hundreds; and now, only he was left. The rest were gone the way of their ancestors . . . or, what was worse in his mind, gone to reservations. As he made his way upward, his moccasins sunk into the sandy soil. At the top of the hill he stopped. It was there, the blue jewel of water shimmering in the morning sun. He crouched down, smiling and taking in the scene below.

The valley reminded him of one of his wedding gifts to his long-ago bride. He had put it inside a parfleche, and when she took it, he reminded her that while the parfleche might seem like only a worthless bit of dried skin, it held a beautiful treasure. As he stood at the top of the hill catching his breath, Going Higher thought it was like that with this valley, hidden away within miles and miles of seeming nothingness, a treasured secret of fresh water and cool grass.

But something had changed in the valley below. There was a small log house. The ancient warrior frowned. The tree was still there, larger even than he remembered, its branches reaching out over the water. But beside the house the earth had been plowed up. Someone was growing a garden. There was a barn and a corral. Inside the corral a handful of horses stood, heads down, their breath rising in steaming clouds. He was old, but his eyes were still true, and the warrior noted that whoever lived in the house had acquired good quality Indian ponies.

A handful of cattle lumbered up the hill behind him. As they passed him, the warrior noted the place on their haunches where white men marked their cattle. The mark was like nothing he had seen before and he was curious who would use a shape like that—the same shape his own mother had painted on their tepee long ago. There were two. Two stars.

Laughter rippled across the valley and a small woman emerged from the house. As the old warrior watched, the woman grasped the hands of the two children at her side. Together they ran towards the tree. They scrambled up its trunk—the warrior realized someone must have made a way—out onto the biggest branch and, screaming with delight, one by one, they dropped into the water.

Presently a man emerged from the house. He shouted something to the people in the water, and the woman swam to shore and climbed out. She ran to the man, who seemed to walk with difficulty. They embraced and then both children and the woman surrounded him and herded him to the water's edge where they doused him thoroughly.

The old warrior smiled when he heard their language. It wasn't Lakota. But it wasn't white man's talk, either. He stood up. At once the man was aware of him. The play ended. The children skittered across the grass and disappeared inside the house. He could tell the man and the woman were talking about him.

The woman smiled as he approached. She was beautiful. Her blue eyes testified to at least some white ancestry, but her face betrayed mixed blood. As for the man, he was pure Indian. He held out his hand in friendship.

As it turned out, Going Higher had come to a good place. Daniel and Genevieve Two Stars lived simply. Their cattle were sold up at Red Cloud Agency, and other than an occasional incident of poaching, life was good. They were visited sometimes by a white soldier stationed up at Camp Robinson. As it turned out, the soldier considered Genevieve his mother. It was a long story, but eventually Going Higher learned it. He lived with Daniel and Genevieve Two Stars for the rest of his life. He was, they told him, an answer to their prayers, because he had come to them just when Daniel needed help from a man with two good legs.

Going Higher learned of Daniel and Genevieve's meeting in the place to the east called Minnesota.

He learned how they were lost to one another and then found again.

He learned how Daniel lost his leg and found a way to heal.

He heard the names of the two children they had lost . . . and played with the three who still lived.

He saw their children grow up.

He met the white soldier Aaron Dane and the people from the East called Leighton.

He helped Daniel raise cattle and break ponies and taught Meg Dane that she didn't need to see to milk a cow.

He was there the day Captain John Willets rode in and, with

a half-embarrassed smile, introduced them to his wife Two Moons.

Going Higher shared what was left of his life with the Two Stars.

And they shared their love, which was considerable, and their faith, which was remarkable, with him.

Acknowledgments

IN THIS, THE MOST DIFFICULT YEAR OF MY EARTHLY LIFE, I have witnessed more than one miracle of God's love. In love, He ended my best beloved's suffering and took him to eternal rest. In love, He provided my children and me with a church family and loved ones and readers and fellow writers who never tired of praying for us and never turned away when we needed them. I owe a debt of love to so many, there is no realistic way to write a traditional "acknowledgment."

This year has taught me something about the irony of being human. When words are most important, they are not sufficient. A songwriter once penned the line that "to write the love of God would drain the oceans dry." It's true. Someday in heaven, when we have all of time and eternity, Bob and I would love to have you stop by so we could tell you what this section of my book would have said . . . had I had the words.

About the Author

Born in East St. Louis, Illinois, Stephanie received her B.A. in French from Southern Illinois University in Edwardsville, Illinois. She has taught high school French, has been both a medical and publications secretary, and became a full-time homemaker in 1980 with the birth of her first child, a daughter. She and her husband and their four home-schooled children founded an inspirational gift company known as Prairie Pieceworks, which supplied a line of character bears to Christian bookstores and catalogs nationwide. Stephanie is an avid quilter.

Stephanie's first book, *Walks the fire*, was written while she and her family lived on acreage in southeast Nebraska. The story was inspired by the lives of pioneers buried in an abandoned cemetery near the Whitson home. Since the introduction of *Walks the fire*, Stephanie has gone on to write eight more inspirational novels. Her titles have appeared on the ECPA bestseller list, and she has been a finalist for the Christy Award for excellence in fiction.

In 1996, Stephanie's husband Bob began battling non-Hodgkins lymphoma. In 1998, the family returned to city living in Lincoln, Nebraska. Widowed in 2001 after nearly 28 years of marriage, Stephanie now pursues a full-time writing and speaking ministry from her home studio in Lincoln, Nebraska. She and her four children are active in their local Bible-teaching church.

⤞

Contact Stephanie at:
www.StephanieGraceWhitson.com
or write Stephanie Grace Whitson
3800 Old Cheney Road #101–178
Lincoln, NE 68516